DO113201

Praise for

The Night Before Thirty

"One of the joys of reading fiction is that it allows you to 'try on' different lives. *The Night Before Thirty* is such a book. It's a tightly structured work that offers a realistic look at the 'life issues' many of us confront. . . . Sweet."—*Upscale*

Praise for

Hand-me-down Heartache

"Butler's second novel [after *Sorority Sisters*] deals sensitively with the impact of domestic abuse on an African-American family and the choices made by a young woman dealing with issues of self-doubt while seeking acceptance in her relationships. . . . Building on the successful formula of her first novel, Butler continues to focus on the lives of sorority sisters as they make the transition from college coeds to young women dealing with life, the job market, love and relationships."
—*Publishers Weekly*

"Tajuana 'TJ' Butler is a hot new author. Don't miss her latest novel, *Hand-me-down Heartache*. It's a winner that you gotta check out!"
—Vivica A. Fox

"Butler hasn't simply written a love story in *Hand-me-down Heartache*. She is also sending a self-esteem message to young women. Through her main character's stumblings and discoveries, Butler subtly weaves a theme of believing in yourself, or not living simply to please those around you but [realizing] we all deserve to be loved and treated well."
—*Fort Worth Star-Telegram*

"A novel of love and resilience . . . [Butler] touches on the strength of relationships among women—be they mothers, mentors, or friends."
—*National Women's Review*

"The publisher is watching this book closely, since Butler's first, *Sorority Sisters*, went into five printings. Here, a young woman fresh from college realizes that her father's abuse of her mother has shaped her own expectations."—*Library Journal*

"Sadly, there are teens who can identify all too strongly with the young woman's struggles to keep her relationship going with her boyfriend, and the desperate measures she takes to try to hold onto something that's not really there. This work is a sequel to *Sorority Sisters*, which deals with college life and love relationships. Teens will find both works worthwhile reading." —*School Library Journal*

Praise for

Sorority Sisters

"Tajuana [TJ] Butler's ripe novel *Sorority Sisters* . . . lifted the veil on life on line. . . . Not since Spike Lee's *School Daze* and the much-loved sitcom *A Different World* has the Black experience on campus been this intriguing and, at times, funny."—*Essence*

"Butler writes a very engaging story about five African American college women struggling with campus life and the rigors of pledging. . . . Each woman matures to confront her insecurities through sheer determination to survive not only the pledging process but also the rite of passage between friends and the unique bonds of sorority sisterhood." —*Booklist*

"Butler's approach to the issues surrounding sororities and fraternities, sex and relationships, friendships and sisterhood, are all genuine and

down to earth. *Sorority Sisters* is a relaxing read that offers a trip down memory lane for some and a heads-up for others."
—*Black Issues Book Review*

"Tajuana 'TJ' Butler scores big with this effort. Serious subtexts involving STDs and loyalty never come across as preachy. Butler keeps her prose light and entertaining, making *Sorority Sisters* an enjoyable page-turner." —*Honey*

"*Sorority Sisters* examines the issues facing women walking a tightrope between their teen years and adulthood. The author's vivid descriptions made me identify with the women's struggle and I felt their emotions keenly. And the fact that the author provided a peek into the pledge process of African-American sororities made the book even more tasty."
—Seventeen.com

"Butler realistically captures the trials and tribulations of African-American college women. . . . Rarely has there been a depiction of African-American college life as vivid and accurate as *Sorority Sisters*."
—Lawrence C. Ross, Jr., author of *The Divine Nine: The History of African American Fraternities and Sororities*

"This is a surprisingly good novel for a first-timer. *Sorority Sisters* keeps the pages turning." —*Rap Pages*

STRIVERS
ROW

During the 1920s and 1930s, around the time of the Harlem Renaissance, more than a quarter of a million African-Americans settled in Harlem, creating what was described at the time as "a cosmopolitan Negro capital which exert[ed] an influence over Negroes everywhere."

Nowhere was this more evident than on West 138th and 139th Streets between what are now Adam Clayton Powell, Jr., and Frederick Douglass Boulevards, two blocks that came to be known as Strivers Row. These blocks attracted many of Harlem's African-American doctors, lawyers, and entertainers, among them Eubie Blake, Noble Sissle, and W. C. Handy, who were themselves striving to achieve America's middle-class dream.

With its mission of publishing quality African-American literature, Strivers Row emulates those "strivers," capturing that same spirit of hope, creativity, and promise.

the night before thirty

the night before thirty

a novel

TAJUANA "TJ" BUTLER

STRIVERS ROW / BALLANTINE BOOKS

NEW YORK

2005 Strivers Row/One World Trade Paperback Edition

Copyright © 2003 by Tajuana Butler
Reader's guide copyright © 2005 by Tajuana Butler and Random House, Inc.
Excerpt from *Just My Luck* copyright © 2005 by Tajuana Butler

Published in the United States by Strivers Row/
One World Books, an imprint of The Random House Publishing Group,
a division of Random House, Inc., New York.

Ballantine, One World, Strivers Row, and Strivers Row colophon are registered trademarks
of Random House, Inc.

Originally published in hardcover in the United States by Strivers Row/Villard Books, an
imprint of The Random House Publishing Group, a division of Random House, Inc., in 2003.

This book contains an excerpt from Tajuana "TJ" Butler's forthcoming book, *Just My Luck*.
This excerpt has been set for this edition only and may not reflect the final content
of the forthcoming edition.

Library of Congress Cataloging-in-Publication Data

Butler, Tajuana.
The night before thirty: a novel / Tajuana "TJ" Butler.
p.   cm.
ISBN 0-8129-6798-4
1. African American women—Fiction. 2. Americans—Bahamas—Fiction. 3. Female
friendship—Fiction. 4. Cruise ships—Fiction. 5. Young women—Fiction. 6. Birthdays—
Fiction. 7. Bahamas—Fiction. I. Title.

PS3552.U829N54 2003
813'.54—dc21   2002044942

Printed in the United States of America
2 4 6 8 9 7 5 3 1

One World Books website address: www.oneworldbooks.net

Book design by JoAnne Metsch

To Tracy,
the youngest of "Raymond's girls."
Your turn is coming.

GET IT GOING!

THE RED LIGHT flashed and Melvin Green began speaking to his millions of fans in over fifty cities throughout the United States. "Good morning! Good morning! Good morning! This is the nonstop morning jock, Melvin Green, and the Morning Show Crew hitting you up with the latest in hip-hop and R and B. Me and the crew are working hard every weekday, Monday through Friday, to help you begin your workday! So get to it! It's six o'clock. It's six o'clock! So wake up, sleepy! Face the day! Face life! Because it's gonna keep going with or without you. Rise and shine, I said! 'Rise and Shine!'"

Melvin leaned back in his chair and took a sip of coffee. "Don't hit that snooze button. That only makes my job more difficult. It's my mission to get you up and going. This morning I brought some help with me. What I'm about to spin for you is going to help get you revved up! That's right, Miss Janet Jackson, help a brother out here," he said, and cut to her latest up-tempo hit.

The song ended and Melvin pulled the mike close. "That song is as hot as Miss Jackson herself. I tell you what, some people are afraid of growing old. They think that as time marches on, it becomes too late to become better, but not Janet. Nobody is working out with the clock better than Janet is. She's like a fine wine. She only gets better with time.

She seems to face each year with bold control, enthusiasm, and class. It's like the older she gets, the better she looks. If it's true that beauty is timeless and ageless, I'm sure Janet's face appears as the picture example of beauty in the dictionary."

One of the crew members, Louisa Montero, cut in. "Excuse me, Melvin. I'm not trying to playa hate Janet, because you are right, she is beautiful, but there are so many other examples of timeless beauties who can't be ignored."

"Like who?" Melvin asked.

"I can go down the list: Oprah Winfrey, Susan Taylor, Lena Horne, Diahann Carroll, Patti LaBelle, and Shelia E, to name a few. Then there are the men: Denzel Washington, Billy Dee Williams, Ossie Davis."

"Okay, you got me there. But Janet is still my favorite. So, follow Janet and the lead of all the other classic beauties that Louisa just named and get up! Get going! Get in the mirror, primp and make it up, shake it up, curl it up, just plain fix it up. Put on your finest threads today. Face the world with confidence and a renewed spirit to be the best you you can be! Good morning, everybody. This is Melvin Green and the Morning Show Crew saying, 'Rise and shine! *Rise* and *Shine!*' "

part one

1

CATARA EDWARDS

EADS OF SWEAT formed on Catara's nose as she moved quickly around her tiny Brooklyn brownstone apartment. Her place was in shambles, and she had only an hour to get dressed and leave for her date.

Depressed during the past week, she hadn't been motivated to pick up around her place. Sketches of her latest designs were thrown all over the dresser, covering her cosmetics, which she'd refused to wear the last few days. Clothes were scattered from the living area to the sleeping space. After a long day of work, Catara would simply undress in whichever spot on the floor was clear, and then walk away, leaving yet another pile. Because the studio was low on square footage, it didn't take much for the place to have a cluttered feeling.

After Rondell had called, Catara was struck with energy and determined to clean her entire apartment. But there was no time. The phone had rung five minutes after she walked in after a long day at Saks Fifth Avenue, and he'd asked her to meet him that evening. It was now six P.M. on a Friday night, and she had to leave at seven.

Whenever Catara called Rondell, he was usually in a rush to get off the phone. After the initial pleasantries, he'd make some kind of excuse to hang up. But when he'd called this time, he was different. He wasn't abrupt and to the point. He actually tried to put a little bass into his voice and seemed careful with the words he chose. She almost hadn't known who he was when she'd picked up the phone.

"Hello," she'd panted, attempting to catch her breath after dashing to answer the phone.

"Hey, lady, how's my girl doing?"

"I'm fine," she'd answered, a little hesitant. "Who is this?"

"Ah, baby, I'm crushed. You mean to tell me you don't know my voice?"

"Oh," she'd responded. "Rondell, is this you?" Her heart began to race as she clenched the receiver, pressing it close to her ear to make sure she'd heard right and that Rondell was actually on the other end.

"Yeah, it's me."

Catara didn't know what to say. Experience had proven that Rondell wasn't interested in spending time on the phone with her. She usually wrote down what she wanted to say to him before she called. Without her script, conversations with him were a complete disaster, and she'd hang up feeling distressed that she hadn't had the opportunity to say everything that she needed to during their brief talk.

She'd felt off-guard and panicked until she realized that if he had something to say, he would eventually say it. No matter how painful it would be to her, Rondell always said his piece.

After a few moments of awkward silence, he spoke. "Hey baby, I was thinking, maybe we ought to go to that bar and grill that's around the corner from my place."

Is he asking me on a date? she asked herself.

"So what's up?" he asked. "Are you down with seeing a brother?"

"That would be cool, Rondell," she'd responded.

"Dig it," he'd replied. "Why don't we meet there around eight P.M.?"

Catara was not in the mood to get back on the subway. If she'd had at least a day's notice, she would have been able to arrange things differently. She had a good friend who lived in his neighborhood, so she could have gone to her friend's place after work and prepared for her date there. Rondell never allowed her the opportunity to be anything more than a friend, but she was still attracted to him. If seeing him meant getting on the A train, then that's what she was going to do.

"Okay, Rondell." The thought of being treated to dinner by a man was a refreshing change from her mundane schedule. Catara hadn't been on a real date in a little more than a year. "I'm looking forward to seeing you."

"Me too," he said and hung up the phone.

Anxious, Catara set out to find something in her collection of By TARA Originals, a line of clothing she had designed and sewn for herself. A graduate of the Fashion Institute of Design and Merchandising in Los Angeles, Catara had relocated to New York to find a designer under whom to apprentice, but somehow found herself working at Saks as a personal shopper. Although there were few things in that store that were in her budget, Catara was an expert at helping others find just the right clothing to create their own unique style. However, in order to find her own, Catara designed her fashions from scratch.

She pulled out the outfit she hoped would not only keep Rondell's attention focused on her through dinner but also convince him to take her back to his apartment for the night, which he had done only once before, in the early stages of their "friendship."

Rondell was a musician, a guitar player. His aspiration was to play for a major act, touring the world with a band and playing nightly at stadiums holding thousands of screaming fans. He had been chasing that dream for eight years, but it continued to elude him. When Catara met him, he was picking his guitar, making pennies at a small coffee shop in the Village. Now, two years later, he was still working at the same place. Sometimes, when he was really hard up for money, he set himself up on a subway platform, opened his guitar case, strapped on his guitar, and played his heart out, while praying to God that enough kind souls would appreciate his music and drop enough change for him to eat that night, pay a bill, or get across town and back.

Although Rondell was usually broke and mostly distant, Catara thought he was talented and gorgeous. And when he did allow Catara inside his world, he could be quite charming, passionate, and sensitive. He stole her heart when he played a song one night at the coffee shop and dedicated it to her. It was the sweetest thing any man had ever done for her. Because of that song, Catara was more forgiving of his moments of inconsideration than she would have normally been.

After laying out her ensemble, Catara turned on the shower and allowed it to warm up while she undressed. The only mirror in her bathroom was on the front of the medicine cabinet, and she turned her back to it as she undressed. She didn't want to be confronted with the rolls of flesh that were now hanging from her once curvaceous and sexy body. Over the years, her underactive thyroid and love of food had somehow added sixty-five pounds to her five-foot-five, 135-pound figure.

She stepped into the tub and allowed the water to hit her body. As she quickly washed, she thought about what she would say to Rondell and how he would react to her when she walked into the restaurant. She was going to do her part to look good. She knew that she had so much to offer him if he'd only give her the chance. She was smart, witty, and thoughtful, and Rondell would be a fool to pass her up.

As she moved the soapy sponge over her breasts, stomach, and thighs, she couldn't help but wish she were thinner. She didn't want to be fashion-model thin; she only wanted to be thin enough not to have to strain when she put on her shoes, or small enough around her waist so that when Rondell hugged her tonight, his hands would connect around her with no effort. But there was no time to pout. She couldn't make any drastic changes in her weight before her date, so she had to work with what she had. Her hands moved back to her breasts. She cupped them and smiled, thinking, *Lots of women wish their breasts were as voluptuous as mine. I am a beautiful woman, and Rondell has finally recognized what he's missing.*

Catara rinsed off and got out of the shower, dressed, put on her makeup, and freshened her shoulder-length, naturally curly hair. She smacked her lips together and smiled. *You look damned good, girl,* she thought. *Now, go handle your business!*

WHEN SHE WALKED into the restaurant, she looked around for Rondell. A couple of tables were filled with people, and there were a handful sitting around the bar. Her heart raced and her palms, nose, and underarms began to perspire. Snow was on the ground, with temperatures below twenty degrees, but Catara had bundled up so well that she had begun to sweat. She took a deep breath and walked over to the redheaded hostess, who seemed overeager to greet her.

"Welcome! We have over twenty-five ales and the best steak north of the Ohio!" she said.

"Hi," Catara said calmly as she pulled off her gloves and unbuttoned her coat. "I'm meeting a friend here."

"I bet you're talking about Rondell. He told me to keep an eye out for you. Nice guy. He's over in the corner booth."

"Thank you," Catara responded, and then rubbed her sweaty hands together. "Would you happen to have a napkin?"

"Sure!" the hostess replied. She walked over to the bar and grabbed a few, then bounced back over and handed them to Catara.

"Thanks," Catara said, then patted her nose.

"By the way, the ladies' room is to your right. You can stop in and freshen up if you'd like before you go over to meet Rondell."

"Thank you," Catara responded, grateful the hostess had keyed in on her need. She walked into the ladies' room and stood in front of the mirror, checking to make sure her face was still made up. Usually when she wore makeup, she applied it lightly, and when it wore off, she didn't fuss about reapplying, but tonight was different; she wanted to make a good impression.

After touching up her makeup she still felt musty, so she unbuttoned her shirt, got a paper towel, wet it, and patted under her arms. She caught a glimpse of herself in the mirror and couldn't help but find humor in her actions. *The things we do for men!* She laughed, then reached in her purse and pulled out a trial-size deodorant and body spray.

She put everything back into place and went out to get her man. As she approached Rondell, she reminded herself again just how special she was: *I am big and beautiful, my hair is fly and my breasts are luscious. I am a fashion designer, and even if Rondell doesn't see my beauty, the world soon will through my clothing line.*

"Catara. Hey lady, you made it," he said, and got up from his seat, waiting for her to come close. He stood six-foot-one and was thin and lanky, with a wild, unkempt sandy-brown Afro, and he had on his signature black pants and white tank top. His leather jacket was draped over the back of the chair.

She walked up to him and smiled wide. "Rondell, it's been too long!"

"I agree," he said and reached out to hug her. She had forgotten how he towered over her. Instead of reaching around his neck to hug him, she opted to squeeze his waist.

"I've missed you," she said while in his embrace.

"Let's sit down," he said as they pulled away. They took their seats.

"I'm starved," he said, and flipped through his menu. "I already know what I want."

"I'm really not hungry," she replied. A combination of being with Rondell again, worrying about what events the evening would bring, and wanting to seem appealing had taken away her appetite.

"You mean to tell me you're not hungry?" he said, sounding surprised and just a tiny bit frustrated.

"Positive," Catara replied with confidence. "But I'll get a side salad and soda."

"Salad?" he shook his head and frowned. "Dig it. Well, it's on you. When the waitress comes you can order for both of us. I want the artichoke and spinach dip appetizer and the rib and fries for the entrée. I'll be back. I need to take a leak." Rondell shoved his fingers in his mane, picked through it, and slid out of the booth.

As she watched him walk away, she remembered just why, when he'd stopped calling, she didn't try to contact him. *Why should he be any different tonight?* she thought. She went ahead and ordered for the both of them when the waiter came. She asked if she could have a side salad as her entrée. The waiter rolled his eyes and said, "A side salad must accompany a meal. Only garden salads can be purchased as entrées."

"Well, I only want a Coke!" she replied matter-of-factly. "Add a side salad to my date's meal."

"Whatever you say," he responded, grabbing the menus from the edge of the table and walking away.

Several minutes passed, and the waiter came back with the appetizer, saying, "I brought two plates so you and your date could share." He looked over at the empty seat, snickered, and walked away.

What a jerk, she thought. *And just where is Rondell?*

By the time the snobby waiter returned with their entrées, Rondell was just coming back to their table. Catara had gotten so bored waiting that she had pulled out her cell phone and was cleaning up her phone book.

"Where have you been?" she huffed in a low and angry voice. "I've been looking over my shoulder for the past fifteen minutes, wondering what had happened to you. Plus, the waiter was being an ass."

"I got a call from Wayne—remember him, the keyboard player I vibe with sometimes? Anyway, he was talking about this gig opportunity."

"You've been on the phone with him this long?"

"I hadn't talked to him in a while, so we were catching up."

"Well, you haven't spoken to me in a while, either," she said in a huff.

"Girl, I see you've still got a mouth on you!" Rondell smiled, picked up his fork, and began digging into her side salad, which the waiter had set on his side of the table.

Catara was getting ready to stop him, but decided against it because he was hovering over his food, going through it like it was the first bite he'd eaten in days.

Then he dipped the tortilla chips into the spinach and artichoke dip. He was shoveling into the dip and devouring every bite with merciless chomps.

"So where's the gig?" she asked.

He looked up at her for the first time since he'd started eating and realized that she wasn't joining him. He looked confused but continued to munch on the chips. With his mouth full, he munched out, "I thought you were going to eat a side salad or something?"

"Well, I was, but you seemed to be enjoying it so much that I didn't want to stop you," Catara responded.

"My bad," he replied nonchalantly and picked up a rib, licking his lips in anticipation.

At that point, Catara was astonished, not only by his devouring of the meal but by his inconsiderate attitude. She stared at him and her jaw dropped as she watched him tear into the rib.

"These things are good!" he sang. Catara continued to sit in silence, watching.

Rondell felt her staring and looked at her, chuckling to himself. "I'm being rude," he said and then pushed the basket of tortilla chips to the middle of the table. "Why don't you eat some of these? The dip is slap-yo'-momma good!"

Catara continued to stare.

"I didn't mean to eat your salad, man."

"Man?" Her questioning was more out of shock than of wanting an explanation. There couldn't possibly be an excuse for his behavior.

"Catara, man . . . I mean, Catara I'm not trying to be rude, or anything." He nervously wiped his hands on his napkin. "Why don't you order another side salad? I'm sure they'll have it here in no time."

"I've lost whatever appetite I walked in here with," Catara said, and she wasn't referring only to the food.

"Listen, I haven't eaten anything all day. And if you don't count that wimpy burger that I ate yesterday, it would be two days." He picked up another rib and consumed it.

Catara didn't like the way this evening was going one bit. Her first inclination was to get up and leave that sorry excuse for a man to enjoy his meal in peace, but she couldn't seem to move. She had to know why he wanted to see her, and she wasn't at all in a hurry to get back on the subway. This trip had to be worth her while.

"So why did you want to see me tonight?" she questioned. "I mean, it's been a while."

"It has been a while. I wanted to talk to you about something."

"Oh, really?" Catara replied. She had no idea what he could possibly want to talk to her about.

"Yeah, really. I'll be finished with this food in no time and then we can talk, okay?"

Rondell seemed so sincere that Catara's heart softened a little. She realized that maybe she was being too hard on him. Maybe he was nervous or had a lot on his mind. "So what do you want to talk about until then?" she asked.

"You," he said enthusiastically. "How's life dressing up the rich and the bougie?"

"The same ol' same ol'. I seem to keep getting these old white women who've had the same style for years and stick to the same designer. Anytime I bring in something out of their usual scheme, they turn up their noses at it."

"Uh-huh," Rondell said, continuing to eat.

"But every once in a while some young chick with new money will come in with her husband's charge card, and she'll be open to whatever. Those are my favorite clients because I can mold them."

Rondell didn't say anything. Catara knew she had lost his attention. As she felt her right hand balling into a fist underneath the table, she knew she was becoming frustrated.

"Did you hear me, Rondell?" she asked.

"Huh?" He looked up from his ribs, eyes wide.

"So what did you want to talk to me about? Let's not wait. Let's get it out of the way."

Rondell devoured his one last rib and began finishing off the chips and dip. "Okay," he said hesitantly. "I'm almost finished eating anyway." He shoved the tortillas in his mouth two and three at a time.

He munched and munched. Then he quickly washed them down with the remainder of his Coke, took a deep breath, then paused as if to get his words together.

"Go ahead," Catara pushed.

"Catara, we're friends, right?"

"I guess you could say that, although you sometimes have a funny way of showing your friendship."

"I mean, I am your friend, and I consider you mine."

As badly as she wanted to believe that Rondell was going in a positive direction with this conversation, she couldn't see how. She made her approach as direct as possible to stop his beating around the bush. "What do you want to talk to me about?"

"Okay, Catara, okay." He took a deep breath. "Can I borrow some money?"

"What?" she screamed. This time she didn't care who heard her outburst.

"Only a hundred dollars. I swear I'll pay you back."

"You mean to tell me that you sweet-talked me into leaving the comfort of my apartment—and you know I don't care to ride the subway late at night, plus it's freezing out there—to come all the way over here just so you could ask me to borrow a hundred dollars? Rondell, you've lost your mind!"

Catara picked up her purse and began sliding out of the seat. Rondell stopped her. "What about the meal?"

"What about it?" Catara turned and cut her eyes at him.

Rondell looked dumbfounded. "Well, I don't have enough to pay. I was hoping . . ."

Repeating what Rondell had said to her before he gave his order, Catara shook her head and whispered, "It's on you."

She stood up and clenched her fist beside her leg. "Lose my number," she lashed. "Don't ever call me again. Act like you never met me."

"Come on, Catara," Rondell begged. "We can work this out."

"Screw you, Rondell!" she barked over her shoulder, and walked past the snotty waiter and out the door, leaving Rondell forever.

2

ALECIA JEWEL PARKER

ALECIA JEWEL PARKER tapped the shoulder of the gentleman standing next to her at the baggage claim carousel, pointed at her Louis Vuitton bag moving closer to her around the carousel, and coyly said, "Excuse me, but could you be a dear and grab my bag for me, it's just too heav—"

Before she could finish her sentence, the guy leaped forward, almost knocking down the woman standing next to him, and retrieved Alecia's bag. He set it on the floor in front of her, pulled up the handle, and through his huffing and goofy grin asked, "Is there anything else that I can do to help?"

Alecia smiled pleasantly and then replied with a short "No, thank you." She was very familiar with that look in his eyes. Most heterosexual men displayed it in her presence.

Her beauty seemed to mesmerize them. She called it "the gift," her ticket to whatever she wanted out of life, and she knew how to use it, when to use it, and on whom to use it. She was convinced that all men wanted a piece of her, and this "Buster" was no exception. If she didn't move quickly, he was going to ask her for her phone number.

She clutched the handle of her bag and proceeded toward the door as quickly as she possibly could, but the guy caught up to her. Alecia continued to walk out of the door as if she didn't notice, then pulled out her cell phone and pretended to be engaged in a heavy conversation. The guy finally caught the hint and walked back toward the carousel to retrieve his own luggage.

Outside of the terminal, she looked over her shoulder to make sure he was gone. He was, but her ride was nowhere to be seen; her sugar daddy of two years was supposed to pick her up. He usually arranged to have a car for her whenever she flew back into town, but since he hadn't seen her in more than a month, he'd decided to pick her up. He personally wanted to see to it that she was properly settled back into her high-rise condominium, located in the Westwood district of Los Angeles, which he had purchased for her a year ago and put in her name.

Neither he nor his car was anywhere to be found. Although she was easily frustrated when put in the position of waiting, Alecia took a deep breath and tried to keep her composure. If William was running late, there had to be a logical reason. Since she'd known William Masterson IV, he'd always been prompt. A high-powered entertainment lawyer, he kept a tight schedule. And despite his being married with two grown daughters and a high-maintenance wife, he always managed to be where he said he was going to be and do what he said he was going to do. That's why Alecia cared for him so much. He was not only reliable but also worldly, intelligent, and knowledgeable about a host of subjects. Married or not, aged or not, the man was refined. Plus, he understood her lifestyle—as long as she was there for him in his times of need, he never questioned her comings and goings.

A bragging member of the jet set, Alecia flew first-class in and out of LAX on a moment's notice. All she needed was for one of her "beaus," as she affectionately referred to all the wealthy men who pursued her, to call and ask if she was interested, and she'd pack a bag and head to the airport. She spent weekends skiing, golfing, sailing, dining, shopping—whatever the adventure, Alecia was up for it.

She was a platinum-miles cardholder with all major airlines and had frequent-flier miles piled high, most of which had been earned with someone else's money. Her passport was well stamped, reflecting evidence of her excursions to some of the most exotic and desirable locations in the world. She secretly delighted in the fact that she had spent time on six of the seven continents—if someone found a way to set up an adventure for her in Antarctica, she'd be there. Alecia spoke Spanish and French fluently and could meet and greet in Japanese, Chinese, Italian, Russian, and the Nigerian languages Hausa and Yoruba. Her motto was "When preparation meets the right opportunity, success is bound to materialize."

An example of her motto paying off was the wonderful week she'd just spent in Paris with one of her suitors, Larry Winston, vice president of a large international marketing firm and pushing to make president. Larry wanted to impress his clients in France and had invited her along to wow them with her good looks, her charming personality, and her ability to speak their language.

When she wasn't schmoozing at parties, dinners, and other social settings with Larry, he gave her his platinum card and sent her to be pampered at the hotel's spa and to enjoy a shopping spree so excessive that she had to have her new things shipped back over to the States. Larry stayed on for a few more days, but Alecia returned alone. That's the way it usually worked, and she was fine with it—juggling so many relationships of convenience meant never knowing when she would run into someone with whom she had an "arrangement."

As much as she enjoyed the company of her beaus, none of the men she dated could ever measure up to William Masterson. He had her heart. She was committed to him, lured by the power he possessed in Hollywood and attracted by his attentiveness to her every little need. She wasn't really worried about his being married, because Alecia eventually got everything she went after. She knew that if she waited out their situation and stuck by William, he would eventually leave his wife and commit to her. Besides, she was still young, just twenty-nine, and enjoying her youth, her beauty, and the perks that came along with both. There was no need to push the issue, not just yet.

For now, she was going to be patient, but today William seemed to be taking forever to get to her. Alecia found herself pacing the sidewalk in her tall heels, just the tiniest bit exasperated. She took off the jacket of her suede pantsuit; even though it was November, it was an exceptionally warm California day. *Where is he?* she thought. She couldn't believe he would have her waiting outside like this. She laid the jacket over her suitcase, and then looked around one more time. No sign, so she pulled out her cell phone, this time to make a real call. She dialed William's mobile number and hoped he would pick up.

She got his voice mail on the first ring. *Maybe he's in a bad area,* she thought, and then dialed again. This time he answered.

"This is William Masterson."

"William, honey, where are you?"

"Oh, it's my Jewel. Alecia, I am close to you, yet so far away. We just passed that huge LAX sign, which means I'll be there before you know it." William's tone reflected a day filled with negotiation. He conducted all of their phone calls as if he were closing a deal. "See you then," he said abruptly, and ended their call.

Alecia never took his businesslike, matter-of-fact manner personally because she knew that when he was in her presence he was as attentive as a little puppy. Excited at the thought of seeing him, she pulled a compact out of her purse and checked her hair in the mirror. It was nearly perfect, as usual, bone-straight and parted down the middle. Then she applied additional powder to her T zone, just in case her forehead and nose had become too shiny. Upon closer observation, she decided she needed to freshen up her lipstick.

She was standing there in the middle of the sidewalk, with passersby moving all around her. She didn't seem to acknowledge or care that the walking traffic would have flown a bit more smoothly if only she had positioned herself either closer to the curb or to the building. No, it was Alecia's world. There was no way she could have possibly been in the way. She applied her lipstick lightly, licked her lips, and then used her fingers to fuss around her eyes, ensuring her appearance was as fresh as it could possibly be after such a long flight.

Satisfied, Alecia pulled out an atomizer and sprayed her neck and the folds of her arms. By the time she'd put away her makeup and moved closer to the curb in anticipation, she saw the law firm's sedan moving slowly toward her. She found herself feeling giddy, but she caught herself. *Wait a minute. I am the shit. He's the one who should be excited.*

The driver stopped the car directly in front of her and rushed out to greet her.

"How are you today, Miss Parker?" he asked, opening the car door for her.

"Charmed, Tony. Thanks. And you?" she asked, slipping into the seat next to William without looking at the chauffeur or waiting to hear a response.

Tony shook his head. He was used to Alecia's antics. He closed the door and grabbed her luggage and jacket. He put the luggage in the trunk and came back around to find Alecia and William in a tongue lock. He cleared his throat to announce his presence. "Your jacket, Miss Parker."

"Oh," she said, turning to face him. She placed the jacket on the seat beside her, pulled the door closed, and went back to kissing up her man.

"How's that for a welcome-home kiss?" she purred.

"Fantastic. But I'm not the one who's been globe-trotting."

"Right you are, handsome, but just know that when you're in my presence, you're home. Your Jewel is here in the flesh," she said, and then cascaded her hands past her breasts and down her waist. "Again, welcome home."

"You are too much," William replied, blushing. Then he grabbed her hand. "I'm glad to be home." He squeezed. "I missed you, Jewel, I missed everything about you." He rubbed her thighs. "I missed your long legs, your small waist . . ." He leaned over and planted a light kiss on her breast. "I missed that killer cleavage that called to me every night in my dreams."

"Stop it," Alecia said, and playfully nudged the back of his neck so his lips would fall back on her breast. Then she crossed her legs with her knees facing him and arched her back to make sure her cleavage was pumped up and in his face.

"I missed your beautiful smile and those hypnotic eyes. You know you can get anything you want from me when I'm lost in those eyes." He put his arms around her waist and pulled her close to him. Then he slowly moved his mouth to her ear. When he was close enough, he whispered, "We could make a beautiful son together."

"Oh stop it, William. You know I'm not ready for that kind of responsibility," she said to him. "And your wife would kill us both," she murmured under her breath.

"What was that?" he asked. She gazed into his eyes, and his words played in her mind and moved through her soul. *What would it be like to build a family with him?* she wondered. Divine was the answer. Their child would be amazing. If it were a boy, he would be distinguished like William, one of the handful of black men Alecia dated.

In Los Angeles there was an abundance of powerful, filthy-rich men, but most of them were either white or foreign. When one of these rich men showed an interest, Alecia responded. But none could compare to William—he was such a man. At forty-seven, William could have easily passed for someone in his late thirties, if he didn't have gray hair on his head and in his mustache. He had soft, fair skin, gray eyes, and nice lean features. His smile and charm were of the kind that distinguished phenomenal salesmen from merely good ones. William was exceptional, with a great mind and an incredibly high sex drive.

"Combined with my beauty," Alecia mused softly, "indeed, our son would be a threat to society and the women whose hearts he'd break, one after another."

"Did you say something to me?" he asked her again.

"Pull me closer," she whispered.

William squeezed her tighter and ever so softly put his hand under her chin to pull her lips close to his. His kiss was warm, passionate.

As in-control as Alecia attempted to be when in his presence, she couldn't deny that she was deeply in love with him. All he had to do was say the word, and she would drop every man in her address book and settle down with him.

"So how much time do we have today?" she asked.

He released his embrace. The question triggered William to fall back into business mode. He sat up straight, pulled out his Palm, and called up his schedule for the day. "We have approximately two hours," he said. "I have two meetings later in the day, and then tonight I have to attend a showcase one of the record labels I represent is putting on with some new talent they're considering. But I've got a surprise for you in the next two weekends. Are you going to be free?" he asked.

Of course I will be free, she said to herself. Then she gave an answer to remind him that she had a life outside of him. "I think I can arrange to be. What do you have planned?"

"If I told you, it wouldn't be a surprise, now, would it?"

"You're right, but can't I get an itty-bitty little hint?" She pouted.

"Little, beautiful city, with a beautiful woman, doing beautiful things."

"More, more!" she playfully begged, and moved close to him. "Tell me more."

"Just know that you're going to be with me, and I'm going to treat you like a princess," he said, and then slid his arm back around her waist while Alecia laid her head on his shoulder.

"You always do," she replied.

Alecia lay in silence in William's arms all the way to her condominium. She knew that her relationship with him was a fairy tale. He was her knight in shining armor. But if she wanted to live happily ever after with him, it meant that she would have to share her throne with his queen, whom he'd rescued and made his bride long before he'd met Alecia.

3

TANYA CHARLES

TANYA CHARLES SAT in her living room, legs crossed and arms tightly clutched in front of her chest, as she waited impatiently by the telephone. She had spent an hour and a half getting dressed, only to sit there for at least another hour. Her microbraided hair was pulled up and away from her made-up face. She was dressed in black two-and-a-half-inch pumps, super-sheer black panty hose that hugged her legs, and a sexy, short black dress. Her nails were well manicured. But it was all beginning to seem in vain because there was a possibility she would be going nowhere tonight. To make it worse, this wasn't the first time she'd found herself stood up by her man, Chris.

Christopher Walker was notorious for arriving hours late or just not showing up at all. He was always on his own schedule, and if Tanya wasn't willing to go along with the program, Chris had made it clear that she could hit the road running, because there were too many women in the greater Chicago area more than willing to take her place.

Although there was a clock in the living room, she got up and walked into the kitchen, to look at the big-faced clock hanging over the stove. She released a long sigh. She didn't really need to look at the time. She had checked it every five minutes. The impulse forcing her to get up over and over again clued her in that it was five minutes later than the last time she had looked at the clock, but she got up and looked nonetheless. She wanted to make sure she was correct and that Chris truly was late again.

Tanya attempted to distract herself by opening the refrigerator and checking to see if there was anything she could snack on while she waited. Too much preparation was required for most of what was inside, so she walked over to the pantry and grabbed a bag of chips off the shelf. As she munched, she realized that a snack wouldn't do—she needed a meal. She was starving. She hadn't eaten since her lunch break, and even then, she'd kept the meal light because when Chris took her out to dinner, they always overordered: champagne, wine, or mixed drinks, two or three appetizers, huge entrées, and dessert. The sky was the limit—whatever Tanya wanted, Chris got for her, and not only at restaurants.

She had all the latest fashions. Most of the clothes she wore were stolen, but they were the top-of-the-line threads nonetheless. Her one-bedroom loft located in Wicker Park was elaborately furnished, and she drove a fully loaded Audi 5000—all gifts from the man who insisted she wait until he was ready to get out of the drug game and begin earning money legitimately before they got married.

"I'm sick of this shit!" she huffed, devouring the chips on her way back to her designated waiting area on the sofa, in front of the big-screen television. But she didn't dare call him, because experience had taught her that when she made contact with him, he felt more justified in extending his arrival time. Using the excuse "We touched base. You knew I was coming, so why you bringing the drama?" he avoided taking responsibility for his lateness.

Tanya felt the urge to check the time again. "Okay, five more minutes have passed," she said. "Time to wash down these chips." She got off the sofa and walked back into the kitchen, where she pulled a bottle of soda out of the fridge. The doorbell rang. "He's here," she sighed, and then put the half-open soda back into the fridge, grabbed a knife to check her lips and teeth in its reflection, and then smoothed her hair and her clothes and rushed to open the door.

Chris was posed on the other side of the door, hiding behind his signature dark shades and tugging away at his goatee. His lips were poked out, as they always were when he wanted to appear sexy. Dressed in

Sean John jeans and jacket, a Karl Kani T-shirt, and hiking boots, her man was looking damned good, as usual.

"Hey, baby. Yo' man is here to take you out on the town. So what's up?"

Tanya smiled.

"Get over here and give Daddy some lovin'," he gently demanded.

Tanya happily stepped to Chris and fiercely tongued her man down, then finished him off with gentle pecks. She loved loving on his lips.

"You know how I like it, baby, don't you?" he said, gently nudging her back into the apartment, following close behind her. "I know you're hungry. What you got a taste for?"

"There's a steak restaurant that some of my coworkers were talking about earlier this week. I thought we could try it out."

"Ah, yeah?" Chris's voice was deep, smooth and, as far as Tanya was concerned, sounded like jazz music.

"Yeah. I hear the food is really good."

"Wouldn't we need a reservation or something?" he asked, pulling a chair away from the dining room table.

"Well, I made one for eight-thirty, but now it's almost ten and I'm not sure what time they close. It should only take us twenty minutes to get there from here," she said calmly. Compromise was the name of the game. Dinner at eight-thirty or eleven was fine, as long as Chris was there with her.

"Why don't you call them and see . . ." His cell phone rang. "Excuse me baby," he said, and answered his phone. "Hello . . . okay . . . hold on a sec." He pulled the phone away from his ear and said to Tanya, "Call the restaurant and see what we can do. I'll only be a moment." Then he continued with his conversation. "Yeah man, it's all good. So what's up?"

Tanya looked at her boyfriend suspiciously. Would this call be one that would prevent them from having a night out together? She prayed not. Not wanting to appear too obvious, she slowly walked away, eavesdropping, hoping to find out if their plans were being changed.

By the time Chris got off the phone, Tanya had gotten them a reservation.

"So what's up, baby?"

"Well, we have an eleven o'clock reservation. The kitchen closes at eleven-thirty and the restaurant at midnight."

"Eleven o'clock. Cool. That gives us a chance to make a stop on the way there."

Tanya pouted. "Why?"

"It won't take long, baby. I promise we'll make it on time. It's just gonna be a quick stop."

"Okay. Well, let me get my coat." Tanya went to the closet, breathing a quick sigh of relief. She selected her full-length fur coat to shield her from the harsh Chicago winds, and then walked toward Chris, who was standing at the door with his cigar holder in his hands.

"Damn, baby, you look good in that coat." He pulled out a Cuban but didn't light it. He liked to play around with it in his mouth. He usually waited until after sex, dinner, or drinks to light up.

"I aim to please," Tanya said proudly.

"If you keep being good to Daddy, like you've been, then I'll get you a mink that same length for Christmas."

Tanya smiled big, walked over to her man, and kissed his neck while palming his penis with her hands. "I'll always be good to you," she said, and then walked by him and opened the door.

Chris lifted his eyebrows and poked out his lips. "Now, that's what I'm talkin' 'bout," he said, following Tanya out the door.

TANYA SAT PATIENTLY in the passenger seat of Chris's Cadillac Escalade. She had long since changed the hip-hop song that was blaring in her ear to something with a softer groove. When he made these runs, she didn't ask who he was going to see about what or why. She knew how her man made his money, by selling drugs and firearms. She was never with him when he was in the midst of an actual firearms transaction but was fully aware that it was part of his MO.

She was present, however, during countless minor drug transactions that were discreetly handled. Chris didn't deal in typical street sales. He dealt with the "rich white boys" in their condos and penthouses, big money sales one huge drop at a time. Tanya tried to stay as far away from his customers' eyes as possible—the less they knew about her, the better, and vice versa.

She and Chris didn't talk about business a whole lot. She knew what she needed to know and would put up with his occupation for a little while longer. He had promised her he'd quit once he reached his goal of being half a million dollars liquid, and he was close. Hidden in various banks and backyards, buried underneath trees and in family members' basements and garages, he had saved more than $260,000 over the past eight years. Just as soon as he made his last few big hits, he was going to give it up completely. They would get married and move to Atlanta, where Chris was going to become legit, open a rims shop, and live off his stash. So he said.

Tanya remained tolerant. Although she wanted so badly for Chris to be more like the guys that her coworkers dated—nine-to-five workers with good corporate jobs, who followed weekly schedules and were reliable—she was forced to face the reality of their situation. She wouldn't dare leave him; they had been together too long and had seen too much together, had experienced too much together. They had become family.

She'd met Chris while she was still a senior in high school. She and her good friend, Angel, got all made up one night and sneaked into a nightclub with their fake IDs. Chris had been one of the first men she'd seen when she walked through the door. He seemed so cool with a cigar in his mouth, so mature. Tanya couldn't help but stare. Her friend was excited they'd actually made it past the bouncer and was tugging at her arm, squealing, "We made it in, can you believe it?"

Tanya didn't join in because she was so taken by the sight that was before her. She was absolutely gaga.

"What are you looking at?" Angel insisted.

Tanya turned away to inform her friend, "Only the finest man in the club." Then she directed Angel's attention toward Chris, who was standing by the bar, talking with two other brothers.

"Let's go speak," Angel said.

"What? Wait."

"Well, we're in here. We've planned this for weeks. So let's at least go over to the bar and get a drink," Angel said, trying to appear mature. "Can you believe we're about to order our first real drinks? Do you remember what we said we'd get?"

"Yes, I remember. We're ordering Long Island iced teas," Tanya answered, with her own air of womanhood. She took a deep breath, forced herself to stop drooling, and made her way over to the bar, close to where Chris was standing. The young ladies grabbed two seats and began signaling the bartender. Before they got his attention, they had attracted the attention of one of the guys who was standing with Chris.

The guy motioned to the bartender, who then walked over to him. After saying something to him, the bartender walked over to them and asked, "What are you having?"

The girls placed their orders.

"These are compliments of the gentleman a few seats down," he said when he returned.

The pair looked up, and the guy raised his glass toward them and nodded.

Her friend slapped Tanya's arm. "Is that the one you were checking out?"

"No. The one I was peeping is not even paying us any attention. He's the one in the shades who's talking to the other guy."

"Good. Because I'm diggin' on this guy's look. He's got that 'I just got out of prison' roughneck look that is stirring up my wild side," she said, raising her glass back at him and smiling.

"That was bold!" Tanya commented.

"I know—now what do I do?" Angel asked nervously.

"We sit here and sip on our drinks, and then we casually get up and make our way toward the dance floor," Tanya answered, as if she had a clue.

"Okay, but what if they don't speak to us before then?"

"That's not gonna be a problem for you. But me, on the other hand, I don't know," Tanya replied, and looked past her friend, whose back was to her pursuer.

"What do you mean?" Angel asked.

Just then the guy edged close and hovered over Angel.

"So do you like your drinks?" he asked. His voice was deep and raspy.

"We do, thank you." Angel looked up at the guy, who was not giving her any room to breathe. She shrugged and adjusted herself in the seat, attempting to find some distance.

"Oh, am I making you uncomfortable?" he asked.

"No, not at all," she lied.

He stepped back anyway and reached out his hand. "I'm Greg," he said. "What's your name, pretty lady?"

"Angel. And this is my friend Tanya," she said. Tanya waved.

He shook her hand then turned his attention back toward Angel. "Peep this. None of these other niggas in here will show you as good a time as I can. So ain't no need in looking around. You stopped at the right spot. Right here by me." He grinned, seemingly pleased at the game he had just dropped.

"That's a bold introduction," Angel responded.

"I'm just keepin' it real."

"Well, as long as we're keeping it real, what's up with your boy over there? My girl is checking him out," she said.

"Oh, so it's like that," he said, and looked over at Tanya. "She's fine enough. All right, I'll put in a word."

Tanya couldn't hear the conversation but wondered why this strange guy was eyeing her. She nudged Angel, who turned back to her, lifting her right eyebrow mischievously.

"What's going on?" Tanya asked.

Angel quickly looked away from Tanya and put her hand on Greg's shoulder. "So what's up?" she asked. "Are you gonna make sure both of us have a good time or what?"

"All right," he reluctantly replied. "I'll check it out and see what's up." He walked away.

Angel updated Tanya while they waited.

"I told you we should have done this a long time ago. Those boys at school don't got nothing on the men here," Angel said.

"Girl, I can't believe I'm going to meet him. He's too fine. I'm telling you right now, I don't care how old he is, Angel, I'm pulling him."

"Do your thing, girl," Angel replied.

Greg returned and walked over to Tanya, "Wave at my boy and smile, so he can see your teeth," he said.

"What did you ask me?" Tanya frowned.

"Dang, girl, just smile and say hi. It's all good," he said, and walked back over to Angel.

Tanya panicked; she began to tap her fingers nervously on the bar. But she knew from the moment she spotted him that she had to meet him, so she leaned back in her seat and looked over to where he was standing. Then she waved and managed the sexiest smile that she could.

Chris smiled back, took a final sip of his drink, set it on the bar, and walked over to her. Instead of introducing himself, he stopped short and stared at her from head to toe. Then he poked out his lips, licked them, and moved closer.

"So you wanted to meet me," he said.

"Yeah, I wanted to meet you," she responded, attempting to appear confident. She looked him directly in his shades. But inside she was shivering with fear. What if he found out that she was only eighteen? What if he asked her age? What would she say? She decided she'd say twenty-one, the age on her fake ID. "So what's your name?" she asked. She figured she'd question him before he could her.

"My name is Chris, but everybody calls me Big C," he said and held up a huge gold C pendant hanging on a thick gold rope around his neck. "But you, sexy, can call me Chris."

"Okay, Chris," Tanya responded. She was really getting into his thug-life persona, when he abruptly changed the flow of the conversation.

"Listen, write down your number on a napkin or something, and I'll call you."

"You're leaving?" Tanya asked, disappointed.

"Well, I got to go take care of some business, and I might not be able to find you when I get back, or you might be gone. If you give me your number now, maybe I can swing by your place later tonight."

Tanya frowned.

"Or maybe I can hit you up later, and we can get together some other time. You know?"

"Okay," Tanya said, "I'll give you my pager number." She didn't want to give him her home number, because she didn't want him to know that she still lived with her mother.

"What? Are you married or something?" he huffed.

"No, I live with my sister," she lied, "and I don't like to give her number out to strangers. Just page me, and I'll call you."

"Okay, I'll page you, but you'd better not be living with no nigga, 'cause I ain't got no time for that kind of drama. You feel me?" he said, and then calmed his posturing a bit. "All right, sexy," he said. He blew her a kiss and strolled out of the door of the club.

Tanya was smitten. She could tell Chris was the kind of nigga that didn't take no shit, but she could also tell he had a gentle side and that he would protect her—that's exactly what she needed in her hood, a down brother who would have your back.

She begged Angel to stay an hour later than planned, hoping to be able to see Chris again. The two closed down the club. Tanya danced a few times but spent most of the evening hoping and waiting for Chris to walk back through the door. Some things didn't change: Eleven years later and Tanya was in the same holding pattern with Chris.

She turned up the heat in the truck, snuggled her chin in the lining of her fur coat, lost herself in the music that was flowing through the speakers, and tried to relax, but the reality of their relationship was hard to swallow. She was still waiting to get the chance to spend time with the man who was still hustling while planning to find time to spend time with her.

4

ELISE ROSS PULLED into the lot of the high-rise elderly-assistance apartments her grandma had resided in for the past seven years. Her grandma was scheduled for a colonoscopy the next day, and Elise had to administer the laxative the doctor had instructed her grandma to take orally, once in the morning and once in the evening. It was time for Grandma's evening dose.

She'd spent the entire day at her new gym, Gotta Flip Gymnastics, where she was preparing for the grand opening in two weeks. Elise felt guilty that she hadn't been spending very much time with her grandma lately, but she was realizing her dream, which was to open a gymnastics center to cater to a predominately black student base. She had worked as a gymnastics instructor for Gym Works, located in the east end of town, and although she'd loved working there, she had been disturbed that she touched the lives of so few black children. She loved the kids she worked with and gave them her all as an instructor, but she longed to have a place filled with beautiful, young, smiling black faces wanting to learn everything they could about the art of gymnastics.

Elise rushed out of the car, forgetting to grab her coat and gloves. It was the first of November and winter had made an entrance. Although it hadn't snowed yet, it was freezing. Trees were bare and the grass had turned brown. Louisville usually didn't see snow until late December or early January. She cuffed her hands in front of her mouth and blew inside to warm them. When she got to the front door, Mr. Buzby, who worked the front desk at night, let her in.

"There's my favorite girl," he said as she walked through the door.

"Mr. Buzby. Hello. It's always a pleasure." Usually she'd stop and talk to him for a few minutes, but not tonight. She breezed past him and toward the elevators.

"So you're in a hurry again," he said, disappointed.

"Yes, sir," she replied. "I gotta be back at the gym by seven-thirty."

"I see things are going well."

The elevator flew open and she stepped inside. "Let's just say I'm moving forward," she said as the door closed.

Elise had the keys to her grandma's apartment, but to respect her privacy, she always liked to knock and allow her grandmother to answer the door.

"Elise, is that you?" her grandma asked.

"Yes, ma'am," she replied, and waited patiently as the old woman made her way to the door and finally unfastened all the locks to open it.

"Hey, beautiful," Elise said, and embraced her.

"I don't feel so beautiful today," her grandma replied as they walked back into her one-bedroom place. "I've been on the toilet all day, and anything that was once in me is now gone."

Elise giggled at her grandma's candidness. She'd always been outspoken. She followed her to the living room and sat next to her on the couch. "Well, I'm here to serve you up round two."

"I don't see why I gotta go through this again. I tell you, that stuff you gave me this morning did the job."

Elise rubbed her grandma's arm. "I hear you talking, but you need to follow the doctor's instructions. I'm sure if he wants you to take this medicine twice today, it's for a good reason." She stood up. "And now, Mrs. Ross, I'm going to serve you the best-tasting laxative you've had in your life."

"Easy for you to say. You're not spending a day eating clear gelatin and sitting on the toilet."

"Well, just look at it this way—after you go through your procedure tomorrow, I'm going to make sure you have your favorite dish: roast beef and potatoes."

Elise walked into the kitchen, mixed together the medication in a mug and then walked it back in to her. "Now, Grandma, you know I can't stay long. I have a meeting that I have to get to back over at the gym."

"I know, Elise. I know you're busy, and I appreciate all that you do for me."

"Grandma, you know I don't mind at all."

"Yeah, I know, but you had to stop doing your work to come and see about me."

"Here, Grandma, take this." Elise handed her the mug.

Grandma Ross sat the mug down on the coffee table. "Okay, but first I have to do something." She pulled herself off the sofa and walked into her bedroom. Elise followed her to make sure everything was all right.

Her grandma's bedroom, as well as the rest of the apartment, was neat. Elise came back home with her every Sunday after church and helped her clean the place. Sometimes they'd go out for dinner afterward, and other times they'd get carryout or rent a movie to watch. Their time spent together after church had decreased lately since she'd been busy with the opening of the gym. Elise would help her grandma clean, but then she'd go back to her own apartment to prepare for the week or try to find a moment to rest.

Her grandma walked around to the far side of her queen-size bed, opened the top drawer of the nightstand, and pulled out a ten dollar bill. Elise just stood there at the door of the bedroom, shaking her head. "Grandma, I hope that's not for me 'cause you know I'm not taking it."

"Oh, don't be like that," Mrs. Ross said as she walked toward Elise. "You've helped me so much, and I know that you've put everything that you have into that gym."

"Yes, I'm putting a lot into the gym, but I also got a small business loan. I'm okay, Grandma."

"I know you're okay, but please let me give you this, just this time." Grandma Ross tried to force the bill into her hand.

Elise gripped her hand closed and responded, "That's what you always say. Now, come in here and take this laxative. I gotta be leaving soon."

Grandma Ross balled the bill into her own hand, walked past Elise over to the coffee table, picked up the mug, and drank down the laxative.

"Remember, Grandma, I'm gonna be here to pick you up at nine o'clock in the morning. I'll call you when I'm on my way." Elise walked over and hugged her grandmother. Grandma Ross put her arms around her granddaughter and stuck the money into the pants pocket of Elise's warm-up suit.

"I felt that," Elise scorned her. "I love you so much, Grandma, but you're gonna have to stop this." She removed the money from her pocket and placed it on the table. "Listen, I've gotta go. I will see you tomorrow." Elise shook her head and walked toward the door.

ELISE PULLED INTO her parking space at Gotta Flip. Hers was the only car there, and although she didn't have her sign up yet, she envisioned the one she'd put up, which would read MISS ELISE'S PARKING SPACE. A huge smile spread across her face. Every time she got close to that place, her energy level increased by volumes, which was a good thing. She needed that extra energy, because in order to be prepared for her opening day, she had to get impossible amounts of work done.

She got out of the car, grabbed her gym bag, and walked up to the door of the huge warehouse, which had gray siding and two huge, garage-style entrance doors on either side of the main door. Elise was glad to have those—she'd open them during the summer months to save on electricity.

By the time Elise turned on the light switch, she heard a car pull up. Her seventy-thirty appointment had arrived. She brushed her hair back with her hands and rummaged through her bag for some lip balm to throw on before Allen walked through the door. The gym was freezing, but she unzipped her warm-up suit so her leotard would show through. She wanted to give him something appealing to look at since her hair was a mess. Elise was short, five-one, with broad shoulders, thick, athletic thighs, and a small waist. She had the body of a gymnast.

Allen rang the bell outside, and Elise bounced over to the door to let him in.

"Hi, sorry I'm late," he said, as he walked through the door and dropped a box beside him.

"It's only seven thirty-five. I just got here myself. Don't worry about it. Did you bring the T-shirts?" she asked.

"Of course I did," he responded confidently. He reached into the box to pull one out and threw it to Elise, who caught it with one hand. "This is an extra one—my way of showing my appreciation for your business."

"Thank you," Elise said, unfolding the shirt to examine Allen's work. "It looks good!" she said enthusiastically. Allen was her all-purpose promotions and marketing go-to man. She'd gotten his information from the guy who eventually installed her alarm system—she'd liked the layout of the flyer promoting his business. When she inquired about who'd made it, he gave her Allen's contact information. Allen had been a part of conceiving and developing Gotta Flip's image ever since.

"You ready to get to work?" he asked, slapping the bag he was carrying on his shoulder.

"Yeah, I am. Let's go over to the tumble track. The desk will be installed tomorrow."

"That's cool. We can work on the tumble track," he said, playfully mocking Elise's voice. Then he looked past Elise. "Whoa, this place is dope!" Allen yelled. "So much has changed since I was here last. It looks like a red, white, and blue playground."

The layout wasn't yet complete, although there were several pieces of equipment properly placed throughout. The walls were painted white, but the back wall was red with the Gotta Flip logo boldly centered on it. Hanging from the ceiling were three flags: on the left was the official USA Gymnastics banner, on the right was a flag of the United States, and in the middle was a banner bearing the Gotta Flip logo. The floor was covered with blue carpet. There were six balance beams of various heights and two sets of regulation uneven bars. Along the length of the carpet was a long path sectioned off with white tape, leading to a vault.

The two walked onto the carpet.

"Why is it so soft and bouncy?" Allen asked, thrown off-guard.

"Well, it's cheaper to create an ultrasoft tumbling area than to buy individual tumbling mats. Imagine kids tumbling from one corner of the floor to the next," Elise said. "The front is going to be the receptionist area and store."

Her eyes lit up as she talked, and the energy surrounding her was contagious.

"You're selling clothes?"

"Yeah! You know, supplemental money—leotards, T-shirts, shorts. Things like that."

"I thought you were giving away the T-shirts we made for you?"

"I am, but only to kids who pay for a full semester of classes in advance."

"You are quite the businesswoman," he replied as he followed her toward the long, rectangular trampoline, which extended the full length of the wall and ran parallel to the vault track.

"Yeah, but my rates are reasonable, affordable. I've had to come up with other ways to make money, like merchandising and the weekend gymnastics-themed parties."

"If you don't watch yourself, you'll soon be like me, without a life outside of work."

"Well, I used to have a life outside of work, but it wasn't that exciting a life."

Allen looked at the trampoline. "I've never seen one like this before. Aren't they usually round?"

Elise laughed. "They can be, but this is called a tumble track. Kids will use this to work on getting over their fear of advanced stunts, and once they're more comfortable they'll move to the floor. But look!" she said, running to the end of the track. Allen followed her to the edge of a deep, perfectly square hole in the floor. It was filled with huge red, white, and blue foam squares.

"What you got going on here, girl?" Allen asked, and moved as far away from the hole as he could in a single leap.

Elise burst into laughter. "This is what is called 'the pit.' Go ahead, jump into it!" she teased.

"Naw, I'm cool," Allen said.

"At least come closer and check it out!" she insisted.

"I can see it fine from here," he replied.

"When the kids get to advanced tumbling passes that they're still uncomfortable with completing, they'll complete the pass into the pit. It builds courage," Elise said.

Allen nodded in agreement as he listened. He said, "That seems good and all, but I can't understand for the life of me how tumbling into a hole in the ground of a building is going to make a child less scared."

He took one more step backward at the thought of falling into it. "Let's get away from the pit so that we can get some work done."

"All right," Elise said, amused that someone like Allen, who always seemed reserved and cool and on top of his business, could break out into a sweat at the sight of a foam-filled playground for kids.

The two sat down on the edge of the tumble track farthest away from the pit. Allen pulled out folders and samples, including the completed flyer that would be mailed throughout neighborhoods nearby and passed out by his street promotions team over the weekend at the West End Winter Festival.

Elise read over the flyer to check for errors. She didn't see any. "This is great," she said.

"So you approve?" he asked.

When he'd first met Elise, she was up-front about how important the image of the gym was going to be. She'd informed him she wouldn't bite her tongue if she wasn't pleased with his work.

"I do."

"Just checking," he replied, and then pulled out samples of custom-designed business cards, letterhead, thank-you cards, and student applications. All were exactly what Elise had asked for.

"I can't believe that all of this is coming together so well and on time," she said. "It all looks great."

"When you work with the best, you get the best," Allen bragged.

Elise couldn't argue with him one bit. She liked his work, but more than that, she was beginning to like him. She even liked his arrogance. She'd been attracted to him from the start but promised herself that for the sake of building and keeping a successful business relationship with him she wouldn't make any indications that she was even the slightest bit interested in him. Then, after he began coming around and consistently producing quality work, she began to like him even more. Covering up how she felt toward him was becoming more difficult a task every time she was in his presence. She liked his laid-back yet professional demeanor. He made her feel like no matter what she requested of him, it could be done.

She found herself smiling at him as he was going through one of the folders in his bag.

"I brought your invoice with me," he said as he passed it to her.

"Oh, let me get my checkbook." When she returned, Allen was pushing down on the trampoline with his hand.

"You want to get on the tumble track?"

"I'm already on it," he responded.

"I mean, do you want to jump on it?"

"Are you crazy?"

"Come on!" Elise yelled as she hopped on behind him and began to jump.

The papers they had laid on the trampoline were bouncing with her. Allen quickly shuffled them together and shoved them back into his bag. Then he stood up off the track and placed the bag on the floor.

"Come on," Elise persuaded.

"No!" he replied.

"I'm not going to give you your check until you get up here."

"That's fine with me. You just won't get your stationery delivered next Tuesday."

She saw his keys were still on the track, so she scooped them up.

"Stop playing, Elise!" he demanded. "I can't believe you're acting like this. What happened to your professionalism?"

"Just jump once, and I'll give you your keys. Or are you too cool to get up here?" Elise was surprised by her own actions, but she had already started, so she continued. It was fun. Plus, she believed that everyone, no matter how old, how cool, or how reserved should experience jumping on a trampoline. "Just one little jump," she begged.

Allen huffed a bit, then gave in and awkwardly mounted the trampoline. He put his hands out to maintain his balance. "This doesn't feel right," he said. "I'm getting off this thing."

Elise threw his keys and check onto the floor, and then bounced over to him and put her hands in his. She said, "Come on. You can do it."

"I guess this is funny to you?" He jumped once, and a smile came over his face. "Man, you got me feeling like a kid or something." He jumped again.

"Isn't it fun?" Elise said, jumping up and down alongside him. Then she let go of his hands. "How often do you get to let go like this?" she asked.

"Never," he answered, giggling.

Elise was glad she'd egged him on. There was a cute and cuddly fun side to Allen. Seeing it was refreshing. He could have reacted in many different ways to her pushing him to let loose, but he was a sport about it, and that turned her on. It was exciting, but a little disturbing, too.

The two jumped and laughed until they both collapsed on the trampoline.

Breathing heavily, Allen said, "Elise?"

"Yeah, Allen?"

"Now can I have my check?"

5

LASHAWNDA DAVIS

*L*ASHAWNDA DAVIS ADJUSTED the volume of her desktop radio. She wanted to make sure the off-the-wall comedy of Melvin Green and the Morning Show Crew wasn't so loud that it could be heard by people who walked in for their appointments with her boss, Dr. Cicely Hayes.

Lashawnda had been working for Cicely as her receptionist and personal assistant for three years. Dr. Hayes was a psychologist, and the majority of her clientele were women dealing with clinical depression. Lashawnda's secretarial duties included light bookkeeping, typing, answering phones, setting appointments, and greeting and signing in patients. She ran errands for Cicely, like keeping regular maintenance on her car and picking up her dry cleaning. She also set up appointments and sometimes joined her boss for manicures, pedicures, and whatever other personal maintenance Cicely required.

For Lashawnda, her job with Cicely was a godsend. Before working for the doctor, Lashawnda had gone through nearly every existing fast-food chain and grocery store, working as a cashier or grocery bagger. She had no real skills and had never expected to be more than a cashier until a chance meeting with Cicely one day when she was working as a bagger at a local grocery and Cicely had come through her line.

Lashawnda had been talking to the cashier about how she was catching the blues from her current boyfriend.

"Girl, we got into it again, and his ass locked me out of our apartment. Can you believe that shit? I had to spend the night with my mom." As painful as the episode had been for her, Lashawnda was joking about it, trying to make the best of the situation. "If I had of known he was gonna kick me out, I wouldn'a cooked dinner for him." She and the cashier laughed.

Cicely didn't say anything. She simply paid for her groceries and followed Lashawnda, who was carrying her bags out to the car. As she always did when she was nervous or upset, Lashawnda talked the whole way to the car. "I don't know how we live with them," she complained.

Cicely didn't say a word but stopped and opened her purse, pulled out a lighter and a pack of cigarettes, and tapped the bottom of the pack on the back of her hand. She pulled one out and put it between her lips. In one continuous motion, she flicked the lighter and lit the cigarette, puffed, pulled the cigarette from her mouth, closed her eyes, and then blew as if relieving all the pressures from her day. But Cicely didn't look like the kind of lady who had any pressure that she needed to relieve. Lashawnda had been around smokers, but never had anyone made what she considered a disgusting habit seem so glamorous.

Lashawnda was for once at a loss for words. Cicely had her total attention. Very few black people came through that grocery store who didn't look beaten down, overworked, or lacking in confidence. But Cicely was different. She seemed refreshed. Long, slim, and graceful, she embodied sophistication. She was about something. Lashawnda wasn't going to rest until she knew more. "So what are you doing getting your groceries from here?"

Cicely puffed on the cigarette. "Why would you ask me a question like that?" she responded nonchalantly.

"Well, you don't look like you're from around here."

"Last time I checked I was black. What are you talking about?"

"You know what I mean. Why are you buying groceries from here?"

"Well, if you must know, I'm coming in from Birmingham, and I needed to get gas. While I was filling up, I noticed your grocery store and decided to pick up some things so I wouldn't have to when I got near my house."

They walked up to her Jaguar. Cicely opened the trunk. "You can put them in here," she said.

"So what do you do?" Lashawnda inquired, placing the bags into the trunk.

"I'm a psychologist," Cicely responded.

"Oh!"

They shut the trunk. "So do you like what you do?" Lashawnda asked, still wanting to know more.

"You certainly have a lot of questions," Cicely responded, sounding a little annoyed. Then she looked Lashawnda in the eye. "Do you like what *you* do?"

"Well, I never thought much about it. I just know that I have to work to pay my bills."

"How much do you make here?" Cicely asked her.

"Minimum wage and not a penny more. No overtime, nothing. How much do you make?"

Cicely laughed. She seemed to find Lashawnda's honest probing quite amusing. "I make seventy thousand dollars."

"A year?"

"Yes, a year." Cicely laughed again. Lashawnda must have seemed so naive to her.

"Seventy thousand dollars!" Lashawnda exclaimed. "If I made that kind of money . . . I don't know what I'd do if I made that kind of money. You know, I wonder how many years I'd have to combine to make that kind of money." She thought long and began to pop her knuckles. Then she looked away into a distant place. "I guess I'd have to win the lottery." She smiled at Cicely and put her hand out to shake. "Well, miss, it was nice to meet you," she said, shook hands with her, and began to walk away.

"Wait a minute," Cicely said. "I can tip you, right?"

Lashawnda turned around and grinned. "Tips are always accepted."

Cicely threw her cigarette on the ground and put it out with the heel of her shoe. She reached into her purse and pulled out her wallet. Then she grabbed a ten dollar bill and handed it to Lashawnda.

"Thank you," Lashawnda said with genuine appreciation. "You know, I'm twenty-six, and I've never gotten a tip like this one before." She turned away again.

"Hey," Cicely said. "Do you have a car?"

Lashawnda turned around slowly, surprised that Cicely was continuing a conversation with her. "Well, my boyfriend—or soon to be ex-boyfriend—lets me use his car whenever I need it. Plus, I take the MARTA sometimes. Why do you ask?"

"How attached are you to your job?" she asked.

"Like I said, it pays the bills, but I'm not making seventy Gs."

"If I give you a job, not making what I'm making, but more than what you're making here, do you think you could get downtown by nine A.M. sharp every morning?"

"You want to give me a job?"

"Can you type?"

"No, not really."

"Are you willing to learn?"

"Are you serious about giving me a job?" Lashawnda asked.

"Yes, I'm serious."

"Well then, yes. I can catch the MARTA, and I am willing to learn to type."

Cicely handed her a business card with her downtown Atlanta address on it. "Just be at the address on that card first thing tomorrow morning."

"You're kidding, right?" Lashawnda said, staring at the card.

"No, I'm not. My assistant quit on me two days ago. Plus I've got a good feeling about you."

Lashawnda continued to stare at the card and then shoved it in her back pocket. A solemn look came over her face, and a wave of fear swept over her. There was no way something this fortunate could happen to her.

"You'll be there tomorrow, right?" Cicely asked, pulling another cigarette out of her purse.

"Yes, I'll be there," Lashawnda replied, unsure what to think. She walked back into the grocery store feeling a range of emotions: happy that she'd met Cicely, but fearful that it was a big joke.

She didn't quit her job that evening but waited until the next day, after she saw that she actually had another real job with Cicely. From that day, Lashawnda had been a loyal assistant to Cicely, and Cicely had trained her or sent her to whichever computer or secretarial classes would make Lashawnda more efficient. Lashawnda absorbed her training and eventually became indispensable to Cicely in more ways than one.

That morning, they were going to be extremely busy with traffic. Tuesdays were one of their group-therapy days, and four groups of up to twelve women each would be in and out before the day was over. Plus, they were getting the office computers networked and linked to their new laser printer. To gear up for her day, Lashawnda enjoyed listening to the Morning Show. The host, Melvin Green, had been in rare form all morning. He was joking with one of his cohosts, Louisa Montero, about being twenty-nine, intelligent, beautiful, and single, with no marriage proposals in sight.

"There has to be something wrong with you that we don't know about," he joked.

Lashawnda laughed along as she pulled out her to-do list for the day. It wasn't too bad. She'd have to send out letters to all of their patients, informing them of a price increase that would go into effect at the beginning of the year. Then she had to write and mail out checks for their operating expenses. She'd also have to order monthly office supplies and call the travel agent to make arrangements for Cicely to go on a weekend vacation with several of her old college friends.

Lashawnda was not at all happy about that item on her list. She was disappointed that Cicely hadn't invited her to join them, for several reasons. The trip was scheduled for the first weekend of December, which was the weekend of Lashawnda's thirtieth birthday. Besides, Lashawnda had never been to a tropical island—as a matter of fact, she had never even been to Florida. Finally, most everybody else was bringing their significant others, so why was Cicely hesitant about introducing Lashawnda as hers?

As she put out the sign-in sheet for the first group, "Women Conquering Manic Depression," she couldn't help but feel a little depressed herself. She had expected her new relationship with Cicely to be a change for the better. After giving in to Cicely, whose sexual advances she'd spent nearly two years dodging and overlooking, Lashawnda had thought that things would be better for her. Once they expressed their feelings for each other, Cicely had asked Lashawnda to move into her four-bedroom house out in Alpharetta. They'd shared that arrangement since the beginning of the summer.

She was confident that sharing a relationship with Cicely, who had been so generous to her, would be better than any of the dead-end abusive relationships, one after another, she had been stuck in—which was why she crossed the line and decided to give Cicely a chance. And why not? She was a much better catch than any of the lowlife, ghetto-assed, trifling, inconsiderate, broke men she'd fallen in love with. And for what? They never gave her anything but a hard way to go, a headache, and a trip to the clinic for penicillin. Since Cicely had been in her life, she'd finally gotten the opportunity to experience what it felt like to be showered with gifts, nice dinners, and new, good-quality clothes.

Her way of thinking and way of living had improved. She could run that office blindfolded. In the spring, she would be taking her first college courses. She was becoming cultured and was actually reading for enjoyment. Before Cicely, none of that would have been possible or worth her time. Back then, she was only trying to survive. So whenever she thought about there not being a "she and Cicely," she thought about who she had been before she met Cicely and remembered how lucky she was to have such a terrific girlfriend. So what if she'd never met any of Cicely's friends or family?

Cicely walked through the doors of her office. "Lashawnda, could you turn the radio down, just a little?"

Lashawnda sighed, certain that she had the volume properly adjusted, but it was Cicely's office, and Lashawnda didn't want to do anything that would be distracting to the environment.

"I asked Mrs. Bland to come in a few minutes before group. She got into it with Bernard again. Could you send her back to my office as soon as she gets here?"

"Okay," Lashawnda said.

"I'm so excited about this trip. Let me know as soon as you get my travel arrangements made, okay? And I do want to fly first-class." Cicely floated back into her office like she was on top of the world.

"No problem," Lashawnda responded, but she cringed inside. She hadn't really been attracted to Cicely since she'd moved in with her. That magical mystique, or whatever it was that had caused Lashawnda to be drawn to Cicely, was gradually wearing off. Some days, Lashawnda couldn't believe they actually shared a bed. She cared about Cicely—it might even have been love at one time—but the thrill was definitely gone. Not even the memory of their first night together worked anymore.

Nonetheless, she would never forget it. Cicely had invited Lashawnda over to her house for a working dinner, but it wasn't the meal or the sexy gown that Cicely was walking around in that enticed her. It was a mixture of the wine and the words that Cicely said to her that touched her heart and opened up her soul to Cicely. After dinner, Lashawnda joined her in the living room, where she put on contemporary jazz music as they sat around talking about relationships and people and life while sipping on good wine.

Cicely continued pouring wine into their glasses. "Lashawnda, I know you've had a tough life," she said empathetically, "but I would like to commend you on the progress you've made over the last two years."

"Thanks, girl," Lashawnda replied.

"I remember when I first met you. You were rough around the edges. But look at you now. You're absolutely transformed. No one would believe that you were ever a grocery bagger." She lit a cigarette.

Lashawnda knew that she had come a long way, but it made her uncomfortable when Cicely talked about it. It always made her feel like she owed Cicely something.

"Look at you—you're so beyond those lowlifes you used to deal with, but they never deserved you anyway." Cicely stared at Lashawnda, who was lounging on the sofa. Cicely eyed her legs, curvaceous figure, and young, pretty-girl face. Most people thought Lashawnda looked like a teenager. She was nicely dressed in a pantsuit that Cicely had bought for her, and her hair and makeup both looked great, thanks to the pointers from her hairdresser, Leon, who Cicely hooked her up with.

"Yeah, I know, and right now I'm not in a hurry to jump into another dead-end relationship. Shit, I'm thinking about becoming celibate."

Cicely laughed. "I don't think you need to go that far. You just need to make sure the next time you give yourself to someone, they appreciate the gift you're offering them."

"Yeah, you have a point." Lashawnda always talked candidly about relationships with Cicely, even though she knew her sexual preference was for women. "But I believe that the emotion or love thing only deals with the way two people feel about each other and is separate from the actual act of sex."

Cicely blew one last puff and put out her cigarette. Then she slid closer to Lashawnda, "From what you're telling me, Lashawnda, you've never made love."

She moved closer, put her arms around Lashawnda's shoulder and whispered, "But that's okay. One day you'll get the opportunity to experience what it feels like to exchange sensual pleasures with someone who will have your heart in mind."

Lashawnda's first thought had been to move away, but the wine convinced her that it would be okay to stay, that there would be plenty of time to get out of Cicely's grip. In the meantime, having a caring body close, even if for a short period of time, felt good.

"Lashawnda, you are a beautiful woman and you deserve to be touched and caressed and kissed in all the right places. You deserve to have someone listen to your body and answer its every call."

Her heart raced. Cicely was right. She did deserve those things, and she longed for them. She took another drink.

Cicely put her other arm around the front of her and rested her hand on her shoulder, allowing her elbow to drape over her breast. She whispered, "Don't you want to feel good? I mean, really good?"

Lashawnda closed her eyes. The answer was yes, but she didn't say a word. She sat there, debating the pros and cons of giving into Cicely's sensual seduction. What did she have to lose? She would give in to Cicely, get it over with, and never go there with her again. Then she would never have to wonder again what it would be like to be with a woman because she would know. It would be her little secret.

But what if she liked it? What would her life be like if she fell for Cicely?

Two glasses of wine later and Lashawnda let go of all inhibition, opening herself to experiencing what Cicely was dishing out. As she promised, Cicely was attentive and pleasing. Being intimate with her was intense, yet soft and endearing.

When Lashawnda had left for her own apartment the next morning, she couldn't get the sweet feeling of being with Cicely out of her mind. She'd never before experienced that kind of intimate closeness with any man. She wanted more of that feeling, and she kept going back to Cicely to receive it. Now she was beginning to wonder if she'd made a mistake.

One of Lashawnda's favorite songs came on over the radio, and she nudged up the volume a bit. Just then, Mrs. Bland walked into the receptionist area. She had a black eye. Lashawnda turned the radio back down.

"Good morning, Mrs. Bland. Dr. Hayes is waiting for you in her office. You can go on back." Trying to ignore how hideous her eye looked, Lashawnda buzzed Cicely to inform her that her patient had arrived. She learned early on that it was better not to ask the patients questions.

"Thank you," Mrs. Bland said, walking to the back.

Lashawnda nudged up the radio volume again and tried to lose herself in the world of the Morning Show. She wasn't sure if she wanted a relationship with her boss; she wasn't even sure if she would prefer to be with a man. She was lost, but Lashawnda was a survivor. She knew for sure that she was way better off than she had been three years ago, and that had to count for something, didn't it?

6

DUTY CALLS

CATARA EYED HER watch as she waited for her client to open the fitting-room door. Mrs. LaRue, her last client scheduled for the day, was usually a breeze to shop for, but today she was being giddy and indecisive. She was a widow and had begun a new affair with a younger man; she wanted to update her wardrobe. Catara had several items waiting for her when she arrived, but anything that made her look five years younger scared her, and the usual clothing lines she gravitated toward were suddenly too stuffy and "just not me."

Normally, such a fashion dilemma was a challenge Catara would have gladly met, but she'd scheduled an interview with a young, trailblazing designer, Frederick Yarborough, who was looking for an apprentice. He liked the designs Catara had sent him. Unfortunately the only meeting time he had available cut into the client schedule she'd already prepared for the day. She attempted to reschedule some of them, but none budged. If she moved Mrs. LaRue along quickly enough, then she would be able to get to her interview on time. Otherwise . . . she didn't want to think about "otherwise."

"Catara, you can come in," Mrs. LaRue said, opening the door to the spacious fitting room.

Catara crossed her fingers and walked inside. "So what do you think?" she asked as she gazed at Mrs. LaRue, who was wearing a full-length ball gown and standing on top of a dressing square, staring at herself in the mirror with a sheepish grin plastered on her face.

"I think this is it!" Mrs. LaRue chirped.

"I knew you'd like this one," Catara said as she sat back on the sofa both to allow Mrs. LaRue the opportunity to admire herself and also to prevent herself from showing that she was truly frantic about ending this session and moving on to her interview.

"It's a good start," Mrs. LaRue said sternly, "but it's only the beginning. I will be attending a number of affairs with Rupert. I'm going to need everything from comfy casual to more of this elegant after-seven to intimate apparel."

Catara gasped. She could barely believe her ears. This was going to take all evening.

"Don't worry, Catara, I know you can do this. You've always done a great job of finding the perfect items for me."

Catara wanted to pass out on the sofa. Her limbs were weak. There was no way around it, she was going to miss her interview.

"Is there a problem?" Mrs. LaRue asked, seemingly concerned.

Although it was taboo for a shopper to cut a meeting short with a client, Catara felt that because she'd been working with Mrs. LaRue since she began at Saks, the woman would be flexible. Catara cleared her throat. "Mrs. LaRue, I hate to ask this of you, but I have a very important appointment scheduled today. How about I work with you for thirty minutes more and get a better feel for what you want. Then I'll put together some things, you can come back in a day or two, and we'll go from there."

Mrs. LaRue came off the dressing platform. "I'm sorry, Catara. I thought I made clear that this all has to be done immediately, especially since some things might need to be altered. Rupert and I are flying to Palm Beach at the end of the week. I don't have a couple of days." She turned back toward the mirror and smoothed the sides of her dress. "I'm sure you can reschedule your other appointment," she said nonchalantly. Then she stepped back up on the platform. "Now, Catara, do you think this hem should be lifted a bit?"

Catara pulled herself off the sofa, walked over to Mrs. LaRue, and examined the dress. "I'll call the seamstress in and get right to finding some more things for you to try on. In the meantime, would you like some more wine?"

"No, thank you. My head is already spinning from the first glass."

Catara walked out of the dressing room, found the seamstress, and sent her in to Mrs. LaRue, then headed toward a telephone to make the dreaded call.

When she asked Frederick to reschedule, he didn't yell. He didn't fuss. His words were nice, even, and sharp as a sword: "I was really looking forward to meeting with you because I like your work. You were one of my top candidates. But Miss Edwards, I know you must be a very busy woman, so I wouldn't dare insult you by rescheduling."

Catara was speechless. She knew she'd blown an opportunity of a lifetime, but she had to get back to the job that was currently paying the bills. She tried not to think about what had just happened, because if she did, she wouldn't have been able to go on. Instead, she rushed to the display floor and began to search the racks for clothes for her client. She braced herself because she knew it was going to be a long afternoon.

CATARA RUSHED UP the stairs and out of the subway station. She was glad to be away from Saks. The dial was already set to her favorite radio station, which she faithfully listened to on her walk home. The evening DJ had a sexy voice and was witty; plus, he played short recaps of what happened on the syndicated show that aired every morning.

She tuned in just in time to catch the end of the update. Melvin Green was announcing the Morning Show's new contest for single women. "Attention all single ladies—listen up because Louisa Montero has special contest details that she'd like to share with you."

Catara adjusted the volume. Although she never called or wrote in, she loved to be informed of the wild and varying giveaways the show always came up with.

"Ladies, this is Louisa Montero. I have a birthday fast approaching, and although we women don't like to give our ages away, I'll share mine if you share yours. I'm going to be thirty on December first! Because it's such a pivotal time in a woman's life, I'd like to share my special day with other women whose birthdays fall on December first. That's right, five others approaching thirty will travel with me to sunny South Beach, where we're going to stay at the lovely Royal Palm Crowne Plaza Resort Hotel and be catered to with spa treatments and a mini shopping spree. Then we're going to stroll down famous Ocean Drive and take in the sights and sounds of the beach. On our special day, we're going to take a one-day cruise to the Grand Bahama Islands, where we'll spend four hours touring Freeport and Port Lucaya, and then we'll cruise back that evening while indulging in fine dining, gambling, and whatever else we can get ourselves into."

Melvin Green cut in. "That's right ladies, it's the Night Before Thirty Relaxation Party Weekend, and you just might find yourself indulging in the beauty of tropical climates while bringing in your thirtieth right! All you have to do is write us one page stating why you deserve to spend your thirtieth birthday lounging in the lap of luxury."

Catara gulped. Finally, a contest just for her. What were the odds of she and Louisa Montero having the same birthday? Plus, after all the hard work she'd put in at Saks, her ordeal with Rondell, and missing the appointment of a lifetime, she mentally claimed her spot at the spa, the shopping spree, and the cruise. As she trekked her way to her apartment, she imagined what hanging out with Louisa Montero would be like. She couldn't wait until she got home to begin scribbling down why she should be chosen for the weekend getaway.

7

ALMOST PARADISE

ALECIA ROLLED OVER and wrapped her arm around William's waist. The San Diego sun was setting over the Pacific Ocean, and the soft, warm breeze blowing from the water onto the terrace of the beachfront suite was turning cool. The two had been lying there in the wide lawn chair for the past few hours and had fallen asleep to the sound of the waves hitting the beach.

Alecia was disappointed—being awake meant that she would again begin counting time. It was their second day alone together, and she didn't want their special weekend to come to an end. She nudged herself closer to him and savored the moment, because William, in that time and space, belonged only to her. She had his undivided attention.

He looked so peaceful sleeping next to her in his swim trunks that she couldn't help but sneak a quick kiss on his cheek. Then she took the back of her hand and stroked his cheek, allowing her hand to brush past his neck, down to his chest. More days of intimate solitude with him would not be enough to quench her desire to belong to him forever.

William awoke with a smile on his face and yawned. "Uumm, this feels good."

"Me touching you?"

"You, the breeze, the beach. All of it."

"I know," she said wistfully. "I could stay like this forever."

"Me too," he agreed.

William eased up in the chair so that he could get a better view of his surroundings. Alecia adjusted her position accordingly.

"Breathtaking," he commented of the red and blue hues that mixed together and surrounded the huge sun as it set, looking as if it were gradually submerging into the ocean.

"Breathtaking," Alecia sighed.

The two remained silent as they watched the sun gradually sink until it was no more. What had been a fairly active beach earlier in the day had now become deserted and romantic, sexy.

"I love it when it's like this. It feels like we're the only two people on our own deserted island," William said.

"Uh-huh," Alecia agreed.

"So do we continue like this, starving, or do we eat?" he asked.

"We starve."

"We could. But I say we eat."

"Let's order room service and stay in all night," she suggested.

"We did that last night. Don't you want to see the city?"

"I've seen the city, several times. We both have."

"But there's a new spot downtown that I have to go to tonight."

"Oh, so this is a business trip?" Alecia was disheartened. She had thought the weekend was only about his wanting to do something special for her.

"Not exactly. Well, kind of—John, a client of mine, recently purchased the club. I just have to make an appearance. We can eat on the waterfront, and then we can go to the club." William squeezed her tight. "You can work me out on the floor, and then we can come back here and you can finish off the job."

Alecia pouted a bit, but she knew there was no way around it. She had to go.

She lay there a while longer then forced herself up. "I'm taking a shower." She yawned. "You can join me if you'd like." She winked at him and posed between the sliding-glass door.

"It's tempting, but if I do that, we'll never get out of here." William reached over to the table next to the chair, picked up his Palm, and began fidgeting with it.

Alecia hated being ignored, especially by William, and it was tough for her to accept that all the stops had been pulled and there was nothing more she could do except get dressed and join him for a night on the town.

DOWNTOWN SAN DIEGO was exhilarating. Once in the midst of the action, she was pleasantly surprised that it was just the change of scenery that she and William needed. There were lots of new buildings, condos, hotels, and restaurants, all nestled in the midst of clean streets and plush green landscaping, only blocks away from scenic views of boats and floating yachts.

The new nightclub was located on Fourth Street, in the heart of downtown. They ate dinner at a quaint little restaurant on the waterfront, and afterward, instead of driving their rental to the club, William motioned for a bike-pulled rickshaw. He and Alecia piled in the buggy.

"Fourth Street and D, near Horton Plaza. I'll tell you when to stop," William said to the driver, who began to pedal down the street. Although he didn't seem strong enough to handle the weight of the two of them, he moved them along at a steady pace. The breeze circulated around them and they sat close, holding hands, taking in the naturally beautiful sights and sounds of the city.

"Some of the men here will have their wives with them. And some of them know . . ." He paused. He struggled saying her name. "Phyllis. There might be a few awkward moments."

"What do you mean?" Alecia demanded.

"Well, there might be moments when . . . well, you know what I'm saying."

"No, I don't, William."

"I'm not going to completely ignore you, Alecia. I'm just saying that I might not be able to hold your hand as much as I normally do."

"I understand." Alecia felt numb. What could she say? Nothing. She knew her place in their relationship. This, however, would be the first time she would have it shoved in her face.

The two sat in silence the rest of the way. Alecia combated her hurt by focusing on her surroundings. Around her the streets were filled with laid-back patrons walking in and out of restaurants and shops. Although the downtown was heavily populated, a feeling of relaxation was in the air.

William seemed a bit uneasy.

"I could catch a cab back," she offered dryly.

"What are you talking about? Sweetheart, I want you with me. Just scratch what I said from the record, and let's have a good time."

Alecia frowned and pouted, attempting to garner sympathy from him. Anytime she could make William feel guilty, she milked it dry.

"Please, don't be upset, Jewel," he said, putting his arm around her and kissing her on the cheek. "Don't you worry about anything. You are my princess and I don't care who knows."

Alecia smiled widely. *I am Alecia Jewel Parker, and men love me. All men love me. And you, William, are no exception,* she thought.

Their driver stopped in front of the club, as directed by William. He hopped off the bike, took Alecia's hand, and gently escorted her out. Then he helped William, who paid him. William then put his hand at the small of Alecia's back and they walked toward the club. He gave their names to the guy at the door, and the two walked right in.

Inside, there was an open, airy feel. The walls were high and the color scheme typical of a nightclub. It was bright, inviting, exciting. The music was upbeat hip-hop, the clientele a mixture of ethnicities and sexual preferences. It was the kind of spot that Alecia thrived in, felt most comfort being in, because of the common link among the majority of the partygoers: most were packing money or power, and she was always up for meeting more people with dinero. It affirmed to her that she was in the right place at the right time. That all was well with her life.

William grabbed her hand. It wasn't as natural as usual, but deliberate. "The VIP room is in the back—let's go." Alecia followed. When they got to the velvet rope, the owner, John, was talking to another guy in front of the entrance.

"William!" he said cheerfully when he spotted them walking up. "I'd like you to meet my good friend Al."

William bear-hugged John and shook Al's hand. "Al, Will is my overpriced attorney. Al is a major contractor out here in San Diego," John said, introducing the two.

"This is the one I've been telling you about, John. This is Alecia."

"Nice to meet you," John said. "Absolutely gorgeous." He took her hand and kissed it.

Alecia smiled, then shook Al's hand.

John said something to William, and then patted Al on the back.

William reached in his pocket, pulled out his platinum card, and placed it in her hand. "Alecia, go inside the VIP room. Order yourself a drink. Start a tab, and I'll be right in."

Alecia sternly eyed William, not sure if she was being brushed off. He slowly and gently kissed her on the cheek. "Baby, I'll be right in. I know you'll have no problem handling yourself. I'm right behind you."

Alecia turned away from him and waved at the guy at the rope. He looked up at John, who motioned for him to let her enter, and Alecia walked in.

Few people were inside. Alecia considered it evidence of the elite clientele—because everybody was on the same social level, there was no one to be separated from. She scoped the scene, and no one stood out or caught her eye. It was a cosmopolitan crowd across the line.

She approached the bar and ordered an apple martini. To the right of her was an African who was intensely watching her every move. He seemed desperate to know her, so she made a more concerted effort to ignore him. To the left of her were three women in cocktail dresses wearing clusters of diamonds on their fingers, reflecting years of marriage. They were too mature and would probably be threatened by her, so she didn't even bother speaking to them.

The bartender came back with her drink. "I'll handle that," the guy standing to her left said in a heavy Nigerian accent.

"It won't be necessary. It's already taken care of," she said and handed the bartender William's card. "I'd like to start a tab with that. He'll be in shortly."

"No problem," the bartender said, and walked away with the card.

"What is your name, pretty lady?"

After checking him out from head to toe, Alecia concluded that although he had some cash, his money was probably not enough. She began going through her limited Nigerian vocabulary, trying to remember if one of her Nigerian beaus had taught her to say "Fuck off" in their language.

"You are a beautiful American lady. They will love you where I'm from. You remind me of the Ethiopian women in Africa."

Alecia knew his type and was not in the mood. She knew that if she moved, he would follow, so she weighed her options and decided it was time to make nice with the married women to her left.

She quickly turned toward them and inched closer, searching for an opening line.

"Cute watch. Van Cleef and Arpels?"

"Exactly," the lady responded, surprised.

"Very nice. I purchased a similar one for my mom for Mother's Day."

"You have good taste." The lady smiled. "My husband got this for me 'just because.'"

She returned the smile.

Alecia's first inclination was to avoid conversing with the women and go back out to where William was, but her curiosity got the better of her.

"This is my first time visiting this club. Have any of you come here before tonight?" She knew it was a corny question, but it was worth the information it would bring.

"The two of us have come here more often than we'd like to admit," another answered, then took a sip of wine. "My husband recently bought this place. It's like a big playpen for him. But it is Phyllis's first time," the woman answered, gesturing at the woman with the Van Cleef & Arpels watch. "She's visiting from Los Angeles."

No way! Alecia screamed inside. *This can't be. She can't possibly be William's wife.*

"By the way, I'm Donna Lake, this is Renee Border, and this is our friend Phyllis Masterson."

So this is my competition, Alecia thought. She sized up Phyllis, not able to find any flaws. Obviously well kept, Phyllis was elegantly and tastefully dressed. Alecia would expect nothing less in the woman William married.

"Nice meeting you, ladies," she said as calmly as possible, and excused herself without bothering to give them her name. Alecia wasn't sure if she should alert William or allow him to be busted and force him to make a choice.

Her adrenaline was flowing overtime. She walked away from the bar so quickly that she left her drink sitting there. Once she got a few feet away, she realized she didn't have a plan; she froze and found herself standing in the middle of the VIP room, looking dumbfounded. She knew this was her one opportunity to find out where she really stood in William's life. If the shit hit the fan and the three of them had a face-off, she would find out who was number one. But her gut told her to leave it alone. Deep down, she knew the real answer: William would choose his wife.

So she forged ahead out of the VIP room and sought William. When she found him, he was standing at the bar, alone, with a drink in his hand. His face was pale, and he looked as spooked as Alecia felt. When he saw her, he downed the rest of his drink, walked quickly toward her, and grabbed her hand. Pulling her along he fought through the crowd, practically dragging her behind him until they got to the front entrance.

He grabbed the guy at the door. "Could you call us a cab?" He turned to Alecia and said in an uneasy tone, "I've got to get you out of here."

"Why, William? I'm having a good time," she responded as if she didn't know.

"She's here, Alecia."

"Who's here, William?"

"It's Phyllis. She wanted to surprise me, so she rearranged her schedule and flew in tonight. She's here, at the club."

"You're going with me, right?" she asked. She moved close to him to make sure he couldn't avoid eye contact.

"Alecia, you know I can't do that." He tried to look at her but quickly turned his face away.

Reality stung and lingered. The tears in her eyes said what her words couldn't.

"I'm sorry."

"So are you coming back to the suite?"

William lightly grasped her arms with his hands. Then he held her in an embrace. "Alecia, I do love you, so I hope you understand when I say that I need you to vacate the room before I get back."

"What?" Alecia cried. She became furious. "Don't touch me," she said, pushing him off her.

"Where am I supposed to go?" she demanded.

"Jewel, calm down. You have my card, right?"

"No, the bartender has your card."

"Well, put a room on your card. I'll take care of it. I always do, right?"

William was becoming antsy, and every time the door of the club opened, he shot a look over his shoulder. He reached into his pocket and pulled out a wad of cash. "This should take care of your cabs between the hotels and your transportation to the airport tomorrow."

He moved closer to her and leaned down. "I'll make sure we're not on the same flight. We'll leave later in the day."

"This is just great," Alecia sulked. She wanted him to feel guilty, but not just guilty enough to buy her more things. She wanted him really to consider life without her. "William, you leave me no other choice but to leave you for good. I'm going to leave L.A. altogether. Don't bother calling, because I don't ever want to see you again."

"Don't do this to me, Alecia—to us. We'll work this out when I get back. I promise. Don't make any irrational decisions."

The cab pulled up, and William rushed to it and opened the door. "I'll call you," he said. Then he told the driver where to take Alecia and put her inside. "I'll call you," he said again, and shut the door.

8

IN THE LIFE

THE MUSIC WAS bumping and everybody in the nightclub had moved into a comfortable party zone. Tanya and Chris were in his favorite booth, flanked with Cristal Champagne and some of Chris's closest homeboys from the neighborhood. Chris had been supporting his boy T-Roy's nightclub, the Palladium, for the past three years.

Tanya used to love being there with Chris, because when they were in the Palladium, T-Roy made sure that they received star treatment. All eyes on them, they usually spent the evening getting pissy-drunk and partying until the lights came on. But lately Tanya had not been in the mood to be around Chris's bullshit-talking, lying-ass, thug friends. There was no substance to their conversations, only bottle after bottle of overpriced champagne, each guy trying to outdo the other with stories of their latest purchase. None of their girlfriends had jobs, and all the women talked about was what their "boos" got for them hot off the streets.

Tanya wanted out of the lifestyle badly. The older she became, the more the world she knew so well and once enjoyed suddenly seemed foreign and scary and unappealing.

"A'ight, my mother-fuckin' niggas, listen up 'cause Big C got some-thing to say." Chris held up his glass to make a toast. All eight people who were squeezed into the round booth held up their glasses except Tanya.

Chris looked at her. "Put your glass up, baby, I'm making a toast."

"I don't feel like it," she said. He couldn't hear her because the music was so loud, but she knew Chris wouldn't rest until everyone had their glasses up, so she raised hers.

"I just want to say . . ." Chris began, and then paused to get his thoughts together.

"Come on with it. Shit, we ain't got all night," T-Roy's girlfriend, Rosario, said.

"Okay, baby, okay. I'm gonna bring it. Listen up. I just want to say I'm deeply honored to be with my boys and all you lovely ladies. Especially you, T-Roy. Man, you been holding it down here at the Palladium. You brought the heat from the jump, and this place is still on fire!" Chris put his glass down and then lifted it again. "Excuse me, I get a little emotional sometimes, but I just want to say that whatever goes down, whenever it goes down, or if ever it goes down, just call me, man. I got yo' back."

"For sho," T-Roy said, and touched glasses with him.

"Word is bond," another friend said. Everybody drank from their glasses.

A new P. Diddy joint with a heavy beat thumped through the club and Rosario said, "That's my jam!"

She moved her way out to the front of their table and began to dance. Only, she took her moving to the beat to an extreme; without removing her clothes, she was basically performing a striptease.

"Okay, Rosario, baby, that's enough!" T-Roy said, and grabbed her by the arm.

"Uh-uh, let me go. That's my song," she said and maneuvered herself away from him, swinging her hips and rolling her body seductively.

"I'm not gonna tell you again. This is my establishment, and these are my friends. Don't be trippin' tonight!" T-Roy demanded.

Rosario kept dancing as if she didn't notice T-Roy becoming annoyed and disgusted. He jumped out of his seat, picked up Rosario, and carried her to a corner in the club. The whole time, she yelled at him, "Let me down! Let me down, T-Roy!"

Chris leaned over to Tanya. "I told T-Roy he needed to let that bitch go. She ain't nothing but a little tramp. Always trippin'. She's fucking up his image around here."

Tanya was zoning. She wanted badly to leave but knew Chris enjoyed being out with his friends like this every weekend. Although there was no thrill for her, being out with Chris was a duty that came with being his girlfriend.

He picked up on her dispirited mood.

"You okay, baby?" he asked her.

"I'm not feeling too well," she replied. "I was thinking about turning in early, but I don't want to interrupt your fun."

"Nah, baby, that's cool with me. I was thinking about blowing this joint early myself. I'm not feeling it tonight. For real," Chris said. He grabbed her hand and squeezed. He poked out his lips and asked, "You think you can drive tonight? I've had a little too much to drink."

"Yeah, I can." Tanya smiled softly at him. Damn, she loved this man; she just hated the element he surrounded himself with.

"Look, let's just wait until T-Roy gets back, pay our respects and then we're out. Okay?" He kissed her on the forehead. "Now, hit me with a little more of the bubbly, bubbly!"

Tanya picked up the bottle and raised it to fill Chris's glass.

Suddenly T-Roy rushed the table and grabbed Chris by his leather jacket. "Come on, man, I need you." There was rage in his voice, and his eyes were frenzied.

Chris jumped out of his seat. "What's up, man?"

"That nigga Payne is out front with about ten of his boys trying to get in. Man, I can't let them in here. You know they start trouble everywhere they go."

"What you wanna do, man?" Chris asked, putting his hand on his piece.

"The bouncers should be able to handle it, but man, we need to be up there for backup so there won't be no question of who has the power."

"I got you, man," Chris said and motioned for their other two friends, who were sitting with them, to get up and follow them.

Chris kneeled in to Tanya. "Stay right here, baby. When I get back let's get the fuck outta here." He took off with his boys.

A chill ran through Tanya, and her fingers tapped against the table. She didn't know what was going on. As badly as she wanted to know, she was going to do what he said and stay put. The other two women at the table scooted over to her.

"What in the hell is going on?" one said, popping her gum between words.

"I don't know," Tanya replied. She thought that if the expression on her face was as filled with worry as the two beside her, then whatever was going down couldn't be good.

"I'm getting ready to go see for myself," the other said.

"No, Chris said to wait here. They'll be all right. . . ." Tanya began trying to convince herself as well, but before she could finish talking, several gunshots were fired from the front of the club, setting off chaos. The music stopped instantly. Women were screaming, and a rush of people on the dance floor moved at once to one end of the floor. Several just fell to the ground in the hope of not being hit by a stray bullet. The people at private tables were seeking cover underneath their tables, including Tanya and the women with her.

Rumbling could be heard near the club's front entrance. Tanya knew Chris was in the midst of the brawling. But there was nothing she could do but wait, panic-stricken, to find out if he was okay.

She was wedged underneath a table with two women she barely knew. There was no comfort in being next to them, so she squeezed her eyes tight and said a short, silent prayer: *Dear Lord, I don't ask much from you, but please protect Chris for me, because I love him and he's all I've got.*

Just then, another shot was fired, more rustling, and then one loud, startling scream.

"That's Rosario!" Tanya said, and instinctively moved from underneath the booth. Her heart was racing, but she couldn't stop herself from going toward the direction of Rosario's cry of distress. She had to see what had happened. The lights flashed on.

The chill from earlier revisited her spine. She moved through the confused and frightened partygoers and pushed her way to the front of the club, where Rosario was bent over T-Roy, who was laid out in a puddle of blood.

"No, no, no!" Rosario was yelling and banging on his chest with her fist. Tears were pouring down her cheeks, and blood was all over her hands and splashed on her halter top.

One of the guys who was at the table with them earlier reached down and pulled her off T-Roy's corpse. "T-Roy, no!" Rosario yelled as the guy carried her outside and away from T-Roy's dead body.

Tanya's stomach bubbled over. She felt like she was going to puke, but she couldn't give in to the feeling. She needed to find Chris.

Nothing seemed real. Everybody and everything seemed to be moving in slow motion. Then Tanya noticed that outside of the opened door were two other bodies. Dead. Tanya was terrified to go near them. *One of them has to be him,* she thought. She couldn't bear to face Chris's death. Her legs grew weak and she heard somebody yell, "The ambulance is coming!"

Scattered, Tanya somehow found a wall to catch her from passing out. There was movement around her, and voices, but Tanya had to pause. She didn't want to move forward and face the inevitable, so she just stood there, allowing the wall to sustain her until she was surrounded by a warm hug.

It was Chris. Tanya fell into his arms and wept. She took deep, heavy breaths to release the energy she'd been reserving to handle the news that he'd been shot.

Chris rocked her in his arms. "I can't believe this shit!" he said. There was anger behind his words. "T-Roy is gone, Tanya," he said. His head fell on her shoulder.

"I know," she said, and embraced him tighter.

"We gotta get outta here."

"What?" Tanya needed a moment. The thought of moving from that spot seemed too much.

Chris grabbed Tanya's face and met her eye to eye. "We gotta go."

She understood. There was nothing more they could do for T-Roy. He was already dead. But Chris was alive and an adversary of the police. He didn't need to be anywhere near such a horrific crime scene.

He hugged her tightly one more time, then took her hand and led her out the back door of the club.

9

GRAND OPENING

ORE CHILDREN AND parents were flowing through the gym than Elise had planned for, but instead of panicking, she delighted in their overwhelming interest and quietly thanked God that people were not only interested but signing their children up for classes.

Every hour on the hour, from twelve noon until six P.M., the five high school and college student instructors walked onto the floor and gave a presentation. They had gotten to the last presentation of the day, and Elise was exhausted from talking to parents, meeting children, and answering questions. Just knowing that the day was winding to an end, however, gave Elise the energy she needed to go on. She asked the parents and potential students to take their seats surrounding the floor, while the instructors stood to the side.

Elise introduced the Gotta Flip staff and their mission to the audience.

"Hello, everyone, and thanks for coming out today. I am Elise Ross, owner and head instructor. At Gotta Flip, where our motto is 'safety comes first in our progressive learning environment,' we offer high-quality instruction while using the best available equipment.

"If you're wondering if I'm qualified to instruct your children, the answer is yes. I am a three-time college national medalist in rhythmic gymnastics. Also, I was privileged to study under international gold medalist Wendy Hilliard, the first African American gymnast to represent the United States on the rhythmic gymnastics national team. I was a member of the U.S. Rhythmic Gymnastics Olympic team, but I couldn't compete because of an unfortunate knee injury during the trials.

"Because of that injury, safety is essential to my coaching method. I, as well as the rest of my coaching staff, have been safety certified by USA Gymnastics. If you are searching for a gym and decide that we are not right for you, for the sake of your child, please make sure that the instructors at the gym of your choice have been safety certified.

"I can't promise that your child will be one hundred percent free of injury—no coach can—but I *can* guarantee that the instructors here will take every measure to prevent accidents from occurring. Speaking of instructors, please allow me to introduce my staff to you!"

As Elise introduced the instructors one by one, each entered the floor with an impressive tumbling pass, garnering oohs and aahs from the audience. When all five coaches were standing next to her, she continued talking.

"I'm going to let our senior instructor, Mike, have the floor. He'll explain to you the various levels of instruction available, and then we'll break out and allow everyone a chance to become briefly acquainted with all aspects of our offerings, including beam, bars, and vault.

"After you've spent time at each station, one of the ladies at the desk will help you get your child registered in the wonderful world of gymnastics. Both ladies are well informed about rates, payment options, and class schedules. Remember, if you register your child for a full semester today, he or she gets a free Gotta Flip T-shirt. If you have any more questions at the end of the hour, please see me and I'll do my very best to answer them for you."

Elise handed the microphone to Mike, who continued with the presentation. She walked over to the desk to check in with the two older women who were helping for the day. While the new presentation was going on, there were still straggling parents with questions or those who wanted to see the presentation a second time before making a decision. Some wanted to speak with Elise personally, to ask her questions that had already been answered more than once during the course of the hour.

"How are you ladies holding up?" Elise asked.

The women were members of Elise's church and recent retirees. When Elise had approached them for their help, they enthusiastically agreed and offered their services. One was a retired accountant and the other a secretary; Hattie helped Elise keep the Gotta Flip finances together, and Darlene helped her remain well organized.

"Whew, child! I tell you what, who would've ever thought that this many black people would be interested in gymnastics?" Hattie said.

"Yeah, if I'd of known you were gonna have this kind of turnout I would have asked my sister to come over and help us," said Darlene.

"Ladies, I apologize. I wasn't expecting such a great response myself."

"I was a little worried about you, to be honest. I didn't think you had a leg to stand on trying to teach gymnastics over here. But I'm glad to say you're proving me wrong," Hattie said.

"Oh, so you've been talking about me?" Elise teased.

"Now, you know Hattie talks about everybody. It gives her something to do," Darlene said as she opened a box of file folders. "Ms. Elise, you see all of those parents standing over there in the store area who seem to be so interested in your merchandise? Well, all of them want to speak with you personally."

"You can't be serious," Elise said, staring at the ten or more parents.

"Here, take a bottle of water with you and get to work. You've got an establishment to build," Hattie said, and smiled. "You know, we're proud of you."

Elise took the bottle. "Thank you, Mrs. Hattie. I'm glad to know I meet your approval," she said with a grin, and headed to speak to the parents.

As Elise walked off she heard Hattie say to Darlene, "Now, let's just see if she can keep it up."

She shrugged the comment off because she knew Hattie, in her own warped way, meant well.

By the time Elise said good-bye to her last family, she was tired, starving, and ready to get off her feet. She walked the couple and their seven-year-old daughter out and assured them that before they knew it, their daughter would be asking when it was time to go back to Gotta Flip every week. She walked them out, locked the door, fell back against it, and breathed a sigh of relief.

"Whew, child, we put some work in here today," Hattie said, as she stood up from her chair to stretch her legs. Darlene was creating the last few files for the students who had registered that day.

"We did, didn't we?" Elise said as she took a look at her worn-out staff. The instructors were all lying around in the middle of the floor. Elise was so pleased at the way things had turned out that she knew she would never be able to show her full appreciation to everyone. Nobody had slacked on the job, and their attitudes were pleasant, despite the chaotic day.

"First, before I forget, your friend Allen called to wish you good luck," Hattie said.

"Awww," some of the staff members gushed, teasing Elise.

"Yeah, he's a nice fella. We had a good conversation. I like him and I think he's right fond of you, Elise."

"He's just being nice," Elise responded.

"Maybe, but he asked a few personal questions about you and I had no problem answering most of them."

"What did he ask?"

"Now, that's between Allen and me," Hattie said firmly.

"Come on, Hattie," Elise begged.

Hattie gave her a firm look.

Elise knew she wouldn't budge, so she let it go. "So how did we do tonight?"

"Can you believe we registered nearly one hundred children today?" Hattie said.

"Wow!" everyone exclaimed.

"One hundred children. Are you sure?" Elise said. She moved away from the door and took a seat.

"Not one hundred. I said nearly one hundred. In this case, it means eighty-six children."

"That's still excellent. And with open registration through Thanksgiving, we should have no problem getting the enrollment number to a hundred. I saw a few kids with T-shirts—how many paid up for the semester in advance?"

"Let me see," Hattie said as she fumbled through the paperwork. "Seventeen."

"Not bad," Elise said. She stretched out along with the other instructors. "That's rent for two months," she joked.

"Or salaries, right?" Mike said.

"Right!" Elise agreed.

THE OFFICE AREA was well organized. All the new folders were in their proper place and everyone had left for the day except Elise and Mike. They had stayed to discuss the best way to schedule the coaches and classes, based on the current and projected enrollment through the end of the year.

The two grabbed their gym bags and slowly made their way toward the door, and Mike put his arm around Elise. "You're doing a good thing here, and everything is going to work out fine," he said.

"Yeah, I know. We'll be in a good position if we can get the enrollment to a hundred kids—or better—and keep it there."

"We will. We've got open house the rest of the week. People will be strolling in, and some who didn't register today will come back around." Mike stood by the door, waiting for Elise to set the alarm.

She punched in the code. Mike opened the door, and she walked out and he followed behind her.

It was a clear night. Elise looked up and she could see the stars shining.

"We can only pray," she said. She knew she'd done all she could to prepare for and promote her grand opening. And that at that point, only God could fill the classes. "I'll see you tomorrow, Mike. By the way, thanks for leaving Gym Works and coming over here with me," she said.

"No problem, believe me. For one, Gotta Flip is closer to my apartment. Two, I believe in what you are trying to do, and just by talking to you over the past month, I knew that you weren't going to half-step. Three, it feels good to be a part of history. I don't know if you realize how big a deal this is, the first gymnastics center of this magnitude in this area of town. How could I not be a part of this?"

Elise knew that what she was doing with her gym was a big deal to her, but she never considered it a historical undertaking.

"Did you hear anything?" she asked. She'd heard a slight noise from around the side of the building.

"No," he said, "but let's move quickly to our cars."

Just then a rush of footsteps came from the side of her building. Elise gasped and reached for Mike's arm. She knew something wasn't right.

The noise got louder. They turned to see what was behind them. Suddenly a man wearing a dark jacket and a black ski mask rushed them.

"Turn around and put your hands up!" he demanded.

"There is no way this is happening! There is no way this is happening!" Elise said, in her mind or out loud, she wasn't sure which. She and Mike stopped instantly and threw their hands in the air.

Mike, who was five-nine and barely heavier than Elise, was as frightened as she was, but he couldn't help looking over his shoulder.

"I said turn around," the man yelled. "You saw, right? It's a gun. Now, both of you get on your knees."

Elise and Mike slowly and carefully fell to their knees and stayed close to each other. Elise did everything within her power to remain levelheaded and calm. She looked at Mike out of the corner of her eye. He was distraught, breathing heavily, his face contorted in fear.

"Drop your bags!" he demanded.

The two removed their bags from their shoulders.

"Empty your pockets."

They pushed their hands into their pockets and pulled out their car keys.

"I don't want your cars. I just want the money!" he insisted. Then he came in close to them, hit Mike on the back of the head with his gun, snatched both bags, and took off running behind the building.

Mike held his head in his hands. He'd fallen forward, barely missing the ground.

Elise looked around to make sure the robber had left. She rushed to Mike.

"Are you okay?" she asked, trying to get a closer look at his injury.

"I'll be okay. I'm not bleeding, am I?"

She moved his hands off his head and examined him. "No, thank God! We need to go back inside to call the police," Elise said.

Mike looked up at Elise with eyes that said, "Why bother?"

"I know there isn't much that they'll do, but we have to report this," she said through the tears that had started to flow from her eyes.

"Damn, Elise. Why?" he moaned.

Elise looked at Mike. He was a sophomore in college, intelligent, talented. He was the type of guy who saw the good in people and in life. The defeat in his voice sent an uneasy vibration through her.

She shook her head. She was without answers. "Let's just go inside," she said quietly through the fog of replaying the robbery in her mind.

The two helped each other up, and then Elise reached over to pick up their keys. She stood up, feeling light-headed and having questions of her own, but she wanted to encourage Mike to ease the anger that was settling into his spirit. She handed him his keys and said, "At least he didn't take our cars. And thank God Hattie took the money with her."

"But, Elise, every book that I purchased for school this semester was in that bag. Plus, I had been saving money to get my girlfriend a watch for her birthday. I just bought it today before coming here this morning. That watch was in the bag, Elise!" he yelled, punching at the air to release some of his frustration. Tears fell from his eyes.

Elise was instantly flooded with guilt. Starting her new business, this was a lean time for her. She had no emergency cash. She didn't have enough to help Mike purchase his books again, let alone purchase another watch for his girlfriend. She knew she had to do something; she felt responsible. A lump formed in her throat. She was without words, without an easy solution, without a way to comfort Mike or herself.

10

WHAT ABOUT ME?

LASHAWNDA OPENED THE dishwasher and pulled out two travel mugs. She poured coffee into them and put one teaspoon of sugar in Cicely's and extra cream in her own. She walked over to the kitchen island, set the mugs down, and picked up her purse. Before she could pick the mugs back up, Cicely came behind her, slid her arms around her waist, and leaned over to kiss her softly on her neck.

Lashawnda cringed.

"You were extra good last night," Cicely said.

"I know I was," Lashawnda said. She had spent the night fantasizing about her favorite movie star, helping her performance with Cicely.

She picked up the coffee mugs and handed one to Cicely. "Just the way you like it."

The two walked through the kitchen to the garage.

"Okay, Lashawnda, what's going on with you?" Cicely asked, unlocking her car door.

"Nothing."

"Don't lie to me. I've noticed that something has been different with you. I just haven't been able to pinpoint what it is."

"It's nothing, Cicely."

They pulled out of the garage. Then Cicely hit the brakes at the end of the carport. "This is the last time I'm going to ask you, Lashawnda."

Lashawnda gave Cicely a blank stare. She knew that saying something to her about not being invited on vacation with her and her old college friends wouldn't help. But she couldn't hold her tongue. She was upset and she couldn't get relief unless she spoke.

"Can you believe that I'm gonna be left alone during my birthday weekend? Yeah, my girlfriend would prefer to hang with her big-time college friends than to be with a grocery bagger turned secretary." Lashawnda's best way of confronting issues was to joke through them. "Yeah, maybe once I get my college degree, maybe then I'll be worthy of attention on my birthday. Or worthy of meeting your old college friends."

"You're being unreasonable," Cicely replied calmly. But Lashawnda knew she'd struck a chord, because Cicely pushed in the car's cigarette lighter and started fumbling through her purse for cigarettes.

"No, I'm not being unreasonable, Cicely. It's my thirtieth birthday we're talking about. It should be my best party. Someone should be pulling out all the stops to make sure I have a good time."

"You're right. And I do want to celebrate with you. It's just unfortunate there's a conflict of dates. Maybe we can do something special the weekend before or after."

"Conflict of dates. Oh, so now the day I was born is a conflict with your life. Oh, so sorry, Dr. Hayes. Maybe I can go back in time and reschedule my mother's labor by a week. Would that allow things to flow better in your calendar of events for December?"

"Is all this drama necessary?"

"Wanting to spend my birthday with my lover is unreasonable?"

"No, but your drama queen antics are," Cicely replied.

"Why did you ask me to move in with you?" Lashawnda demanded.

"Why would you ask me a question like that?"

Lashawnda folded her arms and waited for an answer.

Cicely responded in her always cool, always calm, always collected tone. "If you must be told again, then I will tell you." She paused, and then continued. "I asked you to move in with me because I care about you. My place is comfortable, and I thought you'd be happier in this environment. I want you to be able to build your savings and maybe start investing."

Lashawnda opened her mouth to speak.

"Wait. I'm not finished," Cicely stopped her. "And I like holding you at night. Don't you like being close every night?"

She hated when Cicely flipped their conversations with her psychology manipulated responses but had gotten better at comebacks. "We're not talking about how good our intimacy feels. We're talking about you being too embarrassed of me to take me around your fake-ass friends." Touché.

"See, that's the kind of shit that pisses me off. You don't even know my friends, and you go and call them fake."

"Well, something must be wrong with them if you're keeping them hidden from me." Lashawnda adjusted her seat so it reclined. "Or maybe it's me who's being hidden? Funny, I'm good enough to fuck, but not good enough to accompany you to a tropical island, not good enough to know your friends. But it's cool. Don't even sweat it. I'm tired of talking about it anyway."

"It's not like that, and you know it." Cicely stared ahead of her at the congestion of the Highway 75 morning rush hour. There was no quick way around the traffic to get to the office, no way for either of them to get a breather from the conflict.

Lashawnda reached forward and turned on the radio to listen to Melvin Green and the Morning Show Crew. She knew there wasn't an excuse for Cicely's disregard for her feelings; she wanted to continue the discussion until she got a clearer understanding of why, if there was a why. No man she'd dated had ever explained why he'd abused her or talked down to her. Why should Cicely defend her shame about their relationship? There was too much going through Lashawnda's mind. Melvin Green was just the distraction she needed.

"Ladies, listen up! If you want to join Louisa Montero in tropical paradise, you've gotta get those letters in. But right now, we're looking for caller number twenty to win an all-expenses-paid trip to the New Orleans Bayou Classic for Thanksgiving weekend. Caller twenty, we're waiting."

"Sittin' Up in My Room," a song sung by Brandy on the *Waiting to Exhale* sound track, followed.

Lashawnda heard about the Night Before Thirty contest every day now, but she was sure she had no chance of winning. What would she say in her letter, anyway? But after talking with Cicely and clarifying that she was not going to budge, she thought, *What do I have to lose?*

She closed her eyes and listened to Brandy's voice, letting it relax her as she began to formulate exactly what she would say in the letter. Lashawnda felt a smile inside. Her best revenge for Cicely's blatant insensitivity was to plan a trip on her own. *As a matter of fact,* she thought, *even if I don't win the trip, I'll dip into my savings account and go somewhere by myself.*

She looked over at Cicely, who appeared to be involved in fighting traffic. Was every relationship that Lashawnda had going to be an equal mixture of love and hate? What made her and Cicely so much tougher than any of her other relationships was their secrecy and her uncertainty about what it meant. Lashawnda didn't know if she was a straight woman involved with a lesbian or a lesbian who would not venture back into the world of heterosexuality. She still fantasized about men, but when a woman walked by with nice breasts, she often found herself intrigued with the idea of touching them. Touching her. Wondering, if she approached her, whether she could make her laugh.

But thoughts about all this had to be pushed aside. They were turning into the parking garage and had to go to work. Cicely pulled into their assigned space. Lashawnda adjusted her seat back to its upright position.

"Lashawnda, listen, I know your birthday is important to you. It's important to me too. I'm going to make it up to you—by celebrating it early, I mean. Better yet, I'm going to show you a good time the weekends before *and* after. We can do a monthlong celebration if you want."

Lashawnda opened her door.

"Wait a minute," Cicely insisted.

She closed the door.

"Are we okay, me and you?"

Lashawnda responded with an empty, dry "Yeah."

"Can I get a kiss before we go inside?"

Lashawnda eyed Cicely, who didn't back down from her request.

"Just a little one," she pushed.

Lashawnda leaned toward Cicely, who stuck her tongue inside her mouth and forced an intense kiss on her, showing total disregard for their conversation during the drive over.

She slowly pulled back and stared at Cicely, wondering, *Who is this woman I'm living with?* Then a thought that had never before crossed her mind hit her: *She sees me as her toy.* She hoped her perception was wrong, but Cicely's credibility was beginning to appear shadier than that of a man going through his midlife crisis, looking to find a pretty young playmate to keep around for the sole purpose of stroking his ego and making him feel good about his miserable existence. Was Cicely the same?

Cicely opened her door. "Let's get inside. We have a busy day ahead.

"By the way, remember the flight attendant, Marissa?" Cicely said as they walked through the parking garage. "Well, she's coming in for a two-hour session. She's having a rough time. The girl is a mess. Just make sure we aren't disturbed through the duration of the session."

"No problem."

Cicely was the boss, her employer. Duty called and Lashawnda had to push everything aside and go to work. But in between her secretarial duties, she had a letter to write—and a contest to win.

11

PRETTY GIRL

"YOU'LL BE SLEEPING in here tonight," Catara's favorite cousin, Cheryl, said in her high-pitched, girlish voice. She had just picked Catara up from the train station and brought her to her apartment. "We fly out at seven-thirty in the morning, which means we have to be up and out by five o'clock."

Catara had taken a train to meet her cousin in Maryland. The two were going to be flying to their hometown of Indianapolis for Thanksgiving. Meeting in Maryland allowed them to spend some time together before joining their huge, wonderful, sometimes smothering family.

Most people did a double take when they heard Cheryl speak, but Catara had been around that voice for twenty-nine years. When they had both been five years old, their vocal tones were about the same, but as they grew older Catara's tone matured, but Cheryl's didn't. Cheryl had microbraids, full lips, and soft round eyes. You'd never believe that her squeaky, mouselike voice would come from that adult body.

"That means we have to be up at four A.M.?" Catara said as she took a seat on the futon in the bedroom. She breathed a deep sigh. "Are we catching a cab?"

"No. My friend Lamont is going to take us. You're going to love Lamont. He's something else. I'll pull out sheets for the futon. There are towels already laid out in the bathroom."

Catara looked around and noticed that with the exception of the futon the room was empty. Cheryl never was much on decorating. Then her eyes moved to her cousin, who rambled on as she always did. Cheryl Washington's body was basically the same as it was when they graduated high school; she was five-five, slightly curvier and with a more defined cut in her muscles, the picture of athleticism. Fitness was her life. Cheryl was a manager at a health club and had been since she graduated from college with a degree in marketing. She had gotten into fitness in college and had taught numerous dance and aerobics courses through the years. She'd even considered becoming a weight-training instructor.

"I have bath beads if you want to take a warm bath. Otherwise, the water pressure is incredible in the shower."

"I'll probably take a shower," Catara replied, and then continued to stare at Cheryl as she pranced gracefully around the room. Catara couldn't help but wonder how it could be that she loved Cheryl so much but at the same time felt envy surfacing as she examined her from head to toe. Catara hoped Cheryl wouldn't notice her obvious scrutiny, but she couldn't help it. Catara compared everything about their physical differences.

Both Catara and her cousin shared the same paper-sack-brown complexion, and even the same basic facial lines and eyes. Only, Catara's body was fuller, much fuller. Watching Cheryl made her even more aware of the fact that she too had curves. They both were full-busted, and had "sista" rear ends, inherited from the family's gene pool. Only, Cheryl's curves flowed in and out, while Catara's went out and out.

Cheryl lay back on the futon beside Catara. "I can't believe it, C and C are back together again." They hadn't been able to spend much time together since high school.

"Neither can I—we have so much catching up to do."

"Tell me about it. We have to do it tonight, because once we get home the moms are going to put us to work in that kitchen."

Catara didn't respond.

"You seem a bit preoccupied. What's up?" Cheryl asked.

"Girl, I'm just tired. The day has drained me. It's been a long week with work and trying to get my career together."

"Tara, you've always been a planner. I know everything is going to work out for you. You're taking a risk by delving into the fashion industry, but sometimes the road less traveled is the road to success."

"You're right," Catara said. It was only a matter of time before her talent was discovered.

She knew she was destined for success, only the world wasn't aware of it yet, and neither were her parents. After receiving a degree in marketing, Catara had shocked her family when she told them she had been accepted at the Fashion Institute of Design and Merchandising and would be moving to Los Angeles to get another undergraduate degree and a master's in fashion design. The family always knew she wanted to pursue a career in the fashion industry, but they never expected her to go back to school, especially in California. Catara and Cheryl's was a close-knit Indiana family and no one ever moved west— maybe north, or south, but never that far west.

She left Los Angeles after graduating from FIDM and headed to New York to become a renowned fashion designer, or at least open her own boutique in SoHo. Although she lived in New York, she was far from realizing her dreams. She was having a tough time making it happen. She wasn't sure if it was because of the protective rein her family kept on its members, or maybe because of fear of failure—or maybe it was because of her weight, the one thing she never wanted to admit would ever stop her from pursuing her dreams. Maybe it was a combination of everything that had forced her to temporarily push aside her goals and alter her plans. It wasn't lack of talent—that she was confident of. So she continued to persist in trying to get recognized by a designer, and continued to create new designs.

"I couldn't wait until you got here. I know we have to get up early, but Lamont and the rest of the crew from the health club are going to be hanging out. They asked me to bring you. I always have a good time with them. Do you remember how much fun we used to have when we would sneak out to the clubs back in Indy? Remember the Horseshoe?"

"Uh-huh, but that was nearly ten years and fifty pounds ago."

"I know you're not trippin' on your weight."

"No, I'm not. I'm dealing with reality, Cheryl."

"Girl, I don't care what you say, you look good."

"If I look so good, tell me why the only man that I've dealt with over the past year has been Rondell, and you know the story on him."

"Your being dateless has nothing to do with your weight. When was the last time you went out to a nightclub?"

"A little over a year."

"That's exactly what I'm talking about, Catara. No strange man is just gonna walk up to your apartment door, interrupt you watching TV, and say, 'Excuse me, I know you're trying to get your relaxation on, but I just couldn't help but notice you through your closed blinds. Would you like to go out on a date with me?' "

"You're right, but I do get out. I'm always shopping. I go to work, to the grocery store, the video store, to the fabric shops, the newsstand. I go to the bank. I see men, but they're not looking at me."

Cheryl looked at Catara as if her words were absurd. "It's not about your weight. It's about you stepping outside of that little comfortable box that you've taken residence in within your mind. And Catara, if you want to lose weight, I can set up a workout plan for you."

"That's cool and all, and I want to do that, but I've been in and out of gyms for the past five years. Instead of losing, I've continuously gained."

"I can make some calls to our gym in New York. I know people there. I can get a weight trainer to work you out. Someone owes me a favor, and I'm sure I can get you some free sessions."

"Okay, that'll be good," Catara finally said, more to shut up Cheryl than anything else. She always was a Ms. Fix-it—what did she know about Catara's thoughts, anyway? She wasn't living in a "box." She was much too tired to explain to her cousin that her weight issue couldn't be that easily solved. If that were the case, Catara would have slimmed down by now, with all of the miles she'd put on treadmills, stationary bikes, and stair climbers, not to mention the numerous diets she'd tried with hopeful expectations but failed at. Her weight was like a yo-yo: Just when she thought she had a handle on it, that she was losing the pounds, one setback would send her in reverse, and her weight would go on the incline again.

Catara felt her cousin could never know the pain and struggle she'd endured daily. After all, Cheryl never had a problem getting dates, and never experienced going to a department store to buy an outfit for a special event only to find out that they didn't have anything in a size 20 worth purchasing, let alone displaying in their store. Yes, she was a designer, but who had time to create her own clothes every day?

"I'll make the call as soon as we get back from Indy."

"That's cool," Catara replied, attempting to appear enthusiastic.

"Well, let me show you the rest of the apartment. You have to see the pictures that I have in the living room. You are going to get a kick out of them."

The two got up for the tour. Though Cheryl was not big on interior design, she had nice mix-and-match furniture, a black leather sofa, and a papasan chair with a beige cushion. All were arranged around an elegant glass cocktail table. The walls were bare except for a lone Ansel Adams print, but family snapshots were scattered throughout the house in nice frames.

Catara picked up each frame one by one and stared at the images. There was a picture of her parents, Dorothy and Mack, and Cheryl's, Auntie Earlene and Uncle Joe. Dorothy and Earlene were sisters—Cheryl and Catara called them "the moms." Born and raised in Indianapolis, they both had met their husbands, built homes, and raised their families there. In the photo, the two couples were dressed up and posed around a wicker chair in front of a red Valentine's Day–themed backdrop. It was a scene from their partying days. Several pictures of the four of them at various parties and nightclubs they'd attended throughout the years had circulated between the two families.

Perusing the other photos, Catara came upon a picture of Cheryl and herself. They were wearing matching yellow-and-green bathing suit tops and tacky, cut-off jeans shorts.

"Oh my God, Cheryl, look at us. I remember spending long hours puff-painting our names and other little designs on those shorts." Catara handed the picture to Cheryl. "And remember, I ripped the outside seam and braided them back together with bright-colored ribbon."

"Yep, you had the yellow and I had the green to match our bathing suits. And look at those ponytails. Even our bows matched," Cheryl said, and gave the picture back to Catara.

"We thought we were looking good, and I know you remember why we both had those goofy grins on our faces." Catara laughed.

Staring at all the photos, especially at her and Cheryl as ten-year-olds,

Catara became flooded with memories of the day the picture was taken. It was as if it were yesterday. She'd never forget. She even remembered how she felt about herself back then.

She had always been confident. Her parents praised her appearance, especially when her mother used to dress her up for church or when she had ballet or piano recitals. She had always been recognized for her thick, long, wavy hair and superlong eyelashes. And when she was a kid, all her mom's friends seemed to get a kick out of squeezing her cheeks. Although she didn't exactly love the pinching, she adored the attention.

Cheryl slapped her legs in excitement. "Of course I remember, that was at one of your parents' backyard barbecues. I used to love those things. Uncle Mack would grill on the patio while my dad stood beside him talking shit all day. The moms would hook up the dishes they'd spent all morning sweating over," she said, her eyes glazed over. A reminiscent smile overcame her face. "We were bad, girl. Remember? We came up with that plan to sneak half-empty beer cans from the card table."

"Yeah, girl, I remember walking over to where they were playing bid whist, pretending to be interested in who was winning. I stood next to Aunt Earlene, and she said her usual, 'Hey pretty girl,' and then she pinched my cheek and showed me her cards and said, 'Look at this hand. Your momma dealt me this mess, and we're on the same team.' "

"Momma always complained when she played cards, smoking all the while." Cheryl smiled.

"Dad yelled, 'Up jump the devil from the groundhog's den!' and then threw out his card. When all eyes were on his card, I cued you to crawl under the table and get ready for my next signal to steal a beer. I proudly announced, 'Auntie Earlene, will your king beat Uncle Joe's ace?' "

"The whole table was in an uproar. By that time I had grabbed a beer and taken off. Someone yelled, 'Redeal!' "

"I can hear Daddy now: 'Tara, shit! Come on, now. What are you doing over here in grown folks' business, anyway?' "

"Yeah, but you had him wrapped around your little finger. All you had to do was say, 'Sorry, Daddy,' and give him a kiss on the cheek."

"You're right. Then he'd say, 'It's okay, pretty girl, but next time remember not to share the cards in people's hands with the whole table.' I'd say 'Okay, Daddy,' and tell him I loved him."

"You knew how to make him blush for showing his soft side," Cheryl said. "He'd say, 'I love you too.' Then, to change the subject, he looked at my dad. 'And this hand better be as good as the one I just had!'"

"I remember the look on my face when you pulled the beer can from out of the paper towel you used to cover it. We shared two or three beers." Catara placed the picture back on the table. "We both barfed that night," she said, frowning at the memory.

"The moms immortalized us that day with that picture."

"Yeah, those were the good ol' days, back when I was confident and self-assured. I felt beautiful. I knew I was a pretty girl. Nobody could convince me there was a single problem with my appearance, because there wasn't," Catara said.

"You're still pretty," Cheryl said.

"Maybe. Only, the few additional pounds that I've picked up over the years are covering some of my beauty. Plus, my self-esteem is on vacation, and my ability to flirt has disappeared."

"We have a lot to talk about tonight! I'm gonna get you right before the night is over."

"I'm sure you'll break your neck trying," Catara said. After seeing them in that picture, she appreciated how much her cousin had been in her corner for all those years.

"I'm going to pop us some popcorn, and we can talk about it all, the good, the bad, and the ugly."

"That works, cousin," Catara said, and followed Cheryl into the kitchen.

CATARA WAS AWAKENED early the next morning by the doorbell being continuously buzzed. It was still dark out.

"Cheryl!" she yelled across the apartment. "Someone's at the door."

"I know—it's probably Lamont. If we don't answer it he'll go away."

"Isn't he supposed to be taking us to the airport?" Catara asked.

"Yes, but he's here too early. I'm not ready to get up yet. What time is it anyway?"

Buzz from the bell again and again.

"It's three forty-five."

"But we don't have to be up for another fifteen minutes."

The bell sounded again. So Catara jumped out of bed, put on her robe and slippers, and went to the door. Cheryl obviously had no intention of budging.

When she opened the door a tall, slim attractive guy was standing there. "You must be Catara," he said, with the widest grin on his face. "I'm Lamont." He reached out and gave her a big hug.

She stood there, speechless. Lamont walked past her. "And just where is Ms. Cheryl? I know she's still in bed. Sleeping beauty, time to get up!" he yelled as he walked toward her room. Catara followed. He crawled into bed next to Cheryl, who had thrown the covers over her head. "Come give your daddy a hug," he said, and began tickling her.

Cheryl yelled at the top of her lungs, "Stop, Lamont!"

He continued tickling.

"I'm not playing, leave me alone, I'm trying to sleep."

"You know you want me," he said, then pulled the covers off her face and began kissing her cheeks and forehead.

Catara watched from the door. She wasn't sure if she needed to stay or go. Cheryl never mentioned to her that they were seeing each other. She always thought they were only friends. Plus, from the tone of his voice and the presence he commanded when he entered the apartment, Catara was under the assumption he was gay—attractive, but just a little soft.

The two horseplayed, and as they settled down Cheryl said to Catara, "So, I guess you met Lamont at the door."

"Yeah, we met," Catara said, and became suddenly aware of her appearance. Her hair was wrapped in a scarf, she was in pajamas, and there were still traces of sleep in the corners of her eyes.

"So, ladies, you have a plane to catch, right?"

"That's the plan," Catara responded.

"Well Big Papa's here, and I'm gonna make sure you two get to the airport on time."

"Thank you," Catara said.

"Okay then, my BAPs, let's get you two dressed for the day. Although your pajamas are so nice, Catara, that you could probably get away with wearing them all day."

"Thanks, I made them myself."

"You got a gift," he said casually. "Now, go get dressed!"

Cheryl threw the covers over her head.

"You have thirty minutes or this train is leaving without you," he said, then got out of the bed and turned on the radio full blast. Destiny's Child's "Survivor" was playing, and Lamont started grooving to the beat. He had such energy, such enthusiasm, that Catara's eyes were glued to his every move. She couldn't turn away.

"That means you too, Miss Missy," he said to her, continuing to dance all the while.

Catara smiled and looked away, embarrassed for the way she was gawking at him. Looking for comfort, she glanced at Cheryl, who was getting out of her bed and had caught her glimpse and smiled. Catara shrugged shyly and went to get dressed.

By the time Catara was dressed and in the living room, Cheryl and Lamont were sitting around talking health-club politics.

"You'd better be glad I'm just meeting you today, or I'd be all over your case. You took forever," Lamont said, noticing her.

"My bad. The shower just felt so good that I didn't want to get out," Catara said.

"I told you," Cheryl replied.

"Well, you can't rush beauty. And you made it happen, my dear. You're working it," Lamont commented.

Catara looked down at herself, then back up at Lamont, who was still staring at her with a proud grin on his face.

"Let's do this!" he said.

12

A BLAST FROM THE PAST

ALECIA LAY IN bed, moping. It had been nearly two weeks since she'd spoken to William. Although flowers came every day, he didn't call, probably because he was avoiding the inevitable conversation he knew he couldn't get out of. She, on the other hand, refused to call him. She was determined he was going to have to put in extra time and work to get her back. Flowers were not enough.

It was a few days before Thanksgiving, and for the first time in a long time Alecia didn't have plans. She didn't want to go skiing, and she didn't want to be bothered with the families of any of the men who'd invited her to meet their folks, but she didn't want to be alone, either. She didn't consider Thanksgiving a major holiday, but it was a special day, and she always liked feeling special on special days. That wasn't going to happen if she lay in bed all week.

She knew she'd have to take action if she wanted results. No matter what the day would bring, she had to face it. Reluctantly, she threw back her Sferra Bros. lime-green duvet cover and three-hundred-thread-count lavender sheets and jumped out of bed. Deep purple and lime green were the color scheme of her bedroom. The rest of her condominium was decorated with the same bright California-inspired colors: The furniture was modern and varied, in outlandish sizes and artistic shapes.

After slipping into her Hanro of Switzerland robe and slippers, she sauntered into her living room, past her bright red sofa, to her plush sheepskin rug, and picked up her Louis Vuitton Palm case. Then she walked over to her dining-room table, sat down, and went through her addresses, starting with the letter A. Most of the entries were male. Being in the company of any of the names listed seemed too much of a chore. She only wanted to be with William, but she knew that was not going to happen. William would be spending time with his family, sitting at the head of the dinner table, carving the turkey.

The thought of spending time with her own family crossed her mind. It had been a while since she had spent a weekend with them. Maybe it would do her some good to be home. Instead of thinking too hard about it, she picked up the phone and called the airline. She wasn't going to ask anyone to pay for the trip—she would take care of it herself. She would use some of her frequent-flier miles and book a flight to Dallas to spend time with her mother and sister.

ARMED WITH A bouquet of flowers for her mother and a handful of fashion magazines for her younger sister, Alecia propped her luggage next to her and rang the doorbell to her childhood home. She felt giddy as she thought about how excited her mother and sister would be to see her. It was late in the morning, and, if she knew her family, they were just now starting to get dressed for the day. She looked around at the outside of the ranch-style, three-bedroom home. It needed a paint job, but her mother had done an exceptional job of keeping up the yardwork on their spacious lawn.

The door flew open and Alecia's sister, Tabitha Renee, stood at the door in faded jeans and a T-shirt. She was still wearing her sleeping scarf. After taking one look at Alecia, she let out a screech so loud it could easily have been heard throughout the working-class neighborhood. Tabitha hopped onto the front porch and threw her arms around Alecia, almost causing her to drop her gifts.

"What are you doing here?" Tabitha cried out.

"I was in the neighborhood, so I figured I'd drop by and surprise you guys."

"Well, you've done your job." Tabitha turned around and yelled in the house, "Mom, Alecia is here!"

Before Alecia could catch her breath, her mom, Gloria Marie, was at the door, as excited as Tabitha. "Alecia, honey, what are you doing here?"

"Tabitha asked me the same question. It is Thanksgiving, isn't it? I thought it would be a good idea to spend it with my family. These are for you." She handed the flowers to her mother.

"These are nice, but where's my hug?"

Alecia embraced her mom. She could see their resemblance. She would look like her mother as she aged, only better, she assured herself. Her mother carried extra weight from age, which looked good on her; however, Alecia swore she'd not gain weight when she got older.

"We've been up for about an hour, but we're just now getting dressed. My friend Lou is picking us up in his limo and taking us out to breakfast. He's a limousine driver, by the way. Are you gonna go with us?" Gloria asked.

Before Alecia could answer, Tabitha grabbed at the magazines.

"These are for you," Alecia proudly announced, handing them to her.

"Oh good! Did you bring me anything else?"

"Can I get inside first?"

"Oh yeah," Tabitha said, and held open the door.

Alecia grabbed her suitcase and lifted it inside, and her mom and sister followed her.

"Louisa is gonna be at her mother's today," Gloria commented while pulling at the rollers in her hair. "She asked if you were going to be in town."

"Oh, really? How's she doing?" Alecia asked.

"Well, you know, she's on the radio every day," her mom said.

"Are you going to hang out with her?" Tabitha asked.

Alecia looked at her younger sister. She was an overdeveloped, over-excited teen who hadn't had enough of a childhood, just as Alecia hadn't, because their mother was too busy schooling them on how to get every last dime out of a man's pocket to have ever played with them. "You're growing up much too fast," she said.

"No I'm not. You just don't visit often enough, and you're missing the process."

"Hush, Tabitha," Gloria said. "Alecia, I'm glad you're here. We're going out for Thanksgiving dinner because I didn't feel like cooking this year. Plus, my new friend Caleb owns this hot, new soul-food restaurant, and he wants me to have dinner over there with him."

"The food is good, Alecia—you'll like it," Tabitha said.

"You're not cooking?" Alecia said, disappointed. Some things never changed around that house. Her mother was still exposing Tabitha to too many men, and Tabitha seemed not to mind.

"Well, Alecia, I didn't know you were coming, and everybody else in the family decided to stay home this year."

"It'll be fun, Alecia," Tabitha said. "Caleb is cool, and it's a nice place, and the food is good."

"Whatever," Alecia said, sulking like a child.

"Look at you," her mother fussed. "You always have been spoiled. Think the world revolves around you. We're eating at the restaurant tonight, and that's the end of this discussion. Plus, it's free, and, like Tabitha said, the food is good."

Gloria pulled a few more rollers out of her hair. "I'm getting dressed. Lou will be here soon. Now, Tabitha, if you're coming, you need to finish getting dressed yourself. You know how slow you are." She turned and walked to her room.

"Okay, Mom, I will," Tabitha said. "Why are you tripping, Alecia? You know things don't change around here. Mom has a flock of boyfriends. She always has, always will. How else could we afford this house?"

"I know," Alecia said, disappointed and embarrassed about the circumstances surrounding the place that used to be her home. "So, how have you been?" she asked, changing the subject.

"I'm hanging in there, just waiting on responses from my college apps."

"How many did you apply to?"

"Five. I applied to USC and UCLA so that I can be close to you. But if all else fails, I'll go somewhere around here."

"With your grades, you'll get into UCLA."

"Yeah, hopefully, but it's a scholarship that will make the difference," Tabitha said.

"You just get in. We'll worry about tuition when the time comes."

"So how are things in Cali?" Tabitha asked.

"Great," Alecia replied.

"How's the acting thing coming along?"

"I'm going through the motions. You know, submitting head shots and auditioning," Alecia lied. She hadn't had new head shots made in nearly two years, and she couldn't remember when she'd last auditioned for a part or taken an acting class. Alecia was not much different from her mother: She had also made a career of being a professional girlfriend, only in Alecia's world, the stakes were higher and the rewards greater.

She had dropped out of college after only two years but in that time took classes that would be beneficial in helping her secure a wealthy husband, life-enhancing skills like her foreign language and investment classes. She was very intelligent, just like her mother and sister, but getting a degree and working a nine-to-five job never appealed to her nature.

"Are you still wearing the ring I got you?" Alecia asked her sister. She checked Tabitha's hands, seeing it wasn't on her pinky.

"Tabitha, please don't tell me you—"

"Calm down, big sister. I always take off my ring when I get dressed in the morning. The lotion was dulling the stones. Don't have a conniption. I'm still a virgin, and I'm still trying to get my convertible."

Alecia sighed. She found peace just seeing that ring on Tabitha's finger whenever she visited. She'd bought it for her on her fourteenth birthday and made her vow that she would at least wait until she graduated from high school before losing her virginity. Alecia stressed to her that she hoped she'd wait until she was married, but that she'd be proud of her for holding out until graduating. She further promised her a new car of her choice if she held out through college graduation.

"In that case, I do have something else for you," Alecia said. "Let's go back to your room." Alecia's room had been turned into a TV room when she moved out, but Tabitha's had twin beds in it. Alecia slept in one of them whenever she was home.

The phone rang. "I've got it!" Gloria yelled back to the girls. A few minutes later she announced, "Louisa's on the phone."

Alecia picked up. "Hello?"

"Alecia Jewel Parker."

"Louisa Montero!"

"What's up?"

"Just catching up with Tab. When did you get here?"

"Oh, about an hour ago. I didn't think you'd be here. So what are your plans? How long are you staying? I'd love to catch up with you," Louisa said.

"I have no concrete plans. I'll be here until Sunday night." Alecia opened her suitcase to find some items to give to her sister. "There is a jewelry store that I've been hearing about that I'd like to check out."

"I see that diamonds are still your best friend," Louisa joked.

"Always have been. Probably always will be. Friends are flaky, diamonds stand the test of time."

"I'm not hearing that. I'm always trying to reach out to you, but since you've been in L.A., you've become all incognito."

"I've just been focused, that's all," Alecia replied.

She kept her distance from her handful of friends, like Louisa, because she was the only one of them who didn't have a career or a husband. She didn't want a career, so once Alecia had snagged a husband, she felt that Louisa would be more than welcome to visit them in their mansion in Malibu.

"I know how you are. That's why I'm coming over there right now, because if I don't catch you, I probably won't see you again for another two or three years."

"Okay, Louisa, I'm dying to see you too. Just push the door open—it's unlocked."

Alecia hung up the phone, ran to the dresser, and looked in the mirror. Louisa's mom's house was just next door, so she had very little time to freshen her face.

"Why are you primping? It's just Louisa," Tabitha said.

"Oh hush, and hand me my makeup bag."

TABITHA AND GLORIA went off to have breakfast with Lou, while Alecia rummaged through her mom's kitchen cabinets to find mugs and coffee for her and Louisa to sip on while they chatted, catching up and remembering old times.

"You treat me so bad now, but you forget I'm the best friend you've ever had, that you used to call me your twin. How soon we forget that I slapped Danika for you when she took your lip gloss and didn't want to give it back."

"I remember like it was yesterday. You had my back. But who let you sit by her on the bus when you didn't speak a bit of English?" Alecia stood in the kitchen with a coffee filter in her hand. She couldn't figure out how to work the coffeemaker and didn't want to take the time to learn. "Louisa, could you help me? Mom's coffeemaker is not like mine."

Louisa got up and removed the filter from her hands. "You're right. I was the lone Latina girl that nobody could communicate with, but that's all right."

Alecia watched Louisa work her magic with the coffeemaker.

"Take a seat," Louisa said. "I'll handle this."

"But I didn't care. I thought you were intriguing, exotic. Cute. Not as cute as me, but cute enough to be my friend."

"So vain. Still so vain! But who taught you to speak Spanish?"

"I taught myself. How else was I gonna communicate with you?"

They laughed.

Alecia plopped down in the chair, the same one she'd sat down in day after day, every morning for breakfast and every afternoon to do homework after school. It was comforting to be home. "Well, maybe you taught me a little, but I was a fast learner," Alecia said.

"We both bridged the language barrier pretty quickly," Louisa replied.

"And we were like peas in a pod ever since."

"Yeah, until we graduated high school."

"It's amazing how things change."

"It is, but you're still my girl." Louisa brought over sugar and creamer. She took a seat next to Alecia.

"And you're still my twin. So, how's the Morning Show gig working out? I listen to you every chance I get, but to be honest, you're usually already off the air by the time I wake up."

"I love my job—Melvin Green is a hoot! We're now syndicated in over fifty cities, and if you listened sometimes, you'd know that they've created a Night Before Thirty birthday contest around my thirtieth birthday." Louisa got up to pour the coffee, and then stopped short. "Whoa, whoa, wait a minute. Speaking of being twins, this is perfect. We share birthdays, so you have to enter the contest. Go get some paper and a pen. We have to write your letter!"

"See, there you go with one of your 'brilliant ideas.' Please let me in on what's going on before we get started."

Louisa explained the contest.

"Port Lucaya?" Alecia frowned.

"I know it's not as glamorous as the spots you travel to, but it's going to be a blast. Plus, cruises are always nice."

Alecia gave Louisa the thumbs-down.

"Do you have plans for your birthday yet?" Louisa asked.

"Not yet, but . . ."

"Well, you do now, and I'm not taking no for an answer. Besides, I'm on the selection committee. Go get the paper, diva, while I pour us some coffee."

Alecia looked at Louisa. She knew Louisa would make her a winner of the contest, even if she had to write the letter herself. That's how Louisa was, a go-getter. That's why she and Alecia got along so well growing up. Their attitudes were the same, only their energies were focused in different directions: Louisa on her career and Alecia on men.

13

STAND

TANYA WAS AWAKENED by her telephone ringing and someone knocking on her door. She looked at the clock. It was three in the morning. She sat up and picked up the cordless phone while slipping out of bed to see who was at the door.

"Hello?" she said while sliding into her slippers.

"It's Chris, baby. Come and open the door."

"Okay, I'm on my way," she said.

Because it was still dark out, there was little visibility in her living room as she walked through it to the door, unlocking each of the locks and opening it. A rush of cold Chicago wind gushed inside her apartment and down her gown.

"Get in here. It's freezing out there," she said.

Chris looked at her with tears in his eyes. He stepped inside her apartment and pulled the door closed. Tanya nervously went around him and locked the door. Chris just stood there.

"Come here, baby." Tanya threw her arms around him. The cold clinging to his jacket chilled her, but she didn't let go.

"Are you okay?" she whispered in his ear.

"I couldn't sleep. It's been two weeks since T-Roy was shot, and I still can't sleep," he said. "I'm frustrated because the tears came, but I'm even more pissed that I can't stop them."

"It's all right," Tanya said. She wiped his tears with her fingers. "Chris, baby, you're gonna get through this. We'll get through this together."

Chris wrapped his arms around Tanya. "I love you so much. Thank you for loving every fucked-up thing about me," he said, and then sought comfort in her lips. He slid his hands on both sides of her hips and lifted her gown from her waist up over her head. His mouth found its way to her breasts. Then he kissed her neck and whispered again, "I love you."

Tanya kissed the tears streaming down his cheeks. She unzipped his jacket and pulled it down his arms, allowing it to fall onto the floor. He pulled her arms around his neck, picked her up, and carried her into her bedroom, where he laid her on the bed and stared at his woman, showing visible appreciation.

Taking his time, he fully undressed. Then he went to Tanya, who wrapped her legs around him and created a safe place for him to release his emotional woes, filling him up with her goodness.

As he entered her, he whispered, "I need you, Tanya, and I promise I'm gonna be everything you need in a man. I love you, girl."

"I love you too, Chris," she said, while gripping his back with her hands.

"I'm gonna change, Tanya. I promise," he said.

While he made love to her, he whispered passionate words of promise and hope. Those words traveled to the center of Tanya's heart, and she clung to them while receiving pleasure in the midst of their pain.

TANYA AWOKE TO the sound of her alarm clock. She had reset it to ring at eight A.M. so she could call in sick. She did whatever was in her power to miss days only when it was an extreme emergency, but Chris had asked her to stay in with him, and she'd agreed.

After Tanya hung up the phone, Chris put his arm around her waist and pulled her close to him until they both fell back to sleep.

Tanya woke up two hours later. She was wide awake, so she went to the living room and found her gown and her slippers near the door. She dressed and went into the kitchen to fix her and her man some much-needed nourishment.

To break the silence in the apartment, she turned on the little radio that she kept in the kitchen. Melvin Green and the Morning Show Crew were just closing out. Tanya got a boost just hearing Melvin's voice. She listened to the show every morning on her way to work, and then continued listening in while she sat at her desk.

Louisa Montero began talking: "Remember, ladies, you only have a few more days to get those letters in," she said. "If your thirtieth birthday is on December first, I want to hear from you."

Melvin Green made a few closing remarks, and the show closed out with the old-school jam of the day, "Reasons" by Earth, Wind & Fire.

Tanya snapped her fingers to the beat, but her mind couldn't help but go where it went every time Louisa Montero mentioned that contest. Tanya imagined herself in South Beach or chilling out on the deck of a cruise ship sailing to the Bahamas. Her thirtieth birthday was on December first, but she wanted to spend her special day with Chris. There was no way they'd be anywhere tropical on her birthday. Chris hated to fly, and if he couldn't get there by car in less than five hours, he pretty much didn't bother.

Tanya quickly let go of the idea of entering the contest. *My odds of winning would be slim,* she said to herself. *Whoever won contests, anyway?* She proceeded to cook up bacon, eggs, fried potatoes, and biscuits. Before long, Chris came dragging out of the room and took a seat at the dining-room table.

Tanya opened the refrigerator, pulled out the orange juice, and poured a glass for each of them.

"Breakfast smells good," Chris said.

She kissed him on top of his head and went back into the kitchen to get their plates.

"Thank you, baby," he said, and took a drink of his orange juice. Then he eased into his breakfast.

"How did you sleep?" Tanya asked.

"Like a baby." He looked at Tanya and smiled.

"Good," she said, smiling back.

She could feel his leg rubbing against hers underneath the table.

She took his comfort level as her cue to bring up their leaving town for good. "When are we going to move away from all this madness, baby?"

He cleared his throat. "Soon," he replied and gave her a look that clearly said, *Not now.*

If not now, then when? she thought, but was too afraid to say it aloud. Pushing through his uneasiness, she continued. "There is nothing in this city for us, so what are we waiting on?"

"Tanya, you know what the holdup is," Chris said defensively. Then he relaxed. "Like I said, it'll be soon. As a matter of fact, we're making a big move the first of December."

"What kind of move?" she asked.

"Me and some of my boys are rolling to Texas. I got some contacts there. We gonna come back here, get it out on the streets fast, pull in a quick profit, and by the first of next year you and me will be living in a phat crib in Atlanta and then we'll start our new life."

"Texas—how are you gonna get there? I thought you didn't like to drive long distances."

"This is different. It'll take us a full day, plus we're gonna take turns driving."

"Chris, I don't want you to go."

"I knew you were gonna say something like that. That's why I wasn't gonna tell you."

"I already checked it out, and I can get a transfer with my job. I have money saved. Why do you have to have so much money to move with?"

"Tanya, you know I'm not a nine-to-five kind of person. I'm not like you. I can't kiss ass for a weekly check. I have to have my own business."

Tanya was offended by his comment, but she pushed it aside. "You have enough to get started with your business," she pleaded.

"This discussion is over," he said, and pushed himself away from the table. "I'm outta here." He stormed past her and into her bedroom.

Attempting to catch her breath, Tanya put her hand on her chest as she absorbed his words. She felt backed into the same corner that she'd been in throughout her relationship with him. She never had the courage to take a stand. Now, after witnessing T-Roy's death and going through the emotional process of accepting the possibility of Chris's death, she closed her eyes and summoned the courage to say the words that she'd been contemplating saying for the past few years. She followed him into the bedroom.

"Chris, let's talk about this," she begged, giving him one last chance to change his mind.

"I already said the discussion is over."

"No, it's not over. Listen to me. I mean this. If you go to Texas, I'm leaving you. See, I don't need to live large. I just want to live. I'm sick and tired of this miserable place, and I'm ready to get out *now*."

Chris flashed her a look of disbelief. "Well, if you're big and bad enough to go without me, then you just have to do what you gotta do. But either way, I'm going to Texas." He slid his shirt over his head, grabbed his keys off the corner of her dresser, picked up his boots, and walked into the dining room.

Tanya followed. "So it's just that easy for you to give me up?" she asked.

Chris was tying up his boots. "It looks to me like you're doing the same."

"What if you get caught?"

"That's a chance I have to take. At this point in my life, it's all or nothing."

"But Chris, everything you need is wherever you and me are, together. The money is nothing. Am I not worth more than money to you?"

Chris stood up and slid on his jacket. He eyed Tanya. They both knew there wasn't a compromise to be had. He kissed her softly on her forehead, backed up, and looked her over one more time. Then he turned around and walked out the door.

Tanya realized at that moment that she had to save herself, because Chris couldn't save her. From the looks of things, he couldn't even save himself.

14

COME OVER

ELISE AND GRANDMA Ross pulled up to the church's family-life center, where they would spend the day, along with other members, preparing and serving Thanksgiving dinner to the homeless.

It was a cold, breezy, clear day and Elise had made sure to get there early so they could get a good parking space, close to the front door, to cut down on the walking for Grandma Ross. Just as she was about to open her car door, Elise noticed Hattie pulling in behind them.

"Here comes Hattie," she announced.

"Good, I was hoping she'd be here early to help me get things started. Aside from me, she's one of our best cooks."

Elise walked around the front of the car and opened the passenger door for her grandma.

"Good morning, Hattie!" she yelled across the lot.

"Hey, Elise. Is that Sister Ross with you?"

"Yes, ma'am," Elise replied.

"Good! I'm glad y'all got here early, because she's the only one who knows how to keep the kitchen under control."

Elise helped her grandmother out of the car.

Grandma Ross no longer cooked for the Thanksgiving dinners, but everybody liked having her there. She usually took her own sweet time walking around the kitchen, supervising and adding a positive vibe.

"Hey, Hattie," she said. "We got us some folks to feed today."

"Yes ma'am, and it seems like the number grows every year," Hattie replied.

"Thank goodness the church has grown too, so that we can afford to handle the numbers," Elise said.

As the three ladies walked toward the family-life center, Elise got a warm feeling being between the two of them. Serving dinner at the church on Thanksgiving was a tradition that she had participated in since she could remember. Grandma Ross had been a member of the St. Stephen's Church since back when there were only a handful of people attending. She'd been a vital part of the flourishing membership. Active in whatever capacity the pastor asked of her, she was truly one of the mothers of the church.

She was also the only mother that Elise had known. Her biological mom died during Elise's birth. She never even got the opportunity to hold Elise in her arms. Grandma Ross was there immediately to fill her daughter's shoes as Elise's guardian, sure to tell her stories so that she would know everything there was to know about her deceased mother.

Because Grandma Ross's lifestyle was heavily influenced by church activities, so was Elise's. Most of the ladies of the church, especially the ones who had been there several years, knew Elise well and felt they'd helped raise her. Since Grandma Ross was busy, with her hands in everything, the women both disciplined and praised Elise whenever they saw fit. Fortunately, Elise had been a good child: As soon as she was old enough, she found pleasure in helping out. Whatever the task, Elise pitched in with a smiling face and a good work ethic. She did so through high school, and since she'd stayed in Kentucky and attended the University of Louisville, right in the city, she'd never missed a beat. When she was a kid, the church had raised funds to help pay for Elise to go away to gymnastics competitions or extended practices in other cities with elite instructors. When they found out she was opening her own gym, quite a few offered to help her in any way possible.

Every Thanksgiving, they spent the day serving the homeless. When Elise was younger, Grandma Ross used to cook a separate meal for the two of them to eat at home, but as they'd both gotten older, they ate at the church.

"I love Darlene to death, but don't let her get near the green beans. Remember what happened last year?" Hattie complained as she pushed open the door.

"Let me get that door for you two," Elise said as she held the door open.

"I'm one step ahead of you. I talked to her last night. She's going to be in charge of the drinks."

"Surely she can't mess that up," Hattie replied.

"Surely," Grandma Ross agreed.

ELISE SAT DOWN on her sofa and turned on the television, hoping to catch a football game or two. She was physically exhausted from working in the kitchen. Earlier that day, Elise had found that she was pushing herself to make up for her grandma's disabilities. Grandma Ross was getting older and slower. She was still sharp as ever, but her body just didn't allow her to function as adeptly as her brain wanted her to.

After their full day, Elise had taken Grandma Ross back to her apartment. She said she was tired and going to take a nap, and then would get up later and go downstairs to play bingo. She insisted that Elise go home and rest too. So, for the first time in her life, Elise was home alone early on Thanksgiving. It felt weird at first, but once she got into the football game on TV, being at home didn't seem so bad—as a matter of fact, it actually felt great.

Elise waited for halftime to go to the refrigerator and sneak into the overwhelming amount of leftovers the ladies had forced on her. Just when she pulled out a dish, her cell phone rang. She walked over to her bag and pulled it out.

"Happy Thanksgiving, Elise—this is Allen."

Wow. Allen! she thought. "Happy Thanksgiving to you too. I'm surprised to be getting a call from you," she said, walking back to the fridge.

"I hope I'm not disturbing you, with it being a holiday and all, but I'm actually working on your jackets."

"What are you doing working on a holiday?" Elise asked.

"Well, all my family is in Philly, and all of my friends are with their families. So I figured I'd treat today like a regular workday."

"Did you at least have any turkey and dressing today?" Elise asked, looking at all that she had in front of her.

"No, but I'm cool. Listen, I just wanted to make sure that I have the correct spelling for this little girl's name. I'm in the middle of e-mailing the order over, and the lettering looks weird. I want to make sure I get it right."

"Okay, what does it say?"

"J-A-L-L-N?" he said, unsure.

"Oh, okay. It's Jalyn. J-A-L-Y-N. I'm glad you called to verify."

"Well, I try to be thorough. You know how I do."

"Yeah, Allen. I do."

"All right, then, Elise. I'm not gonna take any more of your time."

"I'm just watching a game."

"Football?"

"Yeah."

"By yourself?" he said, exaggerating his words. "I guess I got so involved here that I forgot about the games today." There was an awkward silence. "Anyway, I'm gonna get back to work."

Elise didn't want to hang up. She wanted to keep talking. More than that, she wanted to see him—but how could she ask?

"How long are you going to be working?" she questioned.

"I'm almost finished here," he replied.

"Allen, I have enough leftovers to last me two weeks. If you want to get some turkey in your system just to say you had some, you can come over here, and I'll warm you up a plate."

"You would do that for me?" he said.

"It's really no big deal. If you want, you can catch the rest of the game here." Her voice softened as she continued. She couldn't believe she was being so forward.

"You sure you don't mind?"

"I'm offering, right? Let me give you my address," Elise insisted.

She gave him her information, hung up the telephone, and rushed to the bathroom to freshen up.

———

INSTEAD OF PUTTING the food in the microwave, Elise put the sliced turkey and dressing into the oven, and other items that needed to be warmed into saucepans on the stovetop. When he walked through the door, she wanted Allen to be greeted with the smell of a home-cooked Thanksgiving meal.

The doorbell rang. Elise took a deep breath and went to open it. Allen was standing there with a carton of eggnog.

"This is for you," he said, a smile covering his face.

"Thanks." She ushered him in.

"Well, it's not exactly just for you. It's for me too. It's for us, to make the whole Thanksgiving meal complete," he fumbled nervously.

"Good, it'll go great with the pumpkin pie in the fridge."

"You have pumpkin pie? I love pumpkin pie. I was hoping you had some, but I wasn't expecting you to. What a bonus," he said as he followed her into the kitchen.

"And it's delicious. Here, have a seat at the table," she said and pulled a chair out for him. He sat.

"Did you make it?" he asked.

"No. One of the ladies at the church did."

"Oh, so the leftovers are from your serving at the church today?"

"Exactly. I didn't cook."

"So, how did it go?" he asked.

"Great. We had more than enough food and more than enough volunteers. It was a success." Elise grabbed two plates from out of the cabinet and began piling his with the edibles. "I just wish we could do more for the homeless year-round."

"I hear you," he replied.

Elise put a small amount of everything on her plate and carried both to the table.

"Do you want iced tea with your dinner? It's sweetened."

"It's like that? I even get iced tea?"

"I take that to mean yes," Elise said, and pulled out glasses from the cabinet.

"If you want," she said, "we can take this into the living room and watch the game."

"Who's playing right now?"

"Well, the game that was playing when you called is over. The Colts lost to the Giants. Dallas versus the Patriots just came on."

"Dallas is my team, but let's eat first . . . and talk. We can catch the second half over dessert."

"Okay," Elise agreed.

"So, how is everything going over at the gym since the robbery?"

"Well, as you know, we've had to budget in a security guard just for the last two hours of the day. An unexpected expense," Elise said, feeling frustrated.

"The unexpecteds always manage to creep in, throwing off the budget."

"Hattie, my accountant, bought another watch for Mike's girlfriend, and the Office of Minority Services assisted him in repurchasing his books. Believe me, Gotta Flip is grateful for the assistance."

"That's a tough break. I hate that it happened to you. But I'm glad that everything turned out okay."

"I just thank God that neither of us got shot." Elise couldn't help but visualize how pitiful she and Mike had felt, kneeling down on the concrete, frightened for their lives.

"Me too, because if you did, I wouldn't have had the opportunity to be sitting here with you, sharing this meal," he said and smiled. "And let me tell you, this dressing is almost as good as my momma's."

Elise laughed. Allen had a great personality. She had gotten comfortable meeting with him at the gym. It was strange having him in her home, in a personal setting, but she liked having him there.

"Hattie really is a nice lady," Allen commented.

"Yeah, she really is. She's been so helpful to me this year."

"Yeah, me too," Allen said underneath his breath.

"What did you say?" Elise asked.

"Oh, nothing. When's your birthday?" he asked.

"My birthday?" The question seemed out of place to Elise, but she answered anyway, assuming that he was making small talk. "December first. Why? When's yours?"

"No reason. But mine's August twenty-first."

"Oh, okay." Elise smiled.

After dinner, they sat on Elise's sofa, watched Dallas clobber the Patriots, ate pumpkin pie, and drank eggnog. They conversed between plays, and Elise found herself daydreaming about them breaking into a passionate kiss. But she knew that wasn't going to happen. Allen and she were business associates, maybe becoming friends. He didn't appear to have ever looked at her as someone he would want to become intimate with. Any idea of a romance with him had to be pushed aside. So Elise forced herself to become even more into the game than usual. If he was interested, he would have to let her know.

15

THANKSGIVING FIASCO

*L*ASHAWNDA PACKED A bag for a weekend at her mother's apartment in Bankhead, Georgia, while Cicely prepared to take a train to Charlotte, North Carolina, to spend the weekend with her parents. Communication between the two of them had been shaky the past few weeks. At work, they were fine, like old friends. At home, things were much different. As Lashawnda attempted to keep up with Cicely's need for intimacy and stroking, she found herself growing emotionally detached. She was glad to have the break from her. Instead of spending the entire weekend with her mother, she was going to spend one night and drive back after dinner on Thanksgiving Day. She wanted to spend the rest of the weekend alone at the house to contemplate how she was going to proceed with their relationship.

After putting her suitcase into Cicely's car, Lashawnda walked upstairs to the bedroom, where Cicely was closing her suitcase.

"Your train leaves at eight, right?" Lashawnda asked. "Do you need a ride?"

"No. I've arranged for a car to pick me up."

"Oh, okay. I'm gonna go ahead and take off. My mother wants me to help her clean the chitterlings."

"Pew!" Cicely said, keeping things light.

"I know. But what would Thanksgiving at my momma's be like without the scent of chitterlings lingering through the apartment?"

Lashawnda looked Cicely over. She was dressed casually in jeans, a T-shirt, and sneakers. Even dressed down, she was as glamorous as the first day Lashawnda met her, only without the mystique. In fact, Cicely was now a bit of a disappointment to Lashawnda, as if she'd met her favorite movie star and found out that her personality wasn't really as great as had been projected by the media.

How did we ever get here? she wondered. She turned to walk out of the room.

"Hey, I don't even get a hug good-bye?" Cicely asked.

As Lashawnda turned around and caught Cicely's eyes, she felt guilty; she was betraying Cicely by having a change of heart about their relationship. She walked over to Cicely, and they slowly and carefully embraced.

"See you when I get back." Cicely smiled.

"Have a good time with the folks," Lashawnda replied. She waved good-bye and walked out.

ON HER DRIVE back through the neighborhood, Lashawnda noticed the increasing number of cars parked in driveways and at the edge of lawns. Her next-door neighbor had so many cars that they were lined up in front of her own lawn. She pulled Cicely's car into the garage and felt a wave of relief when the door came down behind her. Finally, some time alone.

Her mother had been disappointed that Lashawnda left earlier than planned, but she was having her own drama with her new live-in boyfriend, John. Lashawnda was glad to get away from there because the couple had argued all morning long, made up long enough for a civil dinner, and, by the time she was heading out, were at it again.

She stepped outside of the car, stretched, and then looked around. She was a long way from her mother's two-bedroom apartment, where there were broken-down cars in the lot. The grass was balding and there was bound to be a shouting match at any given moment between neighbors, Lashawnda's mother included. The homes in Alpharetta had garages and nicely manicured lawns. The neighbors were quiet and friendly.

Lashawnda wondered what her next place of residence would be like. She knew for sure that she could never go back to Bankhead, not as a resident, anyway. But she wouldn't be able to afford Alpharetta anytime soon.

She slid her key into the door and walked into the kitchen. The aroma of cooked food met her nose. She stopped and looked around through to the living room. Nobody was in there; however, jazz music was echoing through the house.

Lashawnda's first thought was to walk back out. Apparently Cicely had missed her train or decided to stay home alone herself. Lashawnda didn't want Cicely to know she'd come back early. She didn't want to disturb Cicely's moment of aloneness because she would have been disappointed if things were the other way around, if, after getting home first, she'd been ambushed by Cicely.

Where could she go? She surely didn't want to go back to her mother's. There was noplace. *Think, Lashawnda, think!* She scanned her brain for ideas. The only thing that came to mind was a motel, but where she was from, people only stayed in a motel when they were out of town or sneaking to get their freaks on.

Why not? I'm grown. I can afford it. It'll still allow me to be alone, and Cicely wouldn't have to know that I stopped by, she thought.

She turned to tiptoe back to the garage, when, in the silence between songs on the jazz CD, she heard the faint sound of a voice.

Cicely must be on the phone, she reasoned, but couldn't help but want to eavesdrop. Lashawnda turned back around and crept to the edge of the staircase. Cicely's voice was coming from their bedroom. From where she was standing, Lashawnda could see that the door was closed, and she heard a voice. However, she couldn't hear well enough to decipher words. So she took a deep breath, eyed the stairs, and before she could stop herself, her feet moved up the steps. She reached the top and rushed into the guest room across from the master bedroom. Standing just behind the entry, she peeped around to get in better listening range.

The music from the living room was distracting, but Lashawnda concentrated. Cicely was giggling.

"No, that would be you," she said.

Lashawnda tried to steady her body to keep the slightest movement to a minimum.

"Oh, I know I'm sexy. If I wasn't, you wouldn't have invited me to your room," the other voice purred.

Lashawnda's mouth dropped.

"You want to know what I like?" Cicely asked.

"What's that?"

"To feel your soft lips against my skin."

"Oh really?" the other voice chuckled.

"Really," Cicely responded. "Can I get more of that feeling?"

"It would be my pleasure," the voice responded.

Lashawnda pulled herself away from the door and fell against the wall. Her eyes widened and her arms went limp.

Her instinct was right. It was time to move on. Cicely had actually beaten her to the punch—she'd already brought another woman into their bed. *That bitch!* Lashawnda thought. *She's worse than any of the men from my past. At least with them, I knew they were dogs.*

She started to leave, but caught herself. *I've got to confront this.* Lashawnda moved toward their bedroom. She didn't rush, nor did she hesitate; she just moved naturally toward the room that had been partially hers for half a year. Just as casually as she'd open that door any other day, she turned the doorknob and walked inside.

Candles were lit throughout, casting shadows of light on the walls, while cigarette smoke and Cicely's perfume heavily scented the room. She was lying on her back on top of their nice duvet cover as a beautiful woman with long hair and a beautiful lean backside lay draped on top of Cicely, cupping one of her breasts with one hand and playfully licking the other. Cicely's eyes were closed, an expression of pleasure on her face. She didn't even notice that Lashawnda had walked in.

Wait a minute, Lashawnda thought. *Isn't that . . .* She couldn't hold it in. "Marissa?" she said aloud, surprise in her voice.

Marissa, one of Cicely's patients, looked behind her and saw Lashawnda standing beside the bed. She didn't even try to cover herself, just looked Lashawnda directly in the eye and smirked deceitfully.

Cicely jumped up. She turned pale. "Lashawnda?" she questioned, as if to make sure Lashawnda was actually standing there.

"What are you doing here?" Cicely's face filled with guilt. She reached for her gown and fumbled to put it over her head.

"The last time I checked, this was where I lived."

"Calm down," Cicely said.

"Believe me, I am calm. I'm not even mad. How are you doing, Marissa?"

Marissa's mouth moved, but nothing came out.

"Listen, Cicely. I'm going to go to the bathroom and get that nice bubble bath and salt scrub you got for me. Then I'm going to leave. You two can get back to whatever you were doing."

Cicely stood up off the bed, but she didn't move. Lashawnda went into the bathroom, picked up her bath products, and came back out. She planted a smile of disbelief on her face as she looked at Marissa sitting and Cicely standing, both looking dumbfounded.

Before she walked out of the door she stopped and said, "By the way, watch yourself, Marissa, this one lays it on thick. Three years will fly by before you know what hit you."

Marissa rolled her eyes and folded her arms.

Lashawnda looked at Cicely one more time. Cicely no longer looked like the in control, together power figure Lashawnda looked up to. The sight of her there with Marissa was disgusting. Lashawnda couldn't digest the two of them any longer, so she quickly turned away and shot out the door.

She grabbed the rail at the top of the stairs and sat down on the top step. She had to catch her breath, accept the reality of what she'd just witnessed. Lashawnda stared down the steps. She knew that when she walked down them, her life would never be the same. She was struck with fear. How would she ever be able to trust again?

She heard movement from inside the room, so she hopped up and headed down. She didn't know whether to laugh or to cry. She thought about how absurd Cicely looked when she knew she was busted and laughed all the way down the steps. She laughed hard and loud. She knew Cicely heard, she wanted her to hear so she'd know just how big a joke Lashawnda thought she was.

Once she was safe in Cicely's car, Lashawnda sighed, relieved to be out of that house. She acknowledged that she did care about Cicely and that she was pissed off about the episode she'd just encountered. But beneath the feelings of hurt, betrayal, and fear of what her next move would be, she felt a hint of relief. Now she didn't have to make a decision regarding Cicely. It had been made for her. Despite how out of control things seemed, she was going to make it through this, just like she'd made it through every other unfulfilling relationship she had fallen into.

part two

16

*L*OUISA MONTERO HANDED the list of winners of the Night Before Thirty contest to Melvin Green.

"How did y'all ever narrow the list down to five?" he asked on the air.

"Believe me, it wasn't easy," she replied. "It's going to be a while before I can read another letter. I'm burnt out."

"That means you're really going to need this birthday getaway," Melvin Green said. Then he announced, "All right, ladies, grab your suitcases and sunscreen and be prepared to meet Louisa Montero in sunny South Beach if your name is called."

CATARA CLOSED THE door of the dressing room, where her client was trying on clothes. With dresses draped over one arm, she adjusted the volume on her Walkman to make sure she wouldn't miss even one of the names called.

She braced herself for the verdict. She just knew she was going to hear her name. There was no way she couldn't win. She was already packed. If she didn't win, she didn't know what she would do with herself. She had to win because it was the only plan she had for celebrating her birthday.

————

ALECIA LAY IN bed, half asleep, half awake. Louisa had told her that the winners would be announced Monday morning, so she had set her clock radio the previous night to make sure she tuned in.

Even though she knew she had won, she found herself sitting up in bed, wide-eyed. She was excited in anticipation of hearing her name called on the radio. So what—she wouldn't become a famous actress. Hearing her name on the radio would be her fifteen minutes of fame.

TANYA, ALONG WITH three of her coworkers, gathered in the break room and closed the door. Armed with coffee and bagels, the women crowded around a lone portable radio, waiting to see whether Tanya would be flying away for her dream vacation or if they would have to take her out for the usual birthday dinner.

Tanya sat in front of the radio with her eyes tightly shut. Winning this trip meant more to her than she would have ever let on to them. She needed to win this trip as badly as she needed to breathe.

ALLEN SAT IN front of his computer screen, on pins and needles. He could barely concentrate on the flyer he was working on. Once they began talking about the birthday contest, he had to stop working altogether.

With Hattie's help, he'd written a letter to enter Elise in the contest. He wanted to do something special for her. It was a bit drastic, but Allen couldn't garner the courage to let her know that his feelings for her were growing. He was certain that if she could win the contest, knowing that he entered her in it, she would allow him to get closer to her. Maybe in her excitement, she'd do what he couldn't and let him know she cared for him.

LASHAWNDA DRAGGED HERSELF into the office. Cicely had called her on her cell phone earlier that morning, begging her to come in, not only to work but also to return her car. Lashawnda decided that working for Cicely was still a steady paycheck even though she and Cicely were no longer a couple; she really needed the income. She'd endured worse circumstances.

When she sat at her desk, she instinctively turned on the radio. She looked down and found in front of her a small, nicely wrapped box with a card that read: *Please forgive me—Cicely.*

Lashawnda stared at the box in disbelief. She picked it up and put it in the palm of her hand. It was a small box. *Jewelry,* she thought. Unsure if she would even accept the gift, Lashawnda pulled the string on the bow.

MELVIN GREEN READ the first name: "Our first winner is a California girl, Alicia Jewel Parker from Los Angeles."

"It's Ah-*lee-cee*-ah, you cornball, Ah-*lee-cee*-ah!" she yelled at the radio, emphasizing the *e* in the pronunciation. Alecia fell back in her bed. She was perturbed. "I never did like him!" she huffed.

MELVIN GREEN MOVED to the next name. "All right, our next winner is from the Midwest—Louisville, Kentucky, home of the Kentucky Derby. Congratulations, Ms. Elise Ross."

Allen was so excited that he nearly fell out of his seat. He picked up the phone to tell Elise that she had won, and then decided a phone call wouldn't be effective enough. He put the receiver down and looked at the computer. He was supposed to be working. *I'm not getting anything done here anyway,* he thought, jumping up, grabbing his coat and keys, and rushing out the door to tell Elise the good news. Telling her she'd just won a vacation for her birthday would put him one step closer to winning her heart.

"WINNER NUMBER THREE is from the dirty South! Hotlanta to be exact. All you gotta do is hop down one state and begin to celebrate. Lashawnda Davis, congratulations! You're our next winner."

Lashawnda had totally forgotten they would be announcing the winners today. She dropped the gift from Cicely—an ankle bracelet—and her jaw dropped as well. She'd won. She was actually going to be on a plane for the first time. She jumped up and quietly danced around her desk, so as not to disturb Cicely and her client. How would she make it through the rest of the workweek, knowing that come Friday she would be on her way to Florida?

"OUR NEXT WINNER is from my hometown. That's right, the Windy City of Chicago. Please believe I know this lady is going to be glad to get a break from the hawk. Put away your fur and pull out your bathing suit because, Tanya Charles, you're winner number four."

Tanya became physically weak. She was glad that she was sitting down—had she been standing, her legs wouldn't have held her up. She'd never won anything before in her life. Her coworkers were jumping up around her and screaming, causing so much commotion that someone opened the door to the break room. The women froze, but it wasn't their boss, so they relaxed.

"Please hold it down," the older lady said, frowning down her nose at them.

"Excuse us," someone replied.

When she closed the door, everyone laughed and went back to a more toned-down celebration. Tanya smiled along with the ladies but inside she felt fear. She was scared. This trip meant her first step in the direction of becoming independent from Chris. When she returned, Chris would be back from Texas and nothing between them would ever be the same again.

CATARA HUNG THE dresses she'd been holding on the rack beside the dressing-room door. She didn't want anything in her hands. There was one more name left to be called, and she wasn't sure how she'd react, whether hers was called or not. She didn't want to be responsible for paying for damaged merchandise.

"One more name left. I know you ladies out there are anxious to see if you will be the last name on this list, so I'm going to help build the suspense. Can we get a drumroll please?" He pushed the button on his control board to get the effect.

"The final winner of the Night Before Thirty contest—a shopping spree, the Spa in South Beach, and a one-day cruise to the Grand Bahamas—is from the Big Apple! New York. Congratulations, Catara Edwards, you are our final winner.

Catara threw her arms in the air and let out a loud "Yes!" She had known she would win.

Her client opened the door of the dressing room and peeped out. "Did you call me?" she asked.

Catara was so overjoyed that she began sharing her happiness.

"Can you believe it? I just won a trip over the radio. I'm so excited. I won. I really won."

The lady looked at Catara and smiled. "I'm so happy for you," she said. "But while you're celebrating, could I get this dress in an eight?"

"Oh, of course, no problem," Catara said, dancing toward the show-room to get what her client requested.

LOUISA MONTERO ANNOUNCED the winners one more time.

"Alecia Jewel Parker, Elise Ross, Lashawnda Davis, Tanya Charles, and Catara Edwards, I will see you ladies this weekend for a thirtieth birthday celebration you won't soon forget."

17

GETTING THERE

LECIA WALKED OUT of the front entrance of her high-rise building. It was four-thirty in the morning. The doorman followed behind her with her luggage. Parked out front was William's Town Car. Even though they hadn't verbally communicated since the incident in San Diego, Alecia still continued to take full advantage of the amenities that came with being his mistress, including the weekly maid service, laundry, and dry cleaning, and the use of the company car.

Tony, the driver, hopped out of the car when he saw her approaching.

"Good morning, Miss Parker," he said.

"Good morning, Tony." She figured that he was aware of the circumstances surrounding her and William, and felt a bit awkward.

He opened her door and she got in. Inside, on the seat, was a bouquet of roses and an envelope.

"Mr. Masterson asked me to make sure you received that," Tony said as he pulled out and headed toward the airport.

Alecia turned her head away from the flowers and looked out the window. Early-morning rides to the airport were the only time L.A. seemed asleep, the only time that traffic was nonexistent, the only time she ever got a chance to notice the unique beauty of the city. What stood out to her most that day were the mountains surrounding her, majestically standing in the far distance.

"Miss Parker, there is a note attached to the flowers."

"Thank you, Tony." She had already seen the note, she just wasn't sure if she wanted to read it.

"You have a six A.M. flight, correct?"

"Yes," she replied.

"Sit back and relax. We have plenty of time and no traffic to fight to get there."

She sat staring out awhile longer, until her curiosity got the best of her. Reluctantly, she picked up the note and swiped it open. It was brief and straight to the point. It read: *I'm ready to talk. I hope you're ready to listen. Let's have dinner when you return.—William*

Alecia held the note in her hand. A part of her wanted to cancel her trip. She wanted to know what William was thinking; the note gave her no indication. Alecia wasn't getting any younger, and knowing how William wanted to proceed with their relationship would free her, allow her to move out of limbo. She knew that he'd either be telling her he was leaving his wife and she'd fall into a state of bliss, or he'd say he wasn't leaving his wife and they'd need to go their separate ways. Then she'd be miserable. Either way, at least she would be able to move on.

Then, she thought, *It's a good thing that I'm going on this trip. It shows William that I can go on with my life without him, forcing him to make a decision. He'll choose me. He'd* better *choose me.*

As they pulled up to departures, Alecia found herself feeling excited about the weekend for the first time. She looked forward to hanging out with Louisa. She wasn't exactly thrilled about having to be around four other women, because most women usually had a difficult time warming up to her, but however they chose to react to her wouldn't matter. It was her thirtieth birthday. Her own special holiday. So what if she was getting older? Aging was a part of life, and she couldn't stop life, so she may as well join in and embrace the cycle. Whatever it took, Alecia was going to feel special on her birthday.

CATARA TOOK HER assigned aisle seat on the plane. She was the first in her row to sit down. As she watched people take their seats, she wondered who would be next to her. She recalled one flight she'd had about a year ago. They guy sitting next to her apparently had bad nerves, because his left leg shook the entire way, and he passed gas all the while. Catara

couldn't say anything—all she could do was turn her head in the oppo-
site direction, hoping to luck upon some clean air. She was miserable
for the duration of the hour. She prayed she wouldn't have another experience like that again.

Her prayer was answered—she looked up to see a tall gentleman
with a carry-on in his hand. "Excuse me."

"Yes?" Catara replied.

"Oh, well, I have the window seat. Do you mind?" he asked politely
and pointed to the seat.

"Not at all." She smiled. She put her hand on the back of the seat in
front of her to make her getting up appear more effortless than it really
was.

"You know, I hate window seats," he said. "But I got my ticket too
late. There were no aisle seats left. Plenty of middle, but no aisles."

"Why don't we switch," Catara offered, thinking about how awkward
it would be for her to get up during the flight if he had to go to the rest
room. She knew that he'd be looking at her body and sizing her up. If
she didn't have to move during the flight, he wouldn't have any reason
to notice her body.

"You don't mind?" he asked, surprised.

"Not at all," she said and scooted to the window seat. Once she sat
down and buckled herself in, she remembered she'd put a couple of
magazines in the pocket of the seat back.

"Could you pass me the two magazines sticking out there?" she
asked, pointing to them. He handed them to her.

"Thanks," Catara said. She stored one of the magazines in front of
her and thumbed through the other until they were airborne.

"Excuse me," the gentleman interrupted her.

"Uh-huh?"

"Judging from the magazines you're reading, I take it you're in the
fashion industry?"

"I am," she replied.

"I think that's so cool," he said, turning toward her. "I'm intrigued by
people who work in creative fields."

He put his hand out and introduced himself. "I'm Marcus Radford,
by the way."

"Nice to meet you," she replied, and shook his hand.

"My line of work is not as exciting. I'm an accountant and auditor. Here's my card." He pulled one out of his briefcase.

"Cool," Catara said. She wondered what his angle was, what he was trying to gain by talking to her.

"So are you traveling for business or pleasure?" he asked.

"I'm on vacation," Catara said, smiling at the sound of it. But she looked straight ahead, trying to avoid eye contact.

Marcus straightened up in his chair. "I hope you enjoy your vacation," he said and looked down at his watch.

Just then, Catara realized she'd been enjoying the conversation. She turned toward him. "I can be so rude sometimes. I just realized I didn't tell you my name," she said and held out her hand. "Catara Edwards."

Marcus smiled, nearly blushing, and extended his hand to Catara.

TANYA STOOD IN line at the baggage check-in at the Chicago O'Hare airport. Her heart raced as she stepped out of line enough to confirm that yes, although she was running late, nobody cared. She still had to stand in line to check her luggage, and she would more than likely miss her flight. It was freezing outside, and her stiletto-heeled boots were already beginning to bother her feet. *I should have opted for the shorter heel, but they didn't complement my outfit as well as the ones I'm wearing,* she thought.

What she was wearing wouldn't matter if she missed her flight. Something had to be done, but she didn't know what. Surely she couldn't just walk to the front of the line. She had no choice but to wait in hopes that the line would pick up momentum and clear out quickly. She looked around, hoping to find something, anything that would help out her cause. A skycap walked by, and Tanya grabbed him. She wasn't sure how he could help, but she grabbed him anyway.

"Yes, ma'am how can I help you?" he asked.

"Well I'm not sure if you can. See, I'm late, and if I don't get checked in soon, I'll miss my flight. It leaves at eleven-thirty."

"Yeah, you are in a jam. And by the look of this line, you won't be checked in anytime soon."

"Exactly. Do I have any options?" she asked, distressed.

"Well, you could go inside. The line might be shorter, but I doubt it. Or, and keep this on the down-low," he said, lowering his voice, "for the right kind of tip, I might be able to arrange to get you to the front of the line inside."

"Tip? What would be a good tip?" Tanya asked. She'd never flown before and didn't even know there was tipping involved in the check-in process.

"Ma'am, I basically work for tips, and there are a lot of people out here. You tip me what you think is worth my giving you, out of everybody else, personalized time and making sure you don't miss your plane." The skycap was young and full of energy. He was actually charming.

"I can give you fifteen dollars," Tanya said, while trying to add up her spending money in her mind. "I hope that's not an insult," she said.

"It's a start," he said, and loaded her luggage on his cart. "Let's go."

Tanya fell out of line and followed the skycap inside.

"You add your digits to that fifteen dollars and I really won't feel insulted."

"I have a boyfriend, and he's extremely jealous," she shot back.

"If he's so jealous, why ain't he here? If I had a woman as fine as you, I wouldn't let her leave my sight. I'd do whatever it took to make her happy."

He stopped her and her luggage on the side of the check-in counter.

"Wait right here," he said, and walked away.

His words stuck with Tanya. He was right. If Chris really loved her, he would do whatever it took to keep her, even if it meant sacrificing his costly lifestyle. He didn't love her; even though he told her he did, over and over through the years, his actions said otherwise. As scary as it seemed, she was going to have to leave him and move away for good. If she stayed, she'd end up miserable and would probably bury him way too soon, just like Rosario did T-Roy.

"You're all set, pretty lady," the skycap said.

"It's that easy?"

"Yep. Just walk up to that representative right there, and she'll get you taken care of. I'm right behind you with your luggage," he said.

Tanya was checked in with no problem. She slipped the skycap fifteen dollars.

"Hey, pretty lady," he said.

"If things don't work out with your man, you know where to find me," he winked.

Tanya smiled, waved good-bye, and quickly proceeded to the boarding gate.

ELISE AND ALLEN sat at the restaurant right outside the screening area at the Hartsfield airport. Her baggage was checked, and she was ticketed. They'd gotten there early enough to grab breakfast before she had to board her flight, which was scheduled to take off at eleven-thirty A.M.

Elise was bright-eyed and bouncing, still overwhelmed by the events that had occurred over the past week. "Who would've thought that when Mike and I were on our knees on the ground of the parking lot, afraid for our lives, that something so fortunate as this trip could happen for me? Thank you so much, Allen," she said and reached over to hug him.

He blushed.

"I can't take all the credit. Hattie did help. I'm just glad you won. I apologize for forging your name on the letter, but I think it was worth it, don't you?"

"I still feel like I'm dreaming. I've always wanted to go to the Bahamas, even if we're only staying four hours. And a cruise! This is too much. I'll be sure to bring you back a souvenir, I promise."

The last time Allen saw this side of Elise, she had been showing him her gym. Just like then, she was now happy to the core. She was always bubbly, easygoing, and sweet, but even more so now. He was glad to be the man responsible for her happiness.

"You're always doing so much for everybody—your grandmother, the church, the community. I figured it was high time somebody did something for you."

"You're too much. I'm floored that you would take the time out of everything you've got going on to think about me." Elise made the comment lightly, hoping that if there were any romantic efforts behind his actions, he'd let her know.

After she found out he'd entered her into the contest, she was convinced that Allen was the man for her, but Elise was old-fashioned. She wanted him to make the first move, tell her something; otherwise, she could only believe that he wanted just a platonic relationship.

The two went on during breakfast, complimenting each other and waiting for the other to share their true feelings so they could be honest about their own. Before they were ready to leave each other, before either got the courage, it was time for Elise to catch her plane.

"Thanks for breakfast," she said as they stood up.

"It was my pleasure."

They walked over to the screening area.

"You enjoy yourself enough to carry you through the rest of the year," he insisted.

"Oh, I'm sure I will."

They hugged. Elise didn't want to let go. She sensed that Allen didn't either, but they pulled apart.

"See you when I get back," Elise said, pulling out her ticket to give to the first screener.

"Okay," Allen said and turned to walk away.

Elise got in line to go through the metal detector.

"Elise!" Allen yelled to her.

She looked over her shoulder to see what he was going to say. She held her breath—if he said anything romantic, her birthday would be complete.

Allen acted as if he was going to say something heavy.

"If you want, I can pick you up when you get back."

"Okay," she said and forced a smile to hide her disappointment that they still hadn't moved any closer to becoming a couple than when she first realized she liked him.

LASHAWNDA'S MOMMA'S BOYFRIEND was supposed to be taking her to the airport, but when they got into the car and tried to start it, the engine wouldn't turn over.

"Shit!" he said. "It seems like this only happens when I got something important to do."

Lashawnda huffed, but she couldn't say anything, because it wasn't his fault that his vehicle was raggedy.

She was going to catch a cab, but her momma's boyfriend, John, insisted that if she paid him half the price of the cab, he'd get her there on time. Plus, she wouldn't have to worry about dealing with a stranger.

He swore again and popped the hood, rolled down the driver's side window, jumped out of the car, and lifted the hood.

"I think it's the battery!" he yelled from underneath the hood. "Hold tight. I'm gonna get you to the airport. I just gotta get Earl, next door, to give me a jump."

Lashawnda threw her hands up. *Do I have a choice?* she thought.

She was staying at her mom's apartment until she could get back from her trip and find a place of her own. Luckily, she had planned to get to the airport two hours early—she'd had some time to deal with her momma's boyfriend and his unreliable car.

"If he doesn't get it started in fifteen minutes, I'm taking the MARTA," she swore.

John came back. It was ten-fifteen.

"Earl's gone to work. I'm gonna have to find somebody else. Hold tight, Lashawnda." He walked by the car and down the street of the apartment complex.

"I can't trust this," she said to herself, and then took the keys out of the ignition. She got out of the car, opened the trunk, and lugged out her new suitcase and carry-on bag. It was cool out, what her mother called "jacket weather," but the sun was shining. She pulled the handle of the large piece and put the carry-on on top of it. She sighed loudly and set out to walk down the street and up a block to the bus stop.

Her timing was good, because by the time she had gotten to the stop, the bus was in sight. Lashawnda boarded and sat at the front, gripping her luggage. Her hands were freezing, but her nose was perspiring and the liquid foundation on her face was separating and coming off. She could feel it. She reached into her carry-on and grabbed a tissue. She dabbed facial toner on it and began blotting her face. She looked around and noticed that everyone sitting near her was staring. She ignored them—they had no idea of where she was going or what she was trying to do.

She pulled out her compact and patted powder on her face to remove the shine. After she finished, she took a deep breath and lay back in the seat, letting her head fall back. She had so much to deal with when she returned—the first item of business was to look for a new job, which wasn't going to be easy. Working for Cicely had been her first professional position, and the odds of Cicely being a good reference were slim. Then she needed to find a place and eventually try to get a car.

What am I doing vacationing? she wondered. *I have too much to take care of.* Then she concluded that if Cicely could vacation, she could too. Her new life would have to wait until she returned from her thirtieth-birthday celebration.

18

THEY MEET

LOUISA MONTERO, JESSICA, one of the show's interns, and Stan, the limousine driver, arrived at the Miami airport twenty minutes ahead of the first person's scheduled arrival time.

Locating a bar and grill, they found themselves a space, so as each woman arrived, one of them could help them retrieve their luggage and take them to the bar to meet Louisa. Once everyone had arrived, the women would have a long day ahead. There would be thirty to forty-five minutes between each person's arrival time and, contingent on there being no late arrivals, everyone would get to enjoy a brief time meeting and greeting before they got on with their busy day of shopping and being pampered.

Louisa walked to the furthest comfortable corner in the bar and claimed two tables. Then Jessica and Stan went to the waiting area for arriving flights. Stan held a sign that read: "MELVIN GREEN AND THE MORNING SHOW CREW CONTEST WINNERS!" Jessica was prepared, wearing comfortable shoes—as the winners arrived, it was her job to escort them to baggage claim, assist them with their bags, and then take them to meet Louisa.

Lashawnda was the first to arrive. When she saw Stan holding the sign, she breathed a sigh of relief. "Am I ever glad to see you," she said to Stan. "I was so nervous that I'd forgotten where I was supposed to go. Oh, thank goodness."

Jessica moved close to her. "Excuse me, hi. My name is Jessica, and I'll be escorting you to where Ms. Montero is waiting. You must be Lashawnda?" she asked.

"Yes, I am."

"Okay. Follow me, and we'll pick up your luggage first."

"I'm so happy the radio station had sense enough to have you help us. I know that I would have been running around like a chicken with its head cut off otherwise."

"It's my pleasure," Jessica replied.

When Lashawnda saw Louisa, her mouth dropped wide open. She covered it with her hands to contain her excitement.

Louisa stood up to greet her. "You must be Lashawnda," she said.

"Oh my God. Louisa Montero. Girl, thank you for having this contest." Tears began falling from her eyes.

Jessica excused herself.

"You just don't know how much it meant to me to win."

"You're welcome, but it was actually Melvin's idea."

"Louisa, make sure you thank Melvin for me. Oh my God. You just don't know how special this is," Lashawnda said. Then she took a look at Louisa. "You're so pretty!" she squealed.

"Thank you," Louisa said. "Come on, have a seat. You can order an appetizer. Drinks. Whatever."

"Great. I'm starving," Lashawnda said. She sat down and tried to concentrate on the menu, but she couldn't. She was just too excited.

CATARA AND TANYA stood with Jessica and Stan. They'd walked up at about the same time and were waiting for Elise. They were both anxious and wanted to move forward.

"How much longer do we have to wait?" Tanya asked.

"Well, Elise's plane has already landed. She should be coming this way any minute now," Jessica said.

"What about our luggage? Shouldn't we go ahead and try to get it?" Catara questioned.

Jessica became nervous. She knew that the moment that they left,

Elise would walk up. But she didn't want to upset the contest winners. The ladies had every right to be concerned about their luggage, but the timing was important. "Let's just wait a few more minutes," she suggested. "I'm sure your luggage will be okay."

"I don't know about that," Tanya said.

"Why don't Tanya and I walk to baggage claim, and when Elise gets here, the two of you can meet us there and then we'll all go together to meet Louisa and the other lady. What's her name?" Catara said.

"Lashawnda," Jessica replied, biting her bottom lip. "Well, okay. But please don't move once you find your luggage. If I lose you, I'll lose my job."

"Oh, we'll be fine," Tanya said over her shoulder as she and Catara left to go to baggage claim.

"And we'll be down there when you get there with Elise," Catara assured her.

"Yeah, relax," Tanya said, tickled at how nervous Jessica was. It was cute. Most of the women in her hood weren't so quick to let their emotions show, no matter how nervous they were.

She and Catara moved through the airport together like two young girls. They were both giddy and talked like old friends.

"I can't wait to get on that boat and get my party on. It is long overdue. I just hope all the other women who won aren't skinny like you," Catara said.

"What did you say?" Tanya asked, offended. She was hoping to give Catara a chance to clean up her words before she went off on her.

"I don't mean it facetiously. I'm just a little self-conscious about my weight."

"I don't know why. Skinny girls are not in style. They like 'em thick in my hood."

"Well, I need to hang out in your hood, because where I stay, thin is in," Catara replied. "I know everybody is going to be staring at me. But if I'm not the only big girl, it'll take some of the pressure off."

Tanya didn't know how to respond, so she changed the subject. "I'm not getting to my massage quick enough. After the year I've had, I could use one every day for the next year."

"Well, I've been so busy at work that I haven't had a pedicure or manicure in months," Catara said.

"Wait a minute, wait a minute, girlfriend, you gotta find time for the two I-cures."

"I know, but I haven't."

"I thought I needed this, but maybe you need this trip more than me," Tanya said.

They laughed.

By the time they found their luggage and made their way to the front of baggage claim, Jessica and Elise were approaching. The two women smiled when they saw her.

"What took you so long?" Tanya joked.

"I'm so sorry, but there was a mother and two kids on the plane and they didn't have seats together. Two of them were on the same row as I was, close to the front, and one of the seats was in the back of the plane, on the last row. I couldn't let them be separated like that."

"So you gave up your seat," Catara said.

"Yeah, which meant that I was one of the last people off the plane, and it was a full flight."

"That was nice of you," Catara said.

"Oh, by the way, this is Catara Edwards and Tanya Charles," Jessica said, pointing to each. "And, of course, this is Elise Ross."

The women shook hands.

"How was your flight otherwise?" Jessica asked.

"It was fine. Not bad at all," Elise said.

"Elise carried her luggage on the flight, so we can go ahead on over to meet Louisa and Lashawnda."

Jessica touched Elise on the hand. "Lashawnda Davis, the other winner, is already here. The final winner, Alecia Parker, should get here in the next fifteen minutes. She's coming in all the way from Los Angeles."

The women walked into the bar where Louisa and Lashawnda were sitting down talking and sharing a basket of chips and salsa. Jessica introduced everyone. Then they all sat down and placed their orders with the waitress.

"So you're Catara," Louisa said.

"Yeah?" Catara shook her head, unsure of what Louisa was getting at.

"Girl, out of all the letters we received, yours was the best. We *had* to make you a winner."

Catara laughed a sigh of relief. "Oh, thank you!" she responded.

Louisa looked around. "Everybody else's letters were great, but, Catara, yours left such an impression I couldn't wait to meet you."

Catara smiled, but she hated being the center of attention.

"Congratulations on opening your gym. It's not every day that you meet a gymnast."

"Thank you," Elise said. But I have to be honest. I didn't write my own letter. A guy friend of mine wrote it."

"Disqualify her," Lashawnda teased.

"Well, as long as we're playing true confessions, I can't disqualify you, Elise, or else I'd have to disqualify myself and my good friend Alecia. She's the fifth winner."

"I'm telling Melvin Green," Tanya joked.

Everyone laughed.

"Alecia is my girl, but let me warn you ladies, she is a bit of a diva," Louisa admitted.

ALECIA WALKED TOWARD Jessica and Stan. By the way Alecia was eyeing them over her sunglasses, Jessica knew that she was their final winner.

"Hi, you must be Alecia?"

"No. I'm Ah-*lee-cee*-ah."

"Sorry, Alecia," Jessica said, embarrassed that she had mispronounced the woman's name. "How was your flight?"

"Horrible. Why would the show not fly me first-class? Especially coming from L.A. I tried to upgrade, but there were no seats available."

"I'm sorry to hear that," Jessica replied.

"I haven't eaten anything at all today. The food in coach is horrible. I am absolutely famished," she complained, handing her carry-on to Stan.

"So where is Louisa? Am I the first person to arrive?"

"Actually, you're the last. Everybody else is with Ms. Montero. They're all in one of the restaurants getting acquainted. You'll be able to have a bite to eat there."

"Okay," Alecia said.

"By the way, I'm Jessica. I'll be assisting Louisa Montero and the rest of you ladies for the weekend." She looked at Stan.

"Stan, you can bring the car around, and I'll help you to start loading things up once I get Alecia settled."

"Okay. Will you need this?" he asked Alecia, pointing to her bag.

"No, you can take it with you. But I do have another piece to pick up at baggage claim."

"Stan, you might as well walk with us, so you can take her luggage with you when you go to get the car," Jessica said.

"No problem," Stan said.

They picked up Alecia's luggage and gave it to Stan, and then the two women went to join the rest of the group.

Alecia and Jessica walked up to the ladies, who were sitting around making small talk and waiting.

"Excuse me, but I have our final addition to the group: Alecia"—she looked at Alecia for approval for pronouncing her name correctly, and Alecia nodded—"Jewel Parker."

Then she introduced everyone to Alecia one by one. When she got to Louisa, who stood up, she began, "And this is—"

"Louisa Montero," Alecia said, and walked over to her and hugged her.

"Alecia, you made it! So how was your flight?" Louisa asked.

"Let's not talk about it," Alecia huffed.

"Well, come and have a seat. We've just been munching. What do you want to drink?" Louisa asked.

"Apple martini. Ooh, and I'd like some cocktail shrimp to start."

"Sure. Jessica, can you grab a waitress and give her Alecia's order?" she asked. "In the meantime, chips and dip are on the table."

"Cool, because I'm starving. I haven't eaten all day," Alecia said, as she took an empty seat next to Louisa.

"Now that everyone is here and has been introduced, I'd like to welcome you all and say congratulations. This weekend is a special occasion, ladies. All of us are turning the big three-oh. I, for one, have resisted, but this weekend with the company of all of you, I plan to embrace thirty."

"Amen to that," Lashawnda said, lifting her glass toward Louisa.

"We've got a busy day ahead of us. I'm going to go down the itinerary, but first I'd like to do something that came to me last night." She pulled out a small bag from her purse.

"Inside this bag I have five questions. I'd like to have each of you draw a question and, as we spend the day together, I thought it would be nice to have each of you give as detailed an answer as possible."

Louisa shook the bag.

"What I'd like is for each of you to keep your question to yourself. Think about your answer carefully, and then be prepared to share with the group."

"If we don't like our question, can we switch?" Elise asked.

"No, unfortunately you're stuck with your question. I think this will allow for good discussion and help us to really bond this weekend." Louisa smiled, seeming proud of her idea. Everyone else looked skeptical.

"All right, ladies, come on over and draw your question," Louisa requested.

"What if we choose not to participate?" Tanya asked, as she pulled her question.

"You have to participate," Louisa replied.

"What if we don't have an answer to the question?" Catara said after looking at hers.

"I'm sure if you search deep enough, you'll come up with something."

The waitress came with Alecia's drink.

"Okay, ladies, Jessica and Stan are going to load your luggage into the car while we go over the itinerary."

Louisa opened her notebook and began to relay every detail of their packed schedule.

19

LIMO RIDE

THE LADIES LOADED into the limousine and headed for their first destination, Bal Harbour Shops, where they were allotted $1,000 each to spend in any store of their choice on any items they chose.

"This limo is off the hook!" Lashawnda commented.

"Oh, I could get used to this," Catara agreed.

"Oh, me too," Tanya said.

Elise looked at the seats, the bar, and the lighting system, smiling the whole time. "This is nice," she finally said.

"Okay, listen up, everyone, we have two connecting suites at the Royal Palm Crowne Plaza Resort Hotel in South Beach. We're already checked in. Tonight, we're going to spend the evening slumber-party style.

"That should be fun," Elise said enthusiastically.

"We don't get our own rooms?" Alecia asked.

"With the connecting suites, we have four bedrooms with two double beds in each. Each person will have her own bed."

"But that means sharing a room with a stranger," Alecia frowned.

"Believe me, Alecia, you'll be just fine. We're going to stay up pretty late, and we have to be up early to catch the ship. It departs at eight and we have to be checked in by seven-thirty."

"So how do we choose who we'll be sharing with?" Tanya asked.

"We'll figure it out tonight. Maybe we'll draw straws or something to work it out."

"I don't care who I share with as long as they don't snore. I can't sleep through loud snoring, although I have been known to snore myself," Catara joked.

"Well, I don't snore, and I sleep like a rock. I'll share with you," Lashawnda said.

"That's cool," Catara replied.

"Like I said, we'll figure it out. Now, once we get to the mall, you each have only two hours to spend a thousand dollars," Louisa said.

"Here are brochures for the different designer boutiques," Jessica added, handing them out. "Peruse them so you'll have an idea of where you want to spend your time shopping."

"Oh, I already know where I'm going," Alecia said.

Jessica handed each lady a mall gift certificate. "You have to spend your money. What you don't use, you lose," she said.

"I don't know when I went shopping last," Elise said. "I'm getting something for everybody back home."

Everybody stopped going through their brochures and looked at her like she was an alien.

"Seriously, I just opened my own business this year and have been saving over the past few years, in case I have some down times. So, shopping is a luxury that I've had to forfeit for my business," Elise explained.

"Sorry, ladies, no gifts for other people," Louisa interjected. "This is your birthday gift—all the money has to be spent on you."

"Doesn't your man give you money to go shopping?" Tanya asked as if it were some written law.

"I'm single, and even if I had a boyfriend, I don't know if he'd always send me shopping."

"What good is a man to you if he can't take care of you?" Alecia asked.

Elise felt like a foreigner in a strange land. These women saw men as ATMs. "I always thought a man should be loved and would love me in return; that relationships should be based on mutual respect and trust, not a monetary exchange. To me, relationships are two-way streets. He gives a little, and so do I. But my love can't be purchased because it's not for sale."

"In what world?" Lashawnda said, rolling her neck. She thought Elise was about the most naive woman she'd ever met. "The only two-way street I know is where you give your heart and get a hard way to go in return."

"Exactly—that's why all I give a man is time, when it's convenient for me, and heartless attention. In return, he gives me his credit card," Alecia said proudly.

"Well, I'm with Elise. I think relationships should be about an emotional tie between two people," Louisa said.

"But as hard as they try . . ." Tanya began. "Wait a minute; they *don't* try, because they are incapable of making a true emotional connection. That's why you have to get out of him what you can, when you can, before he meets someone younger and prettier who does a better job of stroking his ego."

"And his dick," Lashawnda added.

"Maybe in some cases, with shallow men. But a real man doesn't operate like that," Elise insisted.

"Do they exist?" Louisa questioned.

"I think so," Elise responded with conviction.

"Well, maybe in Kentucky, but I have yet to run into one in New York," Catara said.

"Or L.A.," Alecia agreed.

"Or Chicago," Tanya backed her up.

"And definitely not Atlanta," Lashawnda added.

"That's why you have to get everything you can from them because they really don't give a shit about you or their wives," Alecia said.

"Okay. So maybe some—and I emphasize *some*—men can be foul, but I believe that if we fall into their game of 'if you give me this, then I'll give you that,' we lose our power as women," Elise said.

"No, we gain power," Alecia said defensively.

"I agree, Alecia," Tanya said.

"Yeah, I feel pretty powerful when a man buys me a new car or spends obscene amounts of money on me," said Alecia, "especially when I don't have deep feelings for him."

"But what about when you do?" Catara asked.

"Then it's even better, because eventually he's going to break my heart or move on, and by then I will have sucked his pockets dry," Alecia said.

"Did you even stop to think that maybe that's why he moves on, because he can no longer afford you?" Jessica timidly offered.

"No!" Alecia said with bitterness in her voice. "He moves on because he's a hunter, looking for new prey to devour. But, you see, I am empowered because he might leave with a piece of my heart, but I'm left with a piece of his income."

"But is that true power?" Elise said. "I don't think so—you still aren't getting what you want out of it, because deep down women want the same thing, men's hearts. Your playing that kind of game perpetrates a cycle."

"What kind of cycle?" Louisa asked. She was surprised that Elise had such a strong opinion.

"The kind that forces women to act out of their nature and become just as manipulative and heartless as men supposedly are toward us," Elise said.

"Do we have a choice?" Tanya asked. "This is a dog-eat-dog world. We have to do what we have to do in order to survive."

"Preach on," Lashawnda agreed.

"As long as we operate outside of our loving and caring nature, men will forever control us," Elise said.

"You have a good argument, but I don't see sincere loving and caring flying in the new millennium," Catara said.

"Well, I've broken the cycle, and even though I don't have a man buying me all the latest name-brand fashions, I feel good about who I am, what I stand for, and the goals I am achieving. I am a person who stands alone. When a real man comes along, and I know he will, I will be able to say that I didn't compromise my womanhood just to outdo a man in a relationship. Life is just too short to get caught up in those kinds of games," Elise said.

"I hear you," Catara replied.

"When it's all said and done, I want to leave a legacy that my children and their children can be proud of. No disrespect to either of you, Alecia or Tanya, but manipulating a man for his money doesn't qualify for a legacy in my book," Elise added.

"No, she didn't," Tanya said rolling her eyes.

"You are just a clueless plain Jane from Kentucky, what do you know about anything anyway?" Alecia boldly asked.

Louisa shook her head; she knew how cruel Alecia could be if she in any way felt threatened.

"Yeah, it might seem that way to you, but I know more than you think," Elise said, defending herself. "As a matter of fact, Louisa, if it's okay with you, I'd like to answer the question that I drew."

"Okay, that's cool. Whatever—as long as it'll calm things down a bit."

20

ELISE'S STORY: PROUD OF IT

ELISE PULLED THE slip of paper out of her pocket. "My question is 'What am I most proud of?' Let me see, where do I start?" Elise said.

I USED TO be a pretty well-known gymnast, back when I was in college. I actually made the U.S. Rhythmic Gymnastics Olympic team.

"I'VE NEVER HEARD of you," Alecia interrupted.
 "Shhh, let her talk," Catara retorted.

ANYWAY, BECAUSE I was a member of the Olympic team, I was often invited to events attended by the finest athletes in the country, as well as by coaches and sponsors. And let me tell you, the men who attended those events were fine, physically fit, and wealthy or on their way to riches.

During the Olympic trials that year, I was badly injured and couldn't compete. I was devastated. I would venture to say that it was the lowest I'd ever fallen emotionally. I had no money, no self-esteem, and because that injury marked the end of my gymnastic career, I felt like I had no identity.

"Because I was on the 'in' list at one time, it took a while for my name to fall off, so I continued to receive various invitations to parties and social events that took place up until years after the Olympics."

"WAIT A MINUTE, wait a minute," Tanya interrupted. "It's good that you were this great gymnast, but how are you just gonna change the subject about relationships, just to let us know?"

"I haven't changed the subject. Just stay with me," Elise assured her. "Now, where was I?" she thought out loud. "Okay . . ."

FOR YEARS I had been down in the dumps, with no motivation for getting up. Shortly after graduating from college, I received an invitation to a party that I'd hoped for years to go to. No matter how depressed I felt, I was going to the party. It was right in my city. I had to go. It was during the Kentucky Derby, and anybody who was anybody was in town.

So I did my female thing and got my hair and makeup together and found my best party dress and motivated myself to go. I had convinced myself that if I wasn't going to be a great athlete, then I would find one, marry him, and ride on his thunder.

Just as I'd hoped, I met a guy and instantly fell for his status and position. He was one of the few black men who owned a racehorse. The man was mature, wealthy, and well respected in his circles. I ran into him, literally, when I was coming out of the ladies' room at the hotel.

We hit it off instantly. His ranch was in Lexington, but he also had a home in Louisville. We went out a few times whenever he was staying in Louisville, but it wasn't until our third date that I found out he was married. I was appalled, hurt, and brokenhearted.

There was very little back then to be happy about, but when he was around, my worries seemed to disappear. I felt validated again. Nevertheless, I told him that I couldn't see him again, but he seemed unfazed by his being married. As a matter of fact, I even remember him saying, "I thought you knew."

After that date, I avoided him like the plague. I didn't return his calls,

so he stopped calling. Then one day I heard that his horse had been injured, so I called and left a message on his voice mail to extend my con-
dolences.

The next day he called me, begging to see me. I resisted, but I guess
I gave him just enough to feel like he could call me every day. I finally
gave in and met him for dinner.

Now, let me inform you ladies that I was strapped for cash. My car
was barely rolling, plus I didn't know what I wanted to do with my life.
This man pulls up in a brand-new Benz, and then, during dinner, he
asks me to allow him to take care of me. He offered to lease an apartment for me, and buy me a new car and whatever else my heart desired.
Believe me, back then my heart desired a number of things.

I told him no. I didn't want to disrespect his wife.

Then he asked me, "Can we go out for dinner some time when I'm in
town? That would be harmless, right?"

I said, "I guess you're right."

The next time we met for dinner, he came bearing gifts. He brought
me a suit that totaled two thousand dollars. I knew the cost because I
had to go back to the store and get it altered. I saw it hanging on the
rack and looked at the price. Let me just say that my mind was blown.
I'd never spent too much over a hundred dollars on any clothing item,
and this man paid two thousand for one suit, just because!

After receiving that gift, I found myself dating him more often. I will
admit I crossed over the line a bit. I had begun kissing him at the end
of our dates—I mean really *kissing* him.

You all are women, so I know you can imagine the different scenar-
ios I created in my mind, like being his mistress and not having to worry
about money or success—I'd spend his money and enjoy his success. I
was slowly becoming caught up.

One day I was asked to attend a society women's luncheon with a
group I really admired, and I wore my suit. I felt the positive attention.
I felt the eyes on my attire. I noticed the special treatment. Most of
those women were swimming in money, and they knew that I had spent
a pretty penny on my outfit.

I left that event feeling like a million bucks, but when I got into
my car, it wasn't good enough for my suit. When I got back home to my
apartment, it wasn't good enough for my suit. When I went out with the

guy again, I felt like I didn't have anything good enough to wear. But, I pulled something together.

That evening at dinner, he again offered to take care of me. The part of me that was lacking, which was most of me at that time, wanted to say yes. But I resisted.

That night, after dinner, we got into his car, and he convinced me to ride around with him a bit. His car was so comfortable, so luxurious. We ended up in front of one of the nicest hotels in Louisville.

We parked. We were downtown and everything about being with him felt right. I loved everything about him, except for the fact that he was married.

He took my hand. "Elise, you know I'm crazy about you. There is nothing I wouldn't do for you."

"I do. But you have a wife," I reminded him.

"Listen, I'm not going to beat around the bush. I'm true to my game, but I want to take care of you, fulfill your dreams. I want to be there for you."

Dollar signs were in my eyes. I couldn't think straight—and it was not just the money. This man was handsome and appealing. Without a doubt, I was turned on. Before I knew it, I was upstairs in a hotel room with him. The room was elegant. The bedding was soft. Everything that he offered me was luxurious. When he touched me, I shivered with lust. At that moment, I wanted him more than I wanted to be right. Plus, I hadn't had sex with a man in over a year.

As he undressed me, he painted a picture of all the nice things we would do together, of all the nice things he'd do for me.

I was hypnotized.

Once we were both nude, he asked me to go down on him.

That snapped me out of the trance. First of all, that had never been my thing, and second of all, I was just plain overwhelmed that it was the first thing he'd ask me to do.

"STOP THE PRESSES," Tanya interrupted. "You don't like it?"

"It's okay, but I don't love it," Elise said matter-of-factly. "But that's a whole other conversation."

"Finish the story," Louisa and Catara said in unison.

They laughed.

OKAY. WE WERE in this wonderful hotel room and I was ready to give my-self to this man. Have you ever just needed to be close to a man? Well, that's where I was. I was craving him. I put his wife out of my mind be-cause I had been without for so long, and I was in a need. He stepped to the plate, and I was going to let him give me any and everything he had to offer. That is, until he asked me to go down on him.

I looked around the room. I looked at him. I looked at the situa-tion, and I had to escape. I found myself in a place that I swore I would never be.

I told him, "I can't do this."

"We've got all night," he whispered. "Take your time."

I said, "No. I mean I can't be here like this. I've got to go."

"Don't do this to me," he begged.

"I have to go," I said and got up and began getting dressed.

He reluctantly put on his clothes, and we went back to his car. We were silent during the drive back to my car. Once he pulled next to my car he said—and I'll never forget his words—"You need to decide what you're going to do."

The words clung to me. I needed to make a choice. After that, every time I went into my closet and saw that two-thousand-dollar suit, I began to dream again. I had to pray about it because it was a constant reminder of what I didn't have and what he could give to me, and of what I wanted from him and what I needed to do if I wanted to get it.

Eventually, I decided that I had to be real with myself and do what was best for the whole me. I couldn't let the material things that he of-fered me influence my life choices. One day, when I was so torn after one of our telephone conversations, I hung up from him and pulled the suit out from the closet.

It's amazing the power that he had over me, just by the suit being in my closet.

Y'all are going to say I'm crazy, but I wanted to get my power back, so I rummaged through my drawers and found a pair of scissors. I took those scissors to that suit and shredded it into tiny pieces. I gathered it into a bag and took it outside to the dumpster.

The next morning, when I heard the garbage truck outside my win-dow, I smiled. A feeling of relief came over me. It was that day that I really began to think about who I was, what I wanted to accomplish, and what I wanted to leave behind.

I'm about to turn thirty. I've just opened my own gymnastics center. Every day I step foot in my gym, I touch a child's life. I've met a guy— a good guy—and I like him a lot. There are sparks between us, but we're taking things slow and getting to know each other. I'm not stressed about what I can get from him, not in the way that I used to be.

I'm sure I would eventually like a nice home and a nice car, but right now I am laying a foundation and building on it. I am confident that by taking my chosen route, whatever I involve myself in will not be as easily shattered as if I had taken the shallow route of living a life where nothing is truly pleasing to the heart.

ELISE SIGHED, A serious look on her face. Then she replaced it with a smile. "That's what I'm most proud of."

Silence fell over the car. Elise's story had sent each woman into her own private thoughts. As honest as Elise had been, none felt they could have shared such a truth with complete strangers.

"Wow," Louisa said. "Very well done. Thanks for your honesty and candidness." She inhaled deeply, feeling like she had to say something. She hadn't expected that honest an answer to the question, but she was glad Elise offered it.

"We're coming up to the mall, ladies. I'll let you off out front," Stan said as he maneuvered the limousine in front of the entrance. "Louisa and Jessica, you have my pager number. Just beep me when you're ready."

Stan put the gear in park, then walked around to let the women out so they could indulge in their shopping spree.

21

SHOPPING SPREE

WHEN THE WOMEN walked through the entrance of the mall doors, an atmosphere of elegance and sophistication greeted them. People were going in and out of shops, while others admired the indoor ponds with koi swimming in them.

"I hope everybody has an idea of where they're going to go," Louisa said. "Check your watches. Make sure everyone has the same time. Let's meet back here in exactly two hours. That's five-thirty. If you're not here, you get left. I'm serious, ladies—please be cognizant of the time."

The women adjusted their watches.

"We can stay in a group or split up. It's up to you," Louisa said.

The women compared the shops that they wanted to go to and decided that they would spend the first hour traveling together, and if they needed to, they'd separate during the last hour.

They paraded in and out of the various boutiques, trying on and purchasing clothes and accessories, including shoes, purses, and jewelry. They sampled and purchased perfumes, bath products, and makeup.

The women laughed and joked and gave suggestions to one another about what looked good and what didn't. They shopped well together and didn't want to separate as they began to run out of time, but they decided it would be best if they wanted to meet their deadline.

By five-thirty, everyone began to gather at the entrance. The first person there was Alecia, who had met up with Louisa and Jessica earlier. The two radio show employees had been allotted only five hundred dollars each and had finished fairly quickly. Everyone else fell in one by one. Elise and Lashawnda competed for being loaded down with the most bags. Catara had a handful, Tanya had three, and Alecia had one small bag.

"I can't believe you all made it back with time to spare. Did everybody have a good time?" Louisa asked.

"The best," Elise said.

"Thank you so much, Louisa," Lashawnda said. "You've made my year."

"Girl, don't thank me, thank the station. This was a treat for me as well. I got three pairs of shoes and Jessica got a party outfit. What else?" Louisa asked.

"I got shoes, perfume, a nice pair of shades, and a cute little purse," Jessica said enthusiastically.

"Is that all you got?" Lashawnda asked Alecia, who was carrying one bag.

"Yes," she replied.

"You spent all your money on one item?" Elise asked, surprised.

"Yeah, I got a watch."

"You got a thousand-dollar watch?" Lashawnda asked.

"Well, actually I put a few dollars with it to get it," Alecia responded dryly.

"I couldn't have gone out like that," Lashawnda said. "I got a little bit of everything." She pointed to her bags on the ground beside her.

"So did I—and I caught some great sales," Elise bragged. "What about you, Catara. What did you get?"

"Oh, glasses, a purse, a few pairs of shoes, and some bath products. Things like that," she replied nonchalantly. She was not surprised, but still a bit frustrated, that she couldn't find any clothes in her size that were stylish enough.

"And what did you get, Tanya?" Elise asked.

"I got some clothes," Tanya answered and abruptly looked away.

Jessica looked down at Tanya's bags and said, "Did you know that the store you got your clothes from is a maternity store?"

"Yes," an annoyed Tanya answered.

"Oh, excuse me," Jessica said, embarrassed that she had put her foot in her mouth.

Everybody in the group pretended to be looking out for Stan, except for Lashawnda, who just couldn't bite her tongue, especially in a tense situation.

"So how far along are you?" she asked.

"I just found out. I took a home pregnancy test a few days ago. I was in denial, but when I walked by the store, I couldn't help but go in."

"So you're excited about it?" Lashawnda asked.

"I don't know how I feel about it," Tanya replied.

"Here's Stan," Catara announced.

The ladies gathered their things and walked toward the limousine. They put whatever bags could fit into the truck with their luggage. The rest they put inside with them.

"I'm bushed," Alecia said as she slid into her seat.

"I'm sure everybody else is beat, because I'm tired myself," Louisa said. "We're now headed to the spa. It's less than two miles from the hotel. They're going to stay open late just for us. We'll rotate between two estheticians, two masseuses, two hair stylists, and two nail technicians. You will also be able to get a body scrub as well."

"What about dinner?" Elise asked.

"We'll eat in the hotel restaurant afterward, but they'll have hors d'oeuvres at the spa for us to munch on. So, everybody, sit back and relax until we get to the spa. It's about a fifteen-minute ride," Louisa announced.

The ladies sat back and attempted to relax, with the exception of Lashawnda. She couldn't get Tanya's reaction about her newly discovered pregnancy out of her mind. She had so many questions and knew she wouldn't be able to relax until she asked them. She looked over at Tanya, who was sitting back with her eyes closed, just like everyone else—except Jessica, who was looking out the window at the sights.

Lashawnda kept staring until Tanya opened her eyes.

"I hope you don't mind, but I was wondering if you've told your new baby's daddy?" she asked.

Eyes popped open around the car.

Initially Tanya was offended, but, she figured, why not talk? Elise had. After all, after the weekend she would never see these women again.

"No, I haven't." She sighed.

"Are y'all in a committed relationship? Was it a one-night stand?" Lashawnda pushed.

"Well, if you have to know, he's been my boyfriend since my senior year in high school. I think we just broke up," Tanya said and moved uncomfortably in her seat. "That's why I haven't told him." Tanya could feel tears welling up, so she laid her head back and closed her eyes again.

"Man," Lashawnda said. Her heart went out to Tanya. "So how do you feel about it?"

She couldn't hold back her feelings, "Didn't you ask me that question already?" she snapped.

"I apologize, Tanya. It's just that—"

Before Lashawnda could finish, Tanya interrupted, "How do I feel? I feel like shit! The man I've been with all my adult life chose money over me. Now I'm going to have to make it all alone, with a new baby, and I was hoping to move to Atlanta by the end of the year. Now I might be stuck in Chicago, raising a kid. It's not that I don't love Chicago, because I do—it's my home—but he and I talked about a fresh start in Atlanta, and I'm longing for that. It seems like I keep falling deeper into this situation and I don't see a way out."

Tanya began to bawl uncontrollably. She'd been trying to hold it together, but talking forced the sting of reality on her.

"I'm so sorry, Tanya. I didn't mean to. . ." Lashawnda said.

"It's okay. Does somebody have a tissue?" Tanya asked, wiping away her tears with her fingers.

Louisa knocked on the window to the front seat, "Stan, are there any tissues back here?"

He opened the window, "Here you go," he said and handed her a box.

Louisa held the tissues out for Tanya. She grabbed a few and began to wipe her face.

Tanya blew her nose. "I'm a thirty-year-old woman, and I am scared."

"Tanya, it's okay to be scared," Louisa said, attempting to assure her.

"I know, but I'm petrified because when I go back to Chicago on

Sunday I have not just one, but numerous decisions to make." She balled the tissue in her fist. "Chris, that's my boyfriend, has always been there for me. It's too complicated, it's too much. And on top of that I want to stay, but I can't." Tanya inhaled awkwardly then continued. "It's just like you were saying, Elise, sometimes you have to make decisions that empower you. But I'm scared. I can't believe that I'm admitting it, but I am."

Catara, who was sitting by Tanya, said, "The thing about facing huge problems or obstacles is that they're never as big as they seem. Plus, you're stronger than you think."

Tanya eyed Catara, "Believe me, I haven't begun to scrape the surface. My problems are large and complicated. But you wouldn't be able to understand the place I grew up in or the people I grew up around," Tanya replied.

"Maybe not, but a problem is a problem, no matter where you're from. Living with being overweight for several years has been only one of my many problems," Catara said. "But the problem is not what's important; really, it's how you overcome it that counts."

22

CATARA'S STORY: LIFE-CHANGING

M Y FAMILY IS close-knit, protective. I have always loved fashion design, but my parents wanted me to get a practical degree that would ensure employment for me after graduation. So instead of going away to fashion-design school, I went to Indiana University and got my degree in marketing.

I graduated and had no problem getting a job in Indianapolis. Initially, I was cool with my job. I got my own apartment. Got a brand-new car. I was feeling good about life. But the longer I stayed, the more I longed to go to fashion-design school. The more I got involved with the duties of my position and climbing the corporate ladder, the more I imagined myself with a sketchbook in my hands.

Instead of following my dreams, I started chasing a corner office with a view, a title, respect. It got so bad that I even started coming up with schemes to be noticed around the office, like making sure I arrived earlier and left later than my boss, even when it wasn't necessary.

I didn't even like my job or who I'd become. I had closed myself off from anything that was creative. I purchased the book *Think and Grow Rich,* and that was the only reading that I did. I had dehumanized myself. Nothing mattered except success.

To make a long story short, I had pushed myself so hard and closed myself off to any outlets or releases. I had a mental breakdown. Depression had been creeping up on me, but after I was passed up for that second promotion, I became overwhelmed. I couldn't eat. I couldn't get out of bed.

In my worst state, I missed two weeks of work, causing me to lose my job. I lost my apartment. I lost my car, and I had to move back in with my parents. On top of that, I put on twenty extra pounds. It was a nightmare.

I lived with my parents for three months. I had no direction. I felt like I had no purpose. I had failed. My life was bleak. All those clichés applied to me. I didn't see any hope because I knew that I didn't want to go back to my old lifestyle, but I didn't want to disappoint my family and go off to fashion-design school.

Eventually, I began temping at different companies just so I had a reason to leave the house, but I was emotionally empty. I was scared that if I went to fashion school, my parents wouldn't support me, or that I would fail. I felt like I was starting over, and that was frightening.

This continued on until one day, when I was grocery shopping with my mom. When we left the store, the sky was gray and a huge, thick dark cloud loomed above. As we were driving home, Mom said, "Looks like it's going to storm."

"Yeah, it's gonna be a bad one too, judging from that cloud," I agreed.

When we got into our neighborhood, two boys were walking down the street. I joked and said, "Y'all better take cover because a wreck of a storm is on its way."

The cloud was eerie and intimidating; Mom and I watched it until we pulled up into our driveway. We got the groceries from out of the trunk and walked up to the back door.

On the railing of the patio, close to the door, were two birds. When humans get too close, what do they usually do? Fly away. Well, one of the birds took off as soon as we got close, but the other stayed in place; he didn't move at all. It was the oddest thing we'd ever experienced, so odd that my mother and I walked off the patio and around to the front of the house and went in through the front door.

When we got into the kitchen, I couldn't help but look out the window to see if the bird was still there. I tapped on the window to try to scare it away. The bird didn't budge.

"Catara, leave the bird alone," my mom said. "Its wing is probably broken."

I helped her put away the groceries, but my curiosity got the better of me, so I went back to the window and closely observed the bird. It was looking up at the sky.

"OKAY, ISN'T THIS supposed to be a true story?" Alecia complained.

"Here's my hand to God," Catara said and raised her hand above her head, waving it.

THE BIRD WAS looking up at the sky in the direction of the massive cloud, moving from the left toward the house.

In my mind, I'm saying, *Okay, when this storm hits, I know this bird is going to fly away.* So I'm watching this bird, and the bird is standing there watching this cloud move closer and closer to the house. The closer the cloud gets, the darker the sky becomes.

I said to my mom, "You've got to see this. The bird is watching the cloud."

So my mom comes over and sees for herself.

"Catara, you might be right. I think that bird is watching the cloud," she says, and then goes back to preparing dinner.

I pitch in and help her, but every so often I go back to the window to check on the bird and the dreadful cloud. I notice that the bird has adjusted his position to follow the slow-moving cloud.

Now check this out. That monster of a cloud is right over the house, and instead of pouring down and causing havoc, it lets out a few sprinkles on the patio. The bird kept moving down the rail to get a look at the cloud as it moved to the right of the house. I know y'all are not going to believe me when I tell you this, but once the cloud had moved several houses to the right, the bird flew away.

CATARA PAUSED FOR a reaction.

"So what's the big deal about that? I've seen stranger things happen," Tanya said.

Lashawnda looked at Catara like she was a mental case.

"Well, the question I drew was, 'What one thing influenced or changed your life?' "

"So a bird looking at a cloud changed your life," Tanya said, frustrated. She was in the middle of a crisis, and this crazy woman was talking about a damned bird.

IT SEEMED SIMPLE that night, but after I slept on it, I awoke extra-early the next morning because it came to me. My experience with the bird and the cloud made perfect sense. You see, I was like a typical bird, scared of living life, scared to face anything that was different.

Do you ever see birds around when it's raining? No! Do you ever see birds around people? No! They take cover and hide their faces. That's exactly what I had been doing. I was hiding from life, hiding from the possibility of failure. I was hiding from the possibility of disappointing my family and from seeking out a more fulfilling life.

The first bird that flew away the moment we walked on the patio had no idea we wouldn't hurt it, but it didn't stay around to find out. Just like me, refusing to face my fears and pursue the dreams so close to my heart. I had no idea what possibilities lay ahead for me.

But the second bird stepped out of its comfort zone, faced my mom and me and what threatened to be a horrific storm. It stared that cloud in the face and didn't hide from us. It stood firm, only to realize that that cloud was harmless and so were we.

I'm telling you, that bizarre occurrence with the bird was exactly what I needed at that time in my life to find the courage to take control of my situation. I soon began to take action, and even as frightened or intimidated as I was, I applied to FIDM, a fashion-design school in Los Angeles. And I got accepted. Then I packed up and moved to L.A., even though my family didn't support me wholeheartedly—they were scared too.

I completed my master's and then turned around and moved to New York to pursue my career.

"SO, HAVE YOU been successful?" Alecia asked.

"Well, not in the way that you might consider success. But yes, I am successful. I am pursuing my dreams. I'm no longer obsessed with clawing my way to the top immediately. I work around fashion on a daily basis at Saks. I am enjoying the twists and turns and peaks and dips that come with pursuing my dream. I have created several clothing lines, although they're not on the market yet. Now I have the tools to create fashions, when before I only longed to learn how. I haven't cracked the door open yet to work under a designer, but I am pursuing it every day. Every time I get scared and want to give up, I think of the courage of that little bird on my mother's patio."

"That's sweet," Elise said. "You seeing that bird was like a miracle."

"Yeah, it was," Catara said. "I'm glad I told the story, for myself, because I have to remember to apply that same amount of courage to dealing with life being overweight. I have to break out of my shell again and stop doubting that I can be in a relationship or doubting that I'm beautiful because I'm a big girl."

"I know it's not an easy thing to do," Louisa said. "I have to be honest—after reading the passion behind your letter, I knew you were going to be cool people. The thought of you being overweight never crossed my mind. Now that I've met you and am getting to know you, I like you. I admire your drive."

"Thank you," Catara said. Louisa's words meant a lot to her, especially because they were coming from a woman Catara admired.

"Honey, the man who finds you will be lucky," Louisa said.

"Yeah, he will," Catara said, trying to find motivation in her words. Then she turned to Tanya, who was looking away. "We wouldn't be human if we didn't have problems and ridiculous obstacles to face."

Tanya didn't respond.

"Nobody changes overnight. With all the dieting I've attempted, I know that better than most, but I hope that as I use my bird story to face each day, you'll use it too, or whatever it takes, to confront whatever you'll be met with when you go back home."

Tanya gazed out the window. She didn't say a word, but she appreciated Catara's story and her concern. She wasn't sure if it would help her own life in any way, but she appreciated it.

23

SPA TREATMENT

*S*TAN PULLED UP in front of the day spa. "I got my girlfriend a gift certificate to come here for her birthday last year. You ladies are in for a treat. After her visit, she raved for months."

"Are you still with her?" Lashawnda asked as she stepped out of the limousine.

"You better believe it. I'm going to ask her to marry me this Christmas," Stan announced proudly.

They congratulated him.

"As usual, give me a page when you're ready," he said.

"Of course we will," Louisa replied, and followed the ladies inside.

They entered the spa and took seats. A middle-age woman approached them and greeted them. "Welcome, ladies, and congratulations on winning the Night Before Thirty contest. In addition to the treatment you'll receive here tonight, we have gift bags filled with some of our best-selling products."

"Thank you," Catara said.

"No, thank *you*. This contest has sparked *so* much conversation around here about our own thirtieth birthdays. I tell you, I expected to know it all when I turned thirty, but I got there and realized I had a whole new set of lessons to learn." She laughed. "But the beauty of age is that it brings wisdom. Embrace your life, ladies, and the lessons that it brings with it! If you ignore the lessons, it'll come to you in a different form, but if you pay attention and learn it the first time, you don't have to repeat it again—and you're open to new and deeper truths."

The women nodded.

"At any rate, follow me to the back. And as we walk, please let me know what you would like to drink. We have bottled water, freshly squeezed orange juice, and wine."

Everyone gave her order, and the lady escorted them to a dressing area. "Please change into the robes laid out for each of you, and I will return with your drinks. As you can see, we have light snacks prepared for your enjoyment. Please help yourselves."

As the women set their things aside and changed into their spa robes, they made small talk. They all seemed comfortable getting undressed around one another, except for Catara, who kept her back to the rest of the women so they wouldn't see her stomach. Even though she spoke so passionately about accepting her weight in the car, she still wasn't quite ready to expose her body to the women.

Once they were changed, the ladies checked out the earthy, warm room. There were plush, oversize tawny sofas surrounding a coffee table with burning sandlewood-scented candles. Magazines and books were on the end tables. The walls were a warm chestnut, and the artwork and greenery were well integrated, creating a calm flow of energy.

Each woman found a comfortable seat and soaked in the classical music that was flowing lightly through the room. They enjoyed the soothing party, pleasing to their senses: sight, sound, touch, and smell.

Their hostess returned with their drinks on a tray and passed them out. "We're going to separate you out. The staff will come in and call you for your treatment, and in between you can come back in here and lounge and snack until your next service."

"I've never been to a spa before, unless you count those storefront nail shops a spa," Tanya said.

"Not hardly," Alecia said.

"It's not that I couldn't afford it," Tanya said, eyeing Alecia. "I just never went. I think I'm going to have to change that. I'm enjoying this already, and we haven't even gotten started."

"I really should go more often, but sometimes I get so busy that I don't get around to making an appointment," Catara said.

"And that's when you need it the most, when you're busy," Lashawnda said.

The staff members came in and picked them up for their services. Alecia and Catara left with the nail technicians, Lashawnda with the facialist, Tanya with the masseuses, Louisa and Elise with the hair stylists, and Jessica for her body scrub.

Tanya sat back on a sofa and munched on some fruit while waiting to be picked up for her next service, when Catara walked in admiring her nails.

"I got my I-cures," she joked, borrowing Tanya's slang from earlier that day in the airport.

Tanya smiled. Then asked, "Where's Alecia? Didn't she go in with you?"

"Yeah, but she's giving the manicurist the blues. First she made her completely remove the polish the woman had just put on her toes and start all over again. Then once the lady was almost finished repolishing them, she told her she was incompetent and insisted that my manicurist finish her up." Catara shook her head in disbelief. "Now her first manicurist is outside sneaking a smoke, and the other is trying to get Alecia's pedicure right."

"She is a diva!"

"Louisa did warn us."

"She did, but Alecia is outta control."

"So how was your massage?" Catara asked.

"Girl, my mind is still in that room on that table. It was marvelous," Tanya replied.

"Was the masseuse a man, and did you have to take all your clothes off?" Catara asked.

"Yes and yes. But he used towels to cover the sections that weren't being massaged."

Tanya could see the concern in Catara's eyes.

"When I was in high school and went to the free clinic to get my pap smears, there was a poster on the wall above the table. It had a smiling monkey on it and read, 'Grin and bare it.' Do that when you undress."

"Okay, I'll try that."

"The masseuse is very professional. Plus, you'll be lying on your stomach. If he's checking out the goods, you'll never know. Then before you know it, his magic fingers will be feeling so good that you won't care if he's looking, as long as he continues to release that stress from your muscles."

Catara laughed.

"I'm telling you, girl, if I would've been on that table any longer I would have cried like a baby. It was just that good."

"If it's like that, he'd better hurry up and come and pick me up." Catara got up and put a few pieces of fruit on her plate.

Over the next three to four hours, the ladies indulged in their pamper party and met at the hors d'oeuvres table between rotating treatments.

Alecia was pleased with everything except her session with the manicurist. Catara loved her I-cures. Elise wanted to take the stylist back to Louisville with her just to do her hair every day. Lashawnda went on about her facial, while Tanya raved all night about her massage. Jessica and Louisa's favorites were the body scrub. Jessica went on about how her body never glistened or shined so before now.

At the end of their time at the spa, the entire staff wished them well and sent them away with nice gift bags filled with a body wash and sponge, lotion, foot cream, and a scented candle. The birthday girls walked away breathing deeper and stepping lighter. Yet they didn't allow themselves to get too relaxed. They knew there was still more to come.

24

ROYAL QUARTERS

S TAN PULLED UP to the Royal Palm Crowne Plaza Resort Hotel.
"Nice," Lashawnda said.

"The beach is right behind the hotel," Stan informed them.

"I hope we get a good view from our room," Elise said.

"You're going to love the view," Louisa replied. "Jessica and I already went up to check the suites out."

A guy from the bell stand immediately approached the car and opened the doors. "Welcome to the Royal Palm Crowne Plaza Resort," he said.

Once they stepped into the lobby, their energy level increased. The hotel reflected the art deco look common to South Beach. The lighting and the carefree feel of the people walking through were contagious. Once they got near the front desk, they were welcomed with warm greetings and met by the hotel manager.

"Good evening, Louisa and Jessica, and welcome back."

"Thank you," Louisa and Jessica replied.

"You ladies must be the winners of the Night Before Thirty contest!" They smiled.

"First of all, let me say happy birthday to all of you. I hope you'll enjoy your stay here at our resort. My staff and I will see to it that your visit with us is pleasant and memorable. Also, the owner asked me to extend a special welcome. He left gift baskets for each of you in your suites."

"Wow, happy birthday to us!" Lashawnda squealed.

Everyone laughed.

"You ladies will be dining in the hotel tonight, correct?"

"Right."

"Great. Ladies, have a wonderful weekend and remember—if you need anything, my staff and I are just a call away." He walked toward one of the bellboys, who had been trying to get his attention.

"I like this hotel," Tanya said passionately.

"I do too," Catara agreed.

"And did you know it's black-owned?" Jessica added.

"Shut up!" Lashawnda said. "Now, that's a wonderful thing. I'd like to shake his hand and let him know just how proud I am."

The women rushed up to their suites. Elise quickly went to pull open the blinds so she could get a look at the view. "Wow," she sighed. Everyone joined her by the window.

"I just love the ocean." Alecia sighed too. The sight took her back to the time she'd spent with William in San Diego.

"I can't wait to hit South Beach!" Catara said.

"We're going after dinner, right?" Tanya asked.

"Yeah, were going to take a stroll down Ocean Drive, take in the sights, and then come back here to get some rest," Louisa said.

"Good—I'm gonna need to walk off the meal," Catara added. She stepped away from the window and was about to fall into her usual pattern of dwelling on her shortcomings, when she caught a glimpse of the gift baskets. "Oh look!" she purred.

"Oooh," everyone gushed, and walked over to the baskets to examine their contents. Inside were coffee mugs with the hotel's logo on them and assorted Godiva chocolates and coffees. The notes attached read, *Relax and enjoy your thirtieth birthday—the best is yet to come!*

"This is just too much," Lashawnda gasped.

"Oh, there's more to come!" Louisa said mischievously.

The bellhop brought up their luggage and they quickly changed clothes. The women could hardly wait to head down the elevator to enjoy their evening. When they entered the hotel restaurant, they were promptly greeted and seated. After receiving their drinks and giving their dining orders to their waiter, the ladies began discussing their time at the spa.

"Elise, I must admit, your hair looks so much better," Alecia said.

"I know, girl. Going to the hairdresser is another one of those luxuries I've had to let go. I needed this," she agreed.

"It didn't look bad before, but I like it better this way," Alecia said.

"Thank you." Elise smiled.

"I'd like to get a few more minutes with that masseuse," Lashawnda said.

"Tell me about it. Not only was he efficient and effective, but he was fine too," Tanya joked.

Everybody toasted to the masseuse being fine.

"Am I the only single lady fiending for just one decent evening alone with a man?" Catara complained.

"I don't even remember what it was like to be in the company of a man," Lashawnda said.

Nobody else commented, so Catara turned to Lashawnda. "So what seems to be the problem—is it us or is it them?"

"I don't know what the problem is, but believe me, men aren't the only ones who don't know how to treat a woman," she said before she could stop herself.

Catara laughed, agreeing, and then stopped short when she realized what Lashawnda had said.

"You mean women friends, right?" Catara's tone turned serious.

"Women friends, women girlfriends, whatever. People just don't know how to act in relationships anymore," Lashawnda blurted out.

"Uumph," Catara grunted. She was at a loss for words, second-guessing the sexual preference of the woman she'd agreed to share a room with. She didn't want to be too hasty with her judgment, but she was a little curious. Living in New York had taught her one thing: The only way to find out was to ask. So she did. "Lashawnda, you talk as though you've been hurt by a woman. You're not lesbian, are you?"

"That's a good question, Catara. You know, I ask myself that very question on a daily basis," Lashawnda responded and took a gulp of her wine.

"So you like women?" Alecia asked, frowning.

Lashawnda turned her nose up at Alecia and directed her attention toward Catara. "I don't date women as a lifestyle choice, but I just got out of a relationship with a woman."

"Fascinating!" Jessica said, staring at Lashawnda in amazement.

Elise was outdone. She couldn't remember ever meeting anyone who had owned up to being a lesbian. She wanted to frown like Alecia did, but she waited. She thought Lashawnda was cool—there was no need to turn on her just because she liked women. She asked, "Why did you two break up?"

"I caught her sleeping with another woman," Lashawnda said, trying to laugh it off. "The chick was fine too—I got to give her that. She had nice breasts. I can see why Cicely got with her."

Jaws dropped around the table.

Lashawnda took another drink. "Shit, she was cute. I'll give a sister her props. That doesn't mean that I wanted to jump into bed and join them."

The waiter walked up and began serving the ladies. There was uneasiness within everyone, so Louisa figured it was her duty to change the pace of things.

"Let's take hands and say grace," she said after the last dish was placed on the table.

The women took hands and Louisa led grace. "Dear Heavenly Father, thank you for the food we're about to receive to nourish our bodies. May our time together this weekend as sisters be enjoyable, relaxing, and healing. In your son Jesus' name we pray. Amen."

"Amen," everyone responded in unison.

Louisa looked up and smiled at Lashawnda to comfort her.

Lashawnda took a deep breath and smiled back.

The ladies picked up their silverware and began eating.

Tanya took a bite of her steak and then looked at Lashawnda.

"What?" Lashawnda asked, dropping her silverware. "Why are you looking at me like that?" She was feeling protective, and prepared to defend herself if necessary.

"I might be wrong, but it seems to me that you're going through an identity crisis," Tanya said. "This steak is good!" She took another bite.

Lashawnda relaxed. She was relieved Tanya hadn't spit out a malicious remark at her. "You're right. I am trying to figure it out." She dug her fork into her bow-tie pasta. She was just glad that someone still wanted to talk about it. She didn't want to force the issue on anyone, but she wanted some advice. "I always thought I knew who I was, but I wanted a better life. I wanted to be more than I was. I mean, I was a twenty-something grocery bagger at a supermarket before I met Cicely."

"What do you do now?" Tanya asked.

"I'm an executive secretary. I work for Cicely. She saw to it that I received all the training I needed. She gave me a job. I had no education beyond high school before her. I owe her so much, but I don't know if I'm a lesbian."

"That's deep!" Jessica said.

"Since we've broken up, I've wanted to quit my job."

"Do it. You can always get another job," Tanya said.

Lashawnda sipped her wine, and shook her head, frowning in hopes that her expression would help get her point across. "Y'all don't understand. Working for Cicely was my first real job. She is my only work reference. She's not going to tell another potential employer that I'm a good worker—a damned good worker at that—so how could anybody else know?" She sipped again. "No one is going to hire me at least until I finish college. And that's way down the line because I'll only be going part-time."

"So what you're saying is, you will continue to work for her just because she hired you? And you've built an intimate relationship with her just because she's helped you?" Tanya said.

"Well, kind of," Lashawnda replied. She was still unsure why she'd continued to see Cicely.

"Like I said earlier, you're going through an identity crisis. Cicely knows she's a lesbian. She seems to be proud of it. It's her thing. But you, on the other hand, you don't know if you are, you don't know why you're with a lesbian. You probably don't even know what it truly means to be a lesbian," Tanya said.

She chewed on another piece of steak.

"And you do?" Lashawnda asked.

"Nah, I'm not gay. But I know what it means to be in and try to embrace an environment that isn't your own and doesn't even suit you," Tanya said.

25

TANYA'S STORY: A COSTLY LESSON

IT WAS THE beginning of my senior year in high school, several months before I met Chris. I was a wild child, but smart. I made good grades, but the thought of graduating terrified me, probably because no one encouraged me to go to college or suggested employment options. So I rebelled.

I started smoking weed and drinking every weekend. My friend Angel and I used to put our money together and give it to her cousin at school on Friday mornings. By the end of the day, we'd have two joints. Her mother went out every weekend, so I spent the night with her every time I got a chance. We would get so high!

One night Angel's uncle let her borrow his car, so we went riding around the neighborhood. We ran into some guys who were hanging out on the streets, and stopped and flirted. It turned out they were gang members. One of them, the one who seemed to be the leader, was confident, charming, and he took an interest in me. His name was Steve. Before long we began dating, and I tried to adapt to his way of life. There was always talk of getting somebody back for something they did, or letting people know who's got the juice. You know, things like that.

I was turned on by the control he had over the other members.

Those boys did whatever he said, exactly the way he asked it to be done. He had a temper on him, and I saw it displayed, but I didn't care because he didn't direct it toward me, at first. Plus it felt good to be accepted. That gang was like a family and because I was Steve's lady, they accepted me and let it be known that they had my back no matter what.

I didn't know who I was back then, but it didn't matter, with him being in my life. Whatever he was, I supported and embraced; therefore, I became whatever he stood for. That is, until the night I lied to my mother and told her I was spending the night with Angel, but I stayed with him instead. He had his own place.

We got into bed around eleven-thirty P.M. and started fooling around. I wasn't a virgin, but it was going to be the first time I ever slept with him, so I was nervous but excited. We'd just started kissing when the phone rang. Steve answered and the intensity of the conversation caused him to jump out of bed.

He hung up the phone and said, "We got some business we need to handle, and I need you to go with me."

I looked at the clock. It was midnight. So I asked, "Can't I just stay here until you get back?"

"No, I need you," he insisted.

I hesitantly got out of bed and got dressed. We jumped into the car and headed for the highway. Steve was speeding like a maniac.

I asked him where we were going.

He said, "Don't worry about it—you'll see when we get there. But we have about a two-hour drive ahead of us."

I attempted to sit back and relax, since it was going to take a while to get to where we were going, but he wasn't having that.

"I need you to watch out for five-oh," he said.

I sat up in the seat and tried to spot anything that looked like a cop.

I began to get nervous. "Why don't you slow down a bit?"

He shot a look at me that sent chills through my entire body. Then he said, "Why don't you shut the fuck up and watch out for the motherfucking police, like I told you?"

I went from caring for him to being terrified of him. I didn't know where we were going or when I'd see Chicago again, and I was too frightened to ask. One thing was for sure, I knew that I needed to keep an eye out for the police. I spotted several along the way. I often wondered what would have happened if we had been stopped by a cop, but we weren't.

Anyway, we pulled up to this warehouse, where two guys were waiting for us. Steve opened the car door and jumped out. He went around the corner with them. A few minutes later, they came back, each holding crates, which they put in the trunk of his car. Then they shook hands and dispersed. Steve got back into the car and said, "All right, we're headed home."

Just like that—no explanation, nothing.

At this point, I was fed up with the secrecy and his domineering attitude. On the way home, we were driving fast, but not nearly as quickly as we had been, so I calmed down a bit.

"So what are in the boxes?" I asked.

"You ask a lot of questions," he said.

"You got me up at all times of the night, speeding out of town, and now I'm riding around in a car with you and some boxes in the trunk. After all that, I think I deserve to know what's in the boxes."

"You need to be careful about what you ask for," he said. "Now, sit back. I got everything under control."

We sat in silence until he was ready to talk.

"Don't be mad at me," he said.

I didn't say anything. I realized that night that I didn't like him or anything he stood for. We couldn't get back to Chicago quickly enough. I just wanted to be away from him. I knew that something wasn't right about those boxes.

"Aw, so you're not talking to me!" he said.

"To say what?" I asked.

"Tell me how much you want me, just like you were doing at my place before we left."

"I'm not feeling that right now," I said.

"So what you trying to say?" he demanded.

"I already said it," I replied.

"Nobody, and I mean *nobody,* acts like that with Steve! Don't you know I will bitch-slap you, bitch?" he yelled and threw his hand up as if he were going to, but stopped short.

I was shocked.

"Nah, nah. I ain't gonna hurt you," he snickered slyly.

I didn't know what to think. We were about an hour from town, and I just kept telling myself to try to remain calm until I got home, then get the hell away from this fool.

The next thing I know he pulled off the freeway.

"Why are we stopping?" I asked.

"Because I need to show you something," he said.

"What?" I asked.

"You wanted to know what was in the boxes, right?" he said as he turned the car down a deserted, dark street.

"I did want to know, but I'm cool," I said, trying to sound nonchalant.

"No, you want to know, so I'm going to show you." He turned off his headlights and kept driving slowly down the long street. It dead-ended to an area that looked like a park.

"Get out!" he yelled.

I sat there in shock.

"Get out!" he barked.

I opened the car door. I knew he was going to leave me there, but Steve got out of the car and walked around to me. I was shivering inside, but I tried to appear cool.

"Come on," he said and we walked to the trunk of the car. He opened it and grabbed a screwdriver that was on the floor of the trunk. He used it to wedge open the top of the crate. He got it open—inside were countless numbers of guns.

"That's what's in the crates. Guns," he said calmly. "Now are you satisfied?"

Steve put one of the guns in his hand and gripped it tightly.

"You're not angry with me anymore are you, baby?" he said.

I managed a smile.

"Let's just take a moment to get back to where we were back at my place." He leaned in and started kissing my neck.

I was disgusted.

"You want me, don't you?" he whispered.

I couldn't answer. I didn't want him, and I couldn't form my mouth to lie. I tried to say "Yes," but it wouldn't come out.

"You do want me, don't you?" he whispered again. This time he rubbed the gun on the side of my face.

I knew the gun was probably not loaded, but the idea that it was in that crate and the possibility of a stray bullet being in there—on top of the fact that we were in the midst of a dark nowhere—freaked me out. I couldn't move. I was young, and I couldn't think. I didn't know what to do, so I stood there, speechless.

Steve started slowly unbuttoning my blouse. Then he pulled it down my arms. It was a fall night and kind of cool out. And that hawk attacked my bare skin. I was literally shaking. Then he pulled my skirt and my panties down to my ankles.

"Don't do this," I cried. Tears began to stream down my face because I knew that this man was going to take me and that there was nothing that I could do about it.

He pulled his pants down. Then pointed the gun at the ground. "Lay down," he said.

"On the ground?" I asked.

"Lay down," he said again.

I slowly walked over to the grass and lowered myself onto the ground. I kept saying silently, *I can't believe this is happening. I can't believe this is happening!*

I was being violated, raped; but it wasn't like on television, when some woman is caught alone and is struggling to get away from her attacker. I didn't fight him and there wasn't rage in his voice or his actions. The atmosphere was calm. I could hear crickets chirping. Steve slowly climbed on top of me. He actually caressed me. Then he stuck his dick inside of me, and as much as I loathed him and the situation, after a while it felt good. I had mixed feelings lying on that ground—one part of me wanted to throw up or scream for help, but there was something inside of me that was enjoying his slow, even-paced stroking.

Steve kept the gun right by my face.

"I wanted to be inside you since the day I met you, and I know you've wanted me too. I can tell by the way you touch me and the way that you look at me," he whispered.

I was being raped by a man that at one time I wanted to be intimate with, and he was conjuring pictures in my mind of me wanting him. I had imagined what it would be like having sex with this man, and now he was raping me.

Then he started breathing really heavy and his rhythm became steady and his stroking began to speed up until he came. He fell limp, and I felt limp. Tears streamed down my face. I had been gently raped by my boyfriend. How was I supposed to deal with that?

After a few moments, he got up and pulled up his pants. I just lay there. "Come on, we need to get back to town," he said, and reached over to pick up his gun.

I got up and slowly, ashamedly walked over to the car and picked my clothes up and dressed. We rode back to town in silence. We even went back to his place. I didn't have a way home, so I stayed the rest of the morning with him, in his apartment, until Angel came to pick me up.

When I got in the car with her, I began to bawl uncontrollably, but there was nothing I could do and no way to prove that he'd raped me. I wasn't even supposed to be at his place that night.

It took me a while to get over that night, even though I never saw him again. He called a few times, but I kept the conversations brief and made excuses to get off the phone until he stopped.

"THE QUESTION I drew was 'What was your most costly experience?' My answer is getting involved with a guy I knew from the start was not right for me."

A tear rolled down her cheek. She wiped it away.

"I did it then, and I'm doing it now. Lashawnda, you're doing the same thing."

"We're basically thirty years old, and I'm still trying to find out who I am. If we don't really try to figure it out, we'll stay right there in that cycle of attracting men—or women, in your case—who are wrong for us. Not just wrong for us, but bad for us. I, for one, deserve better. I know I do."

26

OCEAN STROLLING AND HOT-TUBBING

THE WOMEN FINISHED their dinners and then exited the hotel for a short stroll down Ocean Drive. They wanted to get a taste of being on the famous street and experiencing the excitement of its nightlife.

"Oh, it feels so good to be here," Alecia said as they made their way from Collins Avenue to Ocean Drive. "South Beach is one of my favorite places," she said.

Everyone looked at her, surprised. She hadn't said much the entire trip, and most of her comments had been of a condescending nature.

"I do like it here. I have some good memories of this town," she said, and sighed.

"Oh yeah!" Louisa smiled.

"Do tell," Jessica said.

"Well, I've had a few memorable dates right here on this very street with some good guys, men I probably should have been nicer to." She dwelled a bit on her comment. "Plus, we had our senior skip day here in Miami, remember, Louisa? It was the best time I've had in a very long time."

"Oh yeah, I remember," Louisa said.

"You two went to school together?" Lashawnda asked.

"Yes. We've known each other since elementary," Alecia said proudly.

"So are you an imposter or is your birthday really on December first?" Lashawnda questioned.

"Oh, she shares our birthday, and she wrote in," Louisa confirmed.

"I'm just checking, because we've been putting up with your little prissy butt all night, and I just want to make sure there's some justification in it," Lashawnda, who'd had a little too much to drink, blurted out.

"Oh, believe me, spending the day with a lesbian hardly qualifies for one of my most enjoyable moments," Alecia retaliated.

"Fuck you," Lashawnda said, rolling her eyes and her hands and then stumbling and struggling to catch her balance.

"I'm going back to the room," Alecia said, and turned to walk back.

Louisa stopped her and pulled her off to the side. "Now, you know she's had a little too much to drink, and you're not sober your damned self. So just shake it off," she said. "And you do need to apologize."

"For what?" Alecia snapped.

"You did call her a lesbian. You know she's dealing with her sexuality as it is," Louisa said.

Alecia folded her arms and huffed.

"Alecia," Louisa said firmly.

"Oh, all right, but only because you asked me to," she said.

They walked back over to the group.

"Lashawnda, I'm sure if I'd thought about it longer, I would have been able to come up with something nicer to call you than a lesbian," Alecia said nonchalantly.

"Is that supposed to be an apology?" Lashawnda walked in front of Alecia and put one hand on her hip while the other swayed to the side.

"Yes, Lashawnda, I'm apologizing."

"Aw, girl, I know you didn't mean it. If I'm a lesbian, then I'm cool with it, but if I'm not, I'm sure I've been called worse." She turned around and started walking with the group.

Alecia followed but felt guilty. She was sure that Lashawnda meant what she'd said—she probably *had* been called worse names—but that didn't mean it was okay for her to add to the list. Alecia wanted to do a better job of apologizing, but she wasn't sure how, or if it would even be worth it to bring it up again.

They walked down the side of the street all of the restaurants were located on. There was excitement in the air, Latin music coming out of the doors of most of the nightclubs. A few restaurants were still open, and people were dining outside underneath umbrellas, right on the sidewalk. They maneuvered between the different atmospheres and outdoor dining spots. Both sides of the street were heavily populated with people, several of whom dressed in light, airy clothing that flowed in the wind. Women were in halter tops and low-cut jeans. Everyone seemed to be looking for the next thing to get into. After they'd gone so far and seen what seemed to be a repeat of the previous block, they decided to turn around and head back to the hotel. They crossed over to the other side of the street nearest the beach.

"Let's go touch the water," Elise said.

"Let's not!" Alecia said.

"Let's do!" Elise took off toward the beach, stopping short to take off her shoes.

Everyone followed, each woman taking off her shoes. Some rolled up their pants and trekked through the sand.

"I couldn't wait to do this," Elise said. "The only thing I don't like about Louisville is that there isn't a beach."

Tanya took a deep breath. "There's something about being near water."

"I know what you mean," Alecia said under her breath. She couldn't let them know that she was enjoying the beach as much as Elise was.

"I've never been to a beach," Lashawnda said. "I'm so glad you suggested that we walk over here."

"You've never been to a beach?" Jessica asked.

"No. I've never left Atlanta until now. This is the first time I've flown, the first time I've been to Florida, the first time I've been to a beach. Tomorrow will be my first cruise and the first time I've ever gone to a tropical island," Lashawnda said. "I'm happy to have this experience, but I can't believe that it's taken me this long. Everything happens late for me," she sulked. "But the ocean is nice."

"At least it's happening," Louisa said.

"I know, girl." She smiled. "But I'm drunk—you gotta find something to complain about when you're drunk, right?"

"Let's get Ms. Lashawnda back to her room," Louisa suggested through her chuckling.

BACK IN ONE of the suites, the women lounged around.

"I'm tired, but I'm not ready to go to bed," Jessica said.

"I'm not either," Elise said as she stared out the window at the beach.

"My legs are a little tight. Do you think the hot tub is open?" Catara asked.

"Well, it is our birthday celebration. I'm sure that even if it isn't, they'll make an exception for us. I'd like to get into the hot tub myself."

Louisa called down and made the arrangements.

"Anybody else who's interested, let's do it! Don't worry about grabbing a towel, I was informed they'll have them downstairs for us when we get there," she said and grinned with satisfaction.

"I think we should all go," Tanya said.

"Does anyone not want to go?" Louisa asked.

No one responded.

"Okay, then it's settled. We're all going."

The ladies changed into their bathing suits and coverups, pinned up their hair, and then went to the back of the hotel, where the outside bar and swimming pool were located. A member of the hotel staff met them with towels.

"Although the bar is closed, I can arrange to have drinks brought to you ladies," he offered.

"You know, I think a few of us have probably had too much to drink today. Plus, we have a cruise ahead of us tomorrow. Could you bring us some bottled water?" Louisa requested.

"No problem," he said, and rushed off.

The women took their time and sunk into the hot tub. The warmth of the water sent everyone into silence. Once the bubbles began surrounding their bodies and their muscles began to relax, a discussion brewed.

"The funny thing about vacations is that we've done more in this one day than I usually do in a week," Catara said.

"I know. It's like there's this extra energy to go, see, and do," Tanya agreed.

"That's why I spend most of my time traveling," Alecia said. "I become rejuvenated every time I step on a plane and fly to a new intriguing destination."

"After this trip, I'm going to make an effort to go somewhere at least once a year," Lashawnda said.

"I don't know what I would do if I had to wait a whole year to exit L.A. I love my city, but the monotony just has to be broken periodically," Alecia said.

"I would love to travel to Italy and study fashion," Catara said.

"Oh, I love Milan," Alecia said.

"You've been?" Catara asked.

"Twice."

"Where else have you traveled to?" Tanya asked her.

"You name it, I've gone."

"Be more specific," Lashawnda said, rolling her eyes.

"Okay, South Africa, Kenya, Egypt, Japan, China, Australia, Brazil, Venezuela, Peru, and seven different countries in Europe. Not to mention the islands: Jamaica, Bahamas, Virgin Islands, Fiji, Tahiti, French Polynesian Islands . . ." Alecia paused to think of more.

"Bitch," Lashawnda said.

"Well, you asked," Alecia replied.

Lashawnda laughed. "You're right, I did. I'm just jealous. How can I get down with your travel itinerary?"

"Marry well," Alecia said.

"You're not married."

"Not yet, but I'm working on it," Alecia said, thinking about William.

"You think you're all of that, don't you?" Lashawnda said. She couldn't decide if she liked Alecia or couldn't stand her.

"I know I have a lot of positive qualities, if that's what you mean."

"See, that's exactly what I'm talking about. Who acts like you?"

"Me," Alecia said.

"I wasn't sure, but now I *know* I don't like you," Lashawnda said.

Louisa opened her eyes—there was no way she or anybody else was going to be able to relax. "I am sick of you two. What is the deal?"

"I don't have a problem," Alecia said. "She asks me a question and then gets mad at my answer."

"But she's all unnecessarily condescending with her answers," Lashawnda argued.

"Whatever, Lashawnda," Alecia said.

"I mean, you're cool and all, Alecia, you just act like this princess sitting on your throne, looking down on everybody else. You're not any better than anybody else in this hot tub," Lashawnda said.

"I never said I was."

"But actions speak louder than words. You've looked down on all of us at one time or another today."

"Not intentionally," Alecia said, defending herself.

"That's what I mean. You look down on people without even knowing. You have a problem."

"I don't do it intentionally," Alecia repeated.

There was silence all around.

"Well, maybe I do, a little," Alecia said. "But I promise I've been trying to work on it. I don't mean any harm. I can't help it. Maybe I've been in L.A. too long. Maybe I'm just too spoiled. I know that I have a low tolerance for people, but don't you know how miserable I am because of it?

"Louisa has always tried to reach out to me. She's my best friend in the world. I know she loves me unconditionally, and I don't even stay in contact with her. I've been known to go months without calling my mother and my sister. And the only man that I've ever tried to reach out to is a married man who I know is unavailable," Alecia sulked.

"It's like that?" Lashawnda said.

"But I have been trying to change. Especially after the day I met that girl with the tattoos."

"What?"

27

*I*T WAS THE beginning of the summer. I walked out of my doctor's office and over to the elevator. Standing before me was a pale white girl. She looked like she was in her late twenties. You know the type—as if her skin had never been exposed to the sun. She had jet-black, shiny, obviously dyed hair. She wore dark lipstick and eye shadow and dark black eyeliner and mascara. Then she had these small hoop earrings all over the place, at least five in one ear and three in the other, and one in her nose. I'm sure there was probably one in her tongue, but she didn't open her mouth so I couldn't prove it.

I couldn't help but look her over. She was quite a sight. She had on a spandex long-sleeved blouse with a scoop neck, black cotton-spandex pants, and black sandals. Of course her toenails and fingernails were black—what other color would have completed the ensemble? Those elements alone were enough to draw negative attention toward her, make her presence undesirable, but she took her look, the evidence of her lifestyle, one step further. This chick had a dark henna tattoo peeking out of her shirt collar. It was clear, by the traces of the pattern that were visible, that it covered most of her chest area. I knew there had to be more—I could feel it. So I followed her shirt down to where the sleeve ended and there was the same tattoo pattern sneaking out from underneath. It was on both arms. I initially dared not look, but I had to.

I knew what I'd see anyway. So my eyes quickly shot down to the end of her pant legs and sure enough, the same pattern was on her ankles.

The bell for the elevator rang. No one else was around. It was just the two of us boarding this elevator together. I felt a wave of panic overcome me. How dare I be forced to be alone in a small space with her?

But there was nothing else to do, so we boarded the elevator. She pressed the button for the lobby. I was going to the same floor, so I positioned myself in the farthest corner from her and prayed that the elevator wouldn't break down or get stuck, because how would I possibly be able to relate to or work with this girl to bring about a rescue for us? Our signals wouldn't properly connect. She was from another planet, I thought.

I held my breath and the elevator began to descend in what seemed to be slow motion. What was only a seven-flight descent felt like we were going down at least twenty floors.

I tried not to stare, but I couldn't help myself. I questioned what would make a person, especially a woman, want to deface her entire body in such a way. Here I was, pressed about removing a tiny scar from my leg, and she was a body filled with hideous designs and shapes. Believe you me, there was nothing cute about that.

ALECIA TOOK A deep breath as if trying to get her thoughts together.

"I see young white girls like her all the time. Where I come from, we used to call them 'hoods,'" Elise said.

"Well, we used to call them vampires, and I didn't want to be stuck on an elevator with a vampire, of all people," Alecia said.

"So what happened?" Lashawnda asked.

THE DOOR TO the elevator finally opened, and even though she had been waiting for the elevator first and had walked on first, when the door opened, I quickly rushed by her. She was so weird-looking that I couldn't stand to look at her any longer than necessary.

I moved ahead of her as quickly as possible and consequently bumped into this handsome, drop-dead gorgeous, well-dressed Latin guy. I was so taken with him that I barely noticed her walk by me. This brother was fine, with moussed-back dark hair and beautiful dark eyebrows. His name was Dr. Michael DeLeon, and we ended up going out for a while. After we exchanged numbers, I headed to my car. When I got out to the parking lot, that girl was leaning on the back of a car parked next to my Benz.

I was disgusted. Why was she waiting by my car? Was she waiting on me? She didn't know me. I slowed my pace to keep an eye on her— maybe she was planning to jack me for my purse. I got my keys out and clutched my purse tightly, watching her all the while.

I walked right by her, and just when I thought I was home free—I mean, I was putting my key into the car door lock—she spoke to me.

"You think I'm weird, don't you?" she asked.

I pretended that I didn't hear her.

"I see the way you look at me. You think I'm a freak. Don't you?"

I opened the car door so that just in case she tried to attack me, I could get inside more quickly. Then I turned around and caught her eyes.

Tears were slowing streaming down. She looked so sad and alone. As undesirable as she was, I could identify with the pain in her eyes. What- ever fears or uncertainties I had about her disappeared instantly. My feet were glued in place. I couldn't turn away from her, as much as I wanted to. I couldn't escape the look in her eyes.

She said, "You think you're so much, with your rich life, don't you? You probably don't even know what it feels like to want to change your life. Because there's nothing in your high-society life that needs to be changed."

She got off the car and began walking toward me. "I bet men fall over themselves going out of their way for you, don't they?"

"What are you talking about?" I asked her and inched closer inside my car.

"Are you scared?" she asked.

"No," I responded, although I was panic-stricken.

"Women like you annoy the hell out of me. As much as I hate my life, I would never want to be you."

The sadness I saw in her eyes had shifted to hate. Everything about her body language said she hated me so badly that she could hurt me and not think twice about it. Her face tightened, her eyes squinted, and her shoulders tensed up.

I said, "I don't have to listen to this," and lifted one foot up to get into my car.

She reached out and grabbed my shoulder, pulling me backward and turning me toward her. She said, "Not that it's any of your business, but I want this off me as much as you do!" Her voice cracked. She grabbed at the sleeves of her shirt and yanked them up. Then she tugged at her collar to expose her tattoo.

"I hate having this monster stuck to my skin, and the doctor just told me it's going to take no less than twenty grand to have it removed. And even then, because there's so much of it, it's going to take at least a year of repeated surgeries to get rid of it.

"I don't have twenty grand to throw around like you do. And even if I did, I would still have to endure the pain of knowing that that money, which I could use in so many different areas of my life, would be going toward removing something that shouldn't be there in the first place."

"I'm sorry, but I—" I began, but she was so involved that she didn't hear.

"Every time I look in the mirror, every time I glance at any part of my body, I am reminded of everything that is not right in my life. Especially him."

She took a deep breath and fell back onto her car. "I left him, you know."

I looked around to see if one of her friends had walked up because how in the world would I know who *he* was? There was no one there but me, so I listened.

"I moved on. I grew up, but he never did. Probably never will. He'll always be the same rebellious child who never thinks before he acts. But I'm not following him around anymore. I have to think for myself, somehow be my own person, but the only way I'll know who that is, is to get this shit off me." She grabbed at her arms and pulled at her skin as if trying to remove the tattoo.

I was speechless, caught there with a young woman who was desperate, trapped, and wanted so much to change but didn't have the means to.

Thank goodness she continued talking because I didn't know what to say.

"We were both coked out. The mound of coke he had brought that night was the largest we'd ever tried to tackle together. Even when I gave up, he kept snorting. He had already tattooed me at the small of my back and around my belly button. But that night he said he wanted to create the quintessential tattoo for me because he loved me so much. I was stoned and in love, because I lay there voluntarily and allowed him to draw all over my entire body. I didn't even feel any pain."

She dropped her head and all I could do was stare. I looked like I had it going on, but I didn't have a thing to give her: money, advice, or sympathy. Because at that time in my life I was so superficial that I couldn't relate to people who didn't have something to give me.

What was I supposed to do for her? She needed help and I didn't know how to give it. I was incapable of giving. My heart went out to her, but I saw her moment of silence as my cue to escape, to break free from her pain, in order to deal with the complexities of my own life. So I looked her over one last time, got into my car, and drove off as quickly as I could.

"YOU MEAN YOU left her standing there like that?" Jessica asked.

"Wow," Lashawnda said. "That's cold!"

"So you're judging me," Alecia said, shooting a look at her. "I drew the question 'What do you regret the most?' Well, I wish I could undo ever having gotten on that elevator with her. My gut said to let her go and catch the next one, but I didn't listen. I regret not reaching out to her, and I regret leaving her like that."

I GOT A FEW blocks away and turned around to go back, but she had already left. I went back to that office a few times to meet the doctor that I'd met for lunch, but I never ran into her again.

"ALECIA, I'M SO sorry to hear that," Louisa said.

"So that's one of the reasons that I went home for Thanksgiving. And that's the reason that I let you convince me to write in for this contest, because I'm trying to reach out," she said to Louisa.

"Alecia, you know I'm always here for you," Louisa offered.

"I know you are. That's what's so bad about it. I've been a horrible friend to you."

"Maybe so, but you are my friend and I forgive you, Alecia. I love you like a sister."

"I love you too, Louisa," she said, and waded through the water to hug her.

Then she turned to Lashawnda. "I might not be doing the best job of it, Lashawnda, but I am trying."

"I believe you," Lashawnda said. She reached out for Alecia's hand, and Alecia grabbed for hers.

"I'm so sorry about what I said to you out by the beach."

"I know," Lashawnda replied.

28

LAST CALL TILL SLEEP

IN HER PAJAMAS, Elise stood in front of the window and looked out at the ocean.

Tanya walked out of the bathroom, tying her robe closed. She went over to the courtesy bar and pulled out a jar of cashews. "Do you want anything?"

"Nah," Elise said. "The baby must be hungry."

"I guess so. You can't get enough of the ocean, huh?" Tanya asked, quickly trying to change the subject. She didn't want to talk about her pregnancy. It was tough enough for her to push the thought out of her mind; discussing it would only make it worse.

"No," Elise sighed. "Large bodies of water are healing, peaceful. Even to look at from a distance."

"Well, you're going to get plenty of exposure tomorrow on that ship."

"Yeah, and I'm going to fill up, because when I get back home to that gym and the parents and the children, well, I'm going to need to have a peaceful memory to fall back on."

"Tell me about it," Tanya said and stood next to her, munching on the nuts, becoming entranced by the view as well.

Louisa walked out, and Jessica followed. They took seats on the sofa. Jessica had a leather attaché case with her. She pulled out sheets of paper and counted through them. "I need everyone to come in for a short meeting before we turn in."

Lashawnda came in and took a seat on the floor next to the sofa. Alecia walked in with a hairbrush in her hand and sat next to Louisa. Catara walked out with a jar in her hand. She sat in the armchair and began slathering cream all over her face. Everyone stopped and looked at her.

"I love your pajamas. The cut is so unique," Louisa said.

"Thank you," Catara said. She was wearing a wide-lapel white collar top that had a wide cuffed sleeve. The bottoms were black flair-legged pants. The pajamas were like a dressy outfit, only the fabric looked comfortable.

"Where did you get those from?" Alecia asked. "I have a wide collection of pajamas, and I haven't seen any like them around."

"That's because I designed them myself," Catara said.

"Are you serious?" Tanya said, looking skeptical.

"Really, I did."

"Do you have anything else with you?" Louisa asked her.

"Yeah, I have another pair of pajamas in my bag. Oh, and a robe. I also have a few sketches in my book. I take it everywhere I go, just in case I get inspired."

"Go get them," everyone encouraged her.

"Okay."

She returned with her sketchbook, a second pair of pajamas that were lavender and mint green, and a black robe that looked like a trench coat but was the same material as the pajamas she was wearing.

"You gotta model that coat for us," Tanya said.

Catara put the pajamas and her sketches on the chair and slipped on the robe. Then she pulled the cuff from her top over the cuff of the robe.

"That is dope! I'm loving those pajamas!" Louisa said. "You look like you're ready to go out for the day."

"Yeah, if you don't have time to get dressed, you can run out with your pajamas on," Jessica added.

Alecia picked up the other set of pajamas. "Those are one of my favorite color combinations. It's what I used in my bedroom. Can we see the sketches too?" she asked.

The ladies raved over Catara's creations.

"You've really got something there," Tanya said.

"I only hope the fashion industry will embrace them, as well."

"Believe me, it's only a matter of time," Alecia said.

"Okay, I hate to bust up the fashion show, but I need to pass these things out. We've been so busy that I nearly forgot. But being the efficient person that Jessica is, she remembered," Louisa said.

Jessica handed out forms to everyone.

"These are the forms that we need to have ready when we get to the boat. I'd like to have them all together. So if you could fill them out, and get your passport or your photo ID and birth certificate together, I'll return them to you tomorrow night when we come back to the hotel. Now, if I'm not mistaken, we have one more question that needs to be answered before we turn in," Louisa said, looking at Lashawnda.

"Who, me?" Lashawnda said and smiled. "I guess we saved the best for last—at least I've sobered up a bit."

"What was your question?" Elise asked.

"I know you ladies are beat, because I am. But don't fall asleep until I'm finished," she said. "My question was 'What do you appreciate now that you didn't before?' Well, I appreciate adult braces."

"What?" Tanya said, nearly choking on a cashew. "Girl, you are crazy."

"No, really. I got braces shortly after I met Cicely. She was trying to make sure I was completely refined on the outside." Lashawnda cleared her throat. "You know, for a psychologist, she was always a little too concerned about appearances, which was cool with me, because I knew I needed to be polished around the edges."

"Is that it?" Catara said.

"Yes, but no, there's more," Lashawnda said.

29

LASHAWNDA'S STORY: APPRECIATE IT

WHAT I LEARNED from my two years of constant visits with my orthodontist is the reality of something my grandmother used to say to me often before she died. She'd say, "Lashawnda, the problem with young people today is that they want everything *right now*. You don't truly appreciate what you have until you come to realize that life is like planting a seed."

She'd say, "You plant a seed and you watch it grow. It's a process. It doesn't happen overnight. It takes time and patience and nurturing care for that seed to grow up right. That is why I can't give you some money to go to the store just because you ask for it."

EVERYBODY LAUGHED quietly.

BUT SERIOUSLY, IF any of you have had braces, you know that you go in for your initial visit, the doctor X-rays your mouth and then gives you an idea of how long he thinks it'll take to complete your procedure. He might say a year, two years, or three years. Then he'll say something like, "You'll be finished in no time."

Well, that was what happened to me. My orthodontist told me that I would be finished with my braces in one year. That year stretched out to two because of unexpected complications with my teeth. My smile is beautiful now, but I had to go through hell and back to get it.

Cicely knew a lingual specialist who put braces on the back of your teeth, so when I first got those things on, I was so excited. I spent extra time in the mirror, with my mouth wide open, looking to see how they were positioned. Then I'd check my smile every day to see how much it had changed from the previous day. I accepted the pain that came with having the braces on because I knew they were working.

But as time went on, I had to go back and see that man every month. Every time I left his office, I'd leave in pain, pain that would linger on for two or three days. I didn't like having braces so much anymore. I'm a muncher—I love chips, crackers, nuts, anything that I can munch on. But after trying to munch and being met with excruciating pain, I had to alter some of my food choices. I was not happy about that.

Then, as the braces began to work, my smile was changing and not for the better, but for the worse. One day I went to the mirror and looked at my smile, and I swore I saw a horse staring back at me.

"STOP IT, LASHAWNDA, you are killing me," Tanya said. She was bent over in laughter. Everybody else was too.

NAH, SERIOUSLY. I went through some changes. I was a grown-ass woman who had to meet the world every day. Some of the time, I wanted to skip work because I didn't want anybody peeping my new smile for the day. I actually became depressed. Several of Cicely's clients were manic-depressive—I tell you this, I became lower than any of them! At least I felt like I was. As my teeth were being altered by my braces, so was my personality.

I used to walk into the orthodontist's office in a good mood. Then he told me that I was going to have to live with my braces for one more year. I wasn't mentally prepared to hear that. I wanted my braces off, right then. I didn't think I could handle another year. I found myself dreading my appointments. When I sat in the chair, I was no longer nice. I only wanted to know when the braces were coming off, and if the answer wasn't "Today," then there wasn't anything further that we had to discuss. I'd leave frustrated and disappointed because they were never sure how many more months I had to go, plus there was a new pain from the adjustment of my braces that I had to settle into.

I felt ugly some days. I kept my time in front of the mirror to a minimum because I didn't want a reminder that I wasn't finished with my braces. I felt miserable other days. I was angry with my mother for not having the means to get me braces at an earlier age. I was mad at myself for getting them when I did. I was mad! I was just mad!

Then during the last few months of having my braces, I noticed that I talked to my orthodontist a little more. Every time I left the office, I'd get that feeling of dread, but it wasn't as strong as it was before. I started looking into the mirror and began smiling again. The reflection was beginning to look good again, better. Every day I lingered a little longer.

Before long, the orthodontist said, "We're removing your braces today." I tell you what—I cried. I sat in that chair and cried tears of relief. I felt like I had journeyed through a desert and returned. Maybe other people are stronger, but the process of having braces was a struggle for me.

It wasn't until a few months later, when I was at the dry cleaners picking up some items and a handsome gentleman said to me, "You have a beautiful smile," that I associated my journey of getting braces with my grandmother's saying—life is like planting a seed. Then I was able to relate other things in my life to it. Like me going from a grocery store employee to a skilled executive assistant. It took me years to learn and perfect my position.

See, you plant a seed in a ground, and it's buried away from you. You can't even see your seed anymore, but you know where it is, so you water it. Then one day you return and there is a little plant budding out of the ground. Nothing spectacular, but just enough to let you know that you're making progress. Then the seed changes—it is now a plant, and as the plant grows, you have to watch it closely, pick the weeds away from around it. Sometimes you might have to use a stick or something to support it because it's weak and might need a little help in its development. Then maybe one or two of the leaves might die, so you have to cut them off. But the plant is still developing. One day, when you come back to the plant, you realize that it is fully mature and ripe and exactly what you hoped it to be.

So getting my braces helped me to appreciate the process of life. I have grown so much, and it hasn't happened overnight. I have been subjected to love, rejection, learning, failing, rejoicing, and crying, but all of those things have worked to shape who I am.

Like I said before, I am still working on figuring out exactly what that means I am, but there are definitely things about me I have come to like and appreciate.

"I'M NOT WHAT I ought to be, but I'm not what I used to be! Now let the church say 'Amen'!" Lashawnda said, laughing at herself.

"Amen!" the women said in unison and giggled themselves up. Some yawned. Others stretched.

"Lashawnda, you do have a beautiful smile," Alecia said.

They each made their way into their beds, where they reflected on the events of the day until one by one they dozed off into a deep slumber.

30

JESSICA TURNED THE volume way up on her jam box. It was four-thirty A.M., and the women had barely gotten two hours of sleep. Playing was a previously recorded tape that had been made by the radio show both to wish the ladies happy birthday and to make sure that they woke, be it annoyed or grumpy, on time to catch their boat. Blasting from the speaker was Stevie Wonder singing "Happy Birthday to You."

Although no one actually got out of bed, Jessica knew the tape was working because she could hear stirring and groans of aggravation. She let the tape play through as she tried to beat the rush and get herself prepared for the day.

After the Stevie Wonder song ended, Melvin Green and the Morning Show Crew sang their dreadfully funny rendition of "Happy Birthday." Hearing Melvin's voice alone got Lashawnda out of the bed. She bounced to the music while going through her bag to get her toothbrush and toothpaste.

By the time the song ended, everyone else was stirring with quiet smiles on their faces. The Morning Crew then yelled, "Happy birthday, Alecia, Catara, Elise, Lashawnda, and Tanya. Oh, and you too, Louisa, happy birthday, we can't wait until you get back!"

"As a reminder we have to be dressed by five A.M., ladies. Stan will be out front to pick us up. Breakfast will be served on the ship," Louisa said.

Several celebrity voices came on back to back, wishing them happy birthday in their own special way: Sean "P. Diddy" Combs, Queen Latifah, Mary J. Blige, LL Cool J, Busta Rhymes, Babyface, Janet Jackson, and Dr. Dre. The ladies were ecstatic, and everyone took a moment from what they were doing to listen closely to each celebrity's greeting.

"Oh, I just love Dr. Dre," Tanya said.

"LL is my man!" Catara added. "His lips get me every time."

"Is he gonna be on the boat?" Lashawnda asked.

"Nah, girl. No celebrities, just us getting our relaxation on," Louisa said.

"I didn't think so, but I figured it wouldn't hurt to ask," Lashawnda replied.

Still on a high, the women continued to rush to be dressed on time. Then they gathered the things they wanted to take with them for the day.

"I'm so glad we took showers before we turned in, because we really would be late," Elise said.

"Yep, and we need to get a move on it, ladies. We only have five minutes," Jessica announced. She was standing by the door looking at her watch.

Downstairs Stan was waiting for them in front of the car. He grinned and opened the door of the limo for them. "Happy birthday, ladies," he said.

"Thanks, Stan," they replied in unison, cheering.

Inside the limo, he opened the window behind him. "We've got a forty-five minute ride to the Fort Lauderdale port, so sit back and relax. If you don't mind, I'd like to play something special for you to help you start your special day."

"Sure," Louisa said.

Stan adjusted his system then pulled out onto the street.

Out of the speakers came "My Girl" by the Temptations.

"Aahhh," everybody gushed.

"Oh, I love that song. My daddy used to sing that to me all the time when I was a little girl," Catara said.

"That's sweet. You are lucky. I bet that was nice," Alecia said wistfully. "My dad wasn't around."

"Thank you, Alecia. It was nice." Catara smiled. It was good to see a human side of Alecia.

They got to the chorus and everyone sang in unison, *"I guess you say what can make me feel this way? My girl, my girl, my girl, talking 'bout my girl. My girl."*

They giggled and sang along to old-school songs that Stan had prepared for them, including Lionel Richie's "Three Times a Lady," the Isley Brothers' "Who's That Lady?" and the Commodores' "Brick House." By the time they got to the dock, they were pumped up and ready to begin their day at sea.

UPON BOARDING THE ship, the ladies were greeted by the ship's photographer, who urged them to get together so he could snap first a group photo and then individuals of them. Inside, they took a seat in the waiting area while Louisa and Jessica took care of getting them registered. There were all kinds boarding the ship—couples, groups, large families, and people of all nationalities.

"Where are the black people?" Tanya asked.

"There are black people boarding," Elise said.

"I know that, but when I thought about this cruise I imagined that everyone on board would be black."

"I think I did too," Lashawnda agreed.

"You're thinking about a theme cruise like what Tom Joyner has, where they sell the cruise to all of their listeners, most of whom are African American. No, this is your typical run-of-the-mill everyday cruise, a melting pot of people," Alecia commented.

"This is a small ship. I cruised with my family to Nassau, Bahamas, and that ship was a colossal version of this one," Catara said.

"They make them larger than *this*?" Lashawnda asked.

"Much larger."

"You learn something new every day," Lashawnda replied.

Once they were all checked in, they went upstairs for breakfast. Prepared for the passengers was a lavish buffet meal; the ladies joined the line and filled their plates, then found a table.

"I can't wait to get to that deck and fall asleep," Alecia said.

"Me, too. Then I'm gonna spend the rest of the time at the casino at the blackjack table," Tanya said.

"You ladies are party poopers. I'm going swimming and then I'm going to catch a show. Who's interested?" Elise asked.

"I am," Jessica said.

"I'm gambling until lunch," Lashawnda said.

"I'm there," Catara replied.

"I'm with Alecia—I think I'm hitting the deck," Louisa said.

After breakfast, the ladies split up. Alecia and Louisa rested by the pool, while Elise and Jessica swam. Tanya, Lashawnda, and Catara hit the casino. Eventually, everyone ended up in the casino, where Lashawnda was killing everyone at poker. She was on a roll, and the ladies were cheering her on.

"I feel lucky," Lashawnda said, throwing down a few chips onto the table. "Give me two more cards."

The dealer gave her two. Then the other players folded.

Lashawnda laid her cards down on the table. She had a full house. The ladies went wild.

"How did you get so good?" Elise asked her.

"My old boyfriend, the one who used to beat me for breakfast, lunch, and dinner, was a cardsharp. I guess I did get something out of that shitty relationship," she said, then picked up her cards.

Once they'd had enough, they walked to the deck, where the limbo contest had begun. The ladies joined in, dancing underneath the limbo stick, but none of them made it to the final round. They sat around and watched the others while they cooled out and listened to the mellow island music playing on the deck.

Afterward, they walked over to the dining area to find that their lunch was another buffet spread. They filled themselves with seafood, pasta, fresh fruit, and numerous other items.

"The food here is unreal," Catara said. "I had just started a new diet. Now I'm going to have to start over when I get home."

"I'm tired of hearing you talk about your weight. You can diet if you want to, but don't let mainstream society make you think you should lose weight," Tanya said. "Plus, you should capitalize on your weight and create a line of pajamas and lingerie for full-figured women. You have the talent. Girl, use your body to make that money!"

Catara looked at Tanya in amazement. She never would have imagined that going on this trip would help her see her weight as an asset, and not a liability. She smiled because Tanya had a good point, and she took her words to heart. "You're joking, but I might have to consider your plan."

"No. I'm serious. Go for it, girl. Make all the skinny women jealous. Because I know after I have this baby, I'm probably gonna spread, just like my momma, and I'm gonna be one of your main customers." They laughed. After the reaction from the women the night before when they saw her pajamas, and now Tanya's comments, Catara was seriously contemplating putting out her own line of pajamas.

They spent the rest of the cruise relaxing on one of the decks until they docked in the Grand Bahamas. Once at Freeport, they had to show their legal documentation in order to enter the island. Once they got through customs, they were greeted by numerous cabdrivers vying for their business. They chose a driver who had a van. The unsuspecting women piled in, and before long were whisked away at high speeds down a long street going toward Port Lucaya.

The ladies opted to spend the first part of their time on the island shopping at the Port Lucaya Marketplace, located on the waterfront. They browsed in and out of shops, purchasing souvenirs and gifts for their friends and family. Elise was torn about what to get Allen.

"Girl, give him you wrapped in a bow," Tanya joked.

"Yeah, right," Elise replied.

"Well, give him a T-shirt. You can't go wrong with a T-shirt," Catara suggested.

"Yeah, but Elise really wants to let Allen know that she's feeling him. She has to make a definite statement with her gift," Louisa said.

The girls came to a menswear shop.

"I've got it," Alecia squeeled. "Get a pair of silk boxers for him."

"Sexy, sexy," Lashawnda said.

"A hint of sex, but it doesn't scream it. Silk is a nice fabric, so he'll know she wasn't being cheap. Plus, all men need underwear, so it's something he can use."

"It sounds good to me," Elise said.

The women crowded around the boxers and looked through them, debating until they agreed on a pair for Allen.

Then they went to the Perfume Factory, a replica of an 18th-century Bahamian mansion. There they learned how perfume was made—they even had the opportunity to mix and name their own brand.

"I'm going to name mine Jewel," Alecia said. "I always wanted a perfume that no one else would be able to duplicate."

"You've got that," Louisa said, taking a whiff of Alecia's creation.

"And nobody's gonna want to copy that, because it doesn't smell too good. You might want to keep working on it."

Alecia sniffed it again, and frowned. "You might be right."

Back on the cruise ship, the women enjoyed a seven-course dinner in the Grand Bahamas Grill Restaurant, feasting on lamb chops, lobster tail, New York strip steak, and fresh fish. After the main course, the staff members walked out with a huge seven-layer cake filled with candles and sang "Happy Birthday."

"Make a wish, ladies," Jessica insisted.

They closed their eyes, made their individual wishes, and on the count of three blew out the candles. Their waiter cut the cake and served them.

"I am stuffed," Elise said, "But this cake is too good."

"It's your birthday, girl. Go for it!" Tanya, who was on her second piece of cake, encouraged her.

They continued the evening gambling until they either lost all that they could or won just enough to stop. Eventually, they gathered on the deck and reflected on their day while watching the moon reflect off the ocean waves while listening to soothing Caribbean music.

"Please tell Melvin Green that I will always remember my weekend," Lashawnda said. "It has been more than I could have imagined."

"It's been great for me too. I'll never forget it. It's been special, you know?" Catara said.

"Yeah it has been. It's filled me up," Alecia said. "I knew I needed a boost, and this has definitely been it."

Louisa looked at Alecia and smiled. "I'm glad you came," she whispered.

"Yeah, me too," Alecia replied.

Lashawnda began singing the Stevie Wonder song that Jessica played for them that morning: "Happy birthday to you, happy birthday to you . . ." Everybody joined in with the final "Happy birthday!"

part three

31

THE ALLEN FACTOR

ELISE STEPPED ONTO the moving sidewalk leading down the long walkway of the Hartsfield airport, heading toward baggage claim. She stood to the side and allowed those moving faster than her to get by. It was a busy Sunday at the airport, and she felt good about being a part of the hustle and bustle of the day. Smiling all the while, she recapped the time she'd spent in Miami and the Bahamas, thinking of the meaningful friendships she'd developed and of the wonderful gifts she'd brought back with her. Especially the one she'd gotten for Allen. She'd packed everything else, but Allen's gift was right there in the bag dangling from her hand.

There was no nervousness, no jittery feelings of doubt. Elise knew she couldn't remain silent any longer, could no longer wait for him to make the first move. On her plane trip home, she'd decided that she was going to borrow from Lashawnda's boldness and Alecia's way with men and lure Allen, hook, line, and sinker. When she had called that morning, he told her he'd be in the waiting area looking for her, and she intended to give him something to look at. Elise's hair wasn't flying away as usual; it was neat and softly styled. Her makeup was just right—not too much, but just enough to bring out her eyes and accentuate her lips. She knew she looked classy, dressed in one of the new outfits she'd gotten at the Bal Harbour Shops. When Allen got a look at her, he would have to know that she was something special and worth going after. If that didn't work, she would just be honest and let him know how she felt.

Just as he promised, Allen was where he said he would be. Blending in with a group of people waiting for their loved ones, Allen grinned from ear to ear when he saw her approaching.

"You made it back!" he said, and held out his arms to hug her.

Elise fell into his embrace. She didn't want to let go so soon, but he pulled back almost before the hug had begun.

"How was your flight?" he asked, and put his hand out to motion for Elise to head down to baggage claim.

Elise was annoyed. He barely seemed to pay her any attention. There were no comments about her appearance, no indication that he even noticed her hair. Nothing.

"Nice. Relaxing," she replied. Then she stopped walking. "Before we go down. I want to give you a gift." She knew the gift would do the trick.

"Oh, okay," he said shyly. "You didn't have to."

"I know, but I said I would, and I wanted to."

The two moved over to a corner, out of the way of the traffic, and Elise handed Allen the bag. He began to open in, but Elise stopped him.

"Before you open the gift. I want to say something."

"Okay," he said.

"Listen, I could have brought you back a T-shirt or a coffee mug, or some other kind of souvenir, but I wanted to give you something that really showed you my gratitude for all the work that you've done for Gotta Flip and for winning the trip for me. Allen, we've grown to become good friends over the last few months, and since I've opened the gym it seems that we've grown even closer, so I hope that this gift isn't too forward, but I also hope that it will help to bring about a . . ." She stumbled for words, but couldn't find them. "Oh. You'll see what I mean."

Allen looked confused. He held on to the bag but was unsure if it was okay to go into it or not.

"Oh, you can open it now," she said, and smiled.

He put his hand inside the bag.

"Wait."

He stopped.

"I never asked you if you had a girlfriend."

"What does that have to do with anything?" he asked.

She took the bag from him. "Do you have a girlfriend?" she asked.

He laughed. "You are acting strange. Did that tropical sun affect your brain waves?" he joked.

"No," she replied in a serious tone. "Are you avoiding the question?"

"No I'm not, and no, I don't have a girlfriend," he replied.

She let out a gust of air. This was going to be tougher than she thought.

"So, do I get my gift or what?" he asked, making it clear that the grin on his face wasn't going anywhere anytime soon.

You can do this, Elise said to herself.

She handed the bag back to him.

"Can I open it now?" he asked teasingly.

"You can open it," she replied. What seemed to be a good idea initially didn't seem so good anymore.

Allen pulled out the silk boxers with a note attached to them. He blushed and then looked at the note, which read: *I'm looking forward to seeing you in these one day!*

Allen tilted his head and made a face, staring at the boxers.

Elise wanted to hide. She had been too forward with her gift. She knew she was too forward, but she didn't back down. She stood firm and waited for him to respond.

"These are nice," Allen said, and smiled. "I'm just surprised you would give me a gift like this."

"I'm sure," Elise replied.

"So where's your luggage? Didn't you carry it on going to Miami?" he asked.

Elise was crushed. He didn't respond in any way she'd hoped he would, but she wasn't going to embarrass herself further by saying anything else. Maybe she'd misread his signals—maybe he only wanted to remain friends.

"I had to get another bag because I have so much stuff, so I just checked everything."

"Well, I think we should get down to baggage claim and pick up your bags before someone takes them," he said calmly.

"Okay," she replied and turned away from him, walking ahead of him toward the escalator. By the time they got to baggage claim, Elise's luggage was coming around the carousel. She pointed out her bags, and Allen retrieved them.

"You ready to go?" he said nonchalantly.

"Sure," Elise replied.

Allen led the way as they walked toward the door.

"So, that's all you're going to say?" she managed.

"About what?" he asked after turning to face her.

"Allen. I got you a pair of silk boxers as a gift, and you're acting all casual."

He stood there, staring deeply into her eyes.

"I gave you those boxers, Allen, because I wanted you to know that I like you. And it's more than a friendship thing, I—"

Before she could complete her sentence Allen dropped her luggage, grabbed her in his arms, and proceeded to kiss her with all the passion he'd had for her since they first met, the passion he'd held back because he wasn't sure if she felt the same.

Overwhelmed, Elise didn't know what hit her at first, but once she realized that she was being kissed by the man she wanted to be her own, she threw her arms around him and returned his level of passion. The two were all over each other and so caught up in their emotional display that they forgot that anyone was around them until an old lady walked by and said, "Get a room, you two. There are children around, for Christ's sake!"

They stopped long enough to shrug her off and went back to kissing. Then Allen broke off and said, "I've wanted to do that for so long."

"Me too," she replied.

"I was a little embarrassed earlier—flattered and thrilled, but I didn't know what to say when I saw that you'd gotten me boxers."

"Well, you got around to speaking with that kiss. That was nice. I'd like to try that again real soon," she said.

They snickered like schoolkids.

"You ready to go back to your place?" he asked.

They both took a deep breath.

"Yes," Elise replied. "I'm ready."

Allen kissed her one last time then picked up her luggage. He looked at her, "By the way. You are beautiful, and not only because you have your hair all done up today. I think you're gorgeous even when your hair is pulled back and you're walking around in your warm-ups. You're beautiful because you are a special woman, and I admire you. I care about you."

"I feel the same way," Elise replied.

The couple walked out of the airport, laughing and joking and sharing with the destination of togetherness in mind.

32

MOVING FORWARD

TANYA NUDGED THE door closed with her hip and dropped her bags. She looked around at her place. A streetlight was shining through the window, glaring off a picture of her and Chris displayed on the entertainment system. She walked over to the picture and stared at the two of them posing for professional shots that she'd had to beg him to participate in. After they'd gotten the pictures back, he'd told her he was glad that she went through the trouble of convincing him because the pictures were "dope" and he couldn't wait to give one to his mother.

Tanya grabbed the picture and fell back onto her sofa. The photo was a reminder of everything that she had yet to face. She closed her eyes and tried to drift back to her recent trip. Although she'd just gotten back to Chicago, her time spent relaxing in tropical bliss seemed so long ago. She sat there for a moment, going over her options, to decide what her first move was going to be. She'd have to accept her job transfer to Atlanta. She'd already been approved and had thirty days to accept. Then she'd have to pack her things.

The tough part would be telling Chris she was pregnant. She knew he wouldn't want her to leave. *Maybe*, she thought, *it would be better if I never said anything to him, just hired movers to pack up everything and take the long drive in my car to Atlanta.* The drive would give her time to think. She'd have to choose an apartment. She'd already gone through several apartment guides and had an idea of what area she wanted to live in. She'd have to make a final decision based on her single income, and she'd be getting a one-bedroom instead of a two since Chris wouldn't be joining her.

A loud knocking startled Tanya.

She hesitantly got up off the sofa. She knew it was Chris—who else would it be? There was so much she needed to think through. She wasn't ready yet to see him, but he continued to bang on the door. She let him in.

"Where have you been?" he barked as he walked through the door.

"Like you care. Haven't you been gone all weekend?"

"You didn't answer my question, Tanya. Where have you been?" he asked, and slammed the door behind him. Then he looked down at her luggage. "I knew it."

"You knew what?"

"That you went on a trip. Who the hell is he?" he demanded.

"What are you talking about?"

"Who did you go on vacation with?" he asked.

Tanya took a chair at the table. She was feeling a little dizzy.

Chris grabbed the top of the chair next to her and pushed his weight on his arms. Then he eyed her intensely.

"I went on a trip. Me and four other women won a trip over the radio."

"Yeah, right," Chris said, and sat down in the chair.

"Believe me or not—I have no reason to lie. So how was your trip?" she asked. "Wait a minute. Don't even tell me. I don't want to know."

The two sat staring away from one another. Tanya looked at her nails, which were tapping on the table, while Chris was hard-fixed on the wall in front of him.

"I didn't go," he said in such a low voice that Tanya barely heard him.

The tapping stopped.

"What did you say?" she asked.

"I said, I didn't go," he replied.

"Oh."

More silence.

"I'm still moving," she said.

"I figured that," he said, shaking his head. "You still going without me?"

Tanya didn't respond.

"Listen, I'm sorry for walking out on you, but I didn't want to fight. You were seeing things one way, and I was seeing them another," he said.

"Exactly," she replied, crossing her arms.

"But not anymore."

Tanya looked at him.

"I want to move to Atlanta with you. That's if you want me to. I couldn't wait to tell you, but your car was gone all weekend. I've been driving around by your place and calling."

"I know how that feels," Tanya said, and rolled her eyes. "And frankly, Chris, I don't want to deal with it anymore. I'm tired of wasting my life waiting on you to make a move. I've waited on you all of my adult life, and where has that gotten me?"

"Baby, I know you have, and I know I haven't been there for you, not the way that you've needed me to be."

"Well, I'm glad you've finally realized that."

"I have, and that's why I'm here right now."

"Uumph," Tanya replied. It all seemed too easy, his sudden change of heart. "So why didn't you go to Texas, Chris? Why did you change your mind?"

Chris took a deep breath, and then blew out a gust of air.

"I was going to tell you this even if you didn't ask, but the morning I left your apartment, the cops came to my place and started questioning me about T-Roy's murder."

"I thought the case was closed," Tanya said.

"It is, as far as them arresting Payne and his boy. The other two with them were shot. But there were other things involved, so they questioned me, and the low-down bastards locked me up overnight."

"So you were in jail. No wonder you didn't go to Texas."

"I said overnight. They had to let me go because they were holding me on some trumped-up charges."

"Uh-huh."

"Anyway, while I was laying there overnight in that hard, tiny little bed, I had the chance to do some real thinking. I thought about you and me and all the preaching you've been doing to me about not having to have an elaborate life."

"So you got scared. That's why you didn't go," Tanya said, interrupting. She didn't have time for a sob story that was supposed to help him get her back.

"If you would let me talk, I'll be able to tell you what I'm trying to say."

Tanya stared at Chris. She didn't want to continue listening. She didn't need to because she knew the real deal. Chris felt the heat and he was dodging trouble. That's why he didn't go to Texas and was suddenly in a hurry to move to Atlanta.

"Like I said. I had time to think while I was in jail, but I didn't make a decision until I was walking out of my place to meet my peeps to head out to Texas. I saw this couple. They were getting into a raggedy-ass car. But the brother was walking with so much pride, and his girl, you could tell she was in love with him. He opened the passenger door for her. Before she got in they kissed. Them standing there kissing reminded me of us." He stood up.

"Then when I caught up with my peeps, my boy and his girl were outside in front of the car, screaming at the top of their lungs. She was begging him not to go, and he was telling her to get back into the house. Tanya, I got the eeriest feeling, and you know I'm not easily spooked by much. But I had a moment. I could see clear as day that if we went, whether we were caught or not, that I would never see you again. And I couldn't breathe."

Tanya looked at Chris. She was sure that he was saying whatever he needed to get her to change her mind.

"I know you don't believe me, but Tanya, I told my boy it was off. Then I went to my spots to get my money so that we could get ready to be out. One of the stashes is low, way low, but that's all right—I know who took it. I care about my money, but Tanya, instead of me chasing him, I've been looking for you all weekend. The longer it took for me to find you, the more I knew what I had to do."

Chris fell to his knees in front of Tanya.

"I know I've lived a fucked-up life and made a lot of bad choices. I haven't done a whole lot of things I'm proud of. Since T-Roy was shot, nothing has made sense, Tanya, nothing, except for you. You are the only thing that is worth holding on to."

He reached into his pocket and started fumbling around.

"I'm used to living a certain way. I'm not dumb—I know old habits die hard. But I'm making a promise on this ring that I'm going to do whatever it takes to make you always look at me the way that woman looked at her man, even though he was driving a broke-down car." Chris opened the small box and pulled out an engagement ring.

"I'm going to tell you now. I'm not getting a job. I never will, but I am going to open my rims shop, and I'm going to make it work. But I know that it can only work if you are the woman by my side."

Chris held the ring between his fingers while Tanya watched him in disbelief. She didn't budge, but her mind was racing. *Just when I made up in my mind to move on, he has the nerve to try to get it right!* she thought. *Well, it's too late.*

"After all these years, you don't love me anymore?" he questioned.

"Chris, I love you. It's just that—"

"What, you don't believe in me? You don't believe I'm capable of changing, do you? Because if you don't, then I don't need to be here," he said and lowered his head. Then he put the ring back into the box. "I'm sorry. Maybe I'm wrong, but I thought we had something worth fighting for."

Chris got off his knees and sat in the chair, but Tanya's silence was too much. He got up and stood in front of her.

She didn't look at him. She couldn't.

"Well, I won't bother you again, Tanya," he said in a lowered voice. "I see you've already decided to move on with your life." He stood there a while longer to give her a chance to say something, but she didn't. He turned and walked out of the door.

She watched him leave.

But it wasn't right. It wasn't what she wanted. It contradicted everything she'd ever hoped and prayed that they could have, and this time if it didn't come to pass, it was going to be all on her. So she rushed to the door, down the hall, and out of the front entrance and called out to Chris, who was about to get into his truck.

It was freezing out, but Tanya didn't care.

"Chris, you didn't give me a chance to answer your question."

He stopped short. "I'm listening."

"You asked me if I believed in you."

"Yeah."

"Chris, I want to believe in you. I need to believe in you. I've loved you since I first met you, but you weren't ready then. But I have to believe you when you say you're ready now," she yelled to him. "Will you come back inside, please? It's freezing out here."

Chris closed the truck door and walked back over to Tanya. They stepped into the hall.

"Chris, I'm scared. I am very scared," she admitted.

"I know you are, baby, but me and you are going to make it. We're going to be a good team. That's if you're saying yes. Are you saying yes? Please tell me you're saying yes," he said, and poked out his lips.

"Yes, Chris. I am saying yes," Tanya said confidently.

Chris threw his arms around her and wildly kissed her.

"I love you so much and it's gonna work, just you and me," he said.

"Chris, it's not just you and me anymore," Tanya said.

"What?" he replied, fumbling through his pocket again.

"Chris, I'm pregnant," she announced.

He threw his head back in excitement. "Really? Are you serious? Are you really pregnant?" he asked. He lifted her up and swung her around. Then he put her down and tried to compose himself.

"That's all the more reason to do this thing right, starting here and now." Chris kneeled on his knees again and grabbed Tanya's hand.

"Tanya, will you make me the proudest man in the world and say you'll marry me?" he asked.

"I will," she said, and kissed her future husband. She was not sure what their actions on that day meant they would become, or where it would take them, but for the first time in their relationship, she trusted that Chris was going to do the right thing for himself, for her, and for their unborn baby.

33

OH! THE POSSIBILITIES

As SOON AS Lashawnda pulled up at her mother's apartment, she quickly dropped her bags in the guest bedroom that used to belong to her, then she went back to the living room, where her mother was rearranging furniture.

"Making room for the tree, huh?" she said.

"Yeah, we're going to pick it up tonight when John gets home."

"You need some help?" Lashawnda asked.

"Nah."

"I'm getting ready to go to the store. Do you need anything?"

"A pack of cigarettes," her mother replied.

"I got you. And, Mom, I plan to be out by the end of the month," Lashawnda said as she headed out the door.

"I hope so, because it's getting crowded around here," her mother responded, and went back to adjusting the furniture.

Lashawnda came back from the store with her mother's cigarettes, a bag of chips, a drink, the Sunday paper, and an apartment guide magazine.

She'd already narrowed down that she wanted to live in Cobb County, so that she'd be close to downtown by train and also not be too far from her mother. She had good credit, so she knew she'd have no

problem finding a move-in special where there would be either no deposit or the first month of rent would be free. There were tons of pro-
mos like that. She just had to decide which place would be in her price
range.

It was still early on Sunday, so she called the properties she was interested in and found she could visit them that day. She grabbed the
guide and headed out the door to hunt for apartments.

She adored the first place she came to—it was near the bus line and
close to the mall, and the layout was spacious and clean—but she decided to check out the others on her list, just in case. Of the three she
visited, she liked the first best, plus they were offering a waived deposit
and the first month's rent free, so she rushed back to their leasing office and signed the contract for her new place. Provided her credit check
and employment verification would go through on Monday, the place
was hers to move into on the fifteenth.

Lashawnda was so pumped that she drove back to her mother's place
to search the classifieds for a new job. She passed her mother and John
on their way out the door.

"Shawnda, we going to go get the tree. There are some greens and
ham in the oven. Help yourself. Just leave us some for sandwiches."

"Thanks, and Momma, I'll be moving out sooner than I thought."

"Okay, Lashawnda, but it's not that serious," her mother replied.

"Oh yes it is," Lashawnda replied, and walked into the apartment.
She knew her mother needed her privacy as much as she did.

Lashawnda scanned the classifieds with her highlighter pen and
marked every administrative, executive assistant, and office manager
ad she qualified for. Most were through a temporary job placement
service. She cut and taped the ads into her notebook so that she could
discreetly make phone calls and fax out resumes without having the
newspaper on her desk at work. Cicely had watched her like a hawk
the past week, and she didn't want to do anything to draw attention to
the fact that she was actively pursuing another job.

CICELY BOUNCED THROUGH the office, glowing, still on a high from her
vacation. Lashawnda was on a high herself—early that morning, the
apartment she'd applied for called to verify her employment and La-

shawnda validated it herself. So there was an abundance of positive energy bouncing around, only their energies worked hard to avoid each other. Cicely walked around, in and out of her office, humming all day, while Lashawnda attempted to be involved in her duties. She'd actually gotten a lot done, but whenever she found herself alone because Cicely was in with a patient, she pulled out her notepad and made phone calls and sent out several faxes. She put her cell phone number as her contact number on her resume; she put the phone on vibrate and answered as many of the incoming calls as possible. By lunch, she had some promising interviews set up. Several of the temp agents she'd spoken with assured her that she would have no problem finding a new job.

Cicely finished with her last client before lunch. It was Mrs. Bland. Her black eye had cleared up, and she seemed to be in good spirits. After she walked out the door, Cicely buzzed Lashawnda.

"Yes, Cicely," Lashawnda said through the intercom.

"Could you come in for just a minute?" she asked.

"I'm on my way," Lashawnda replied. She picked up a small pad and a pen just in case she needed to take notes and walked into Cicely's office. When she walked in, her mind flashed to all of the lunch breaks and late evenings they'd spent in there, fooling around on the therapy couch. They were fun times, but Lashawnda didn't want a part of them anymore.

"Have a seat," Cicely said. Lashawnda took a seat in a chair across the desk and waited for her to speak.

"What are your plans for lunch?" Cicely asked.

"I was thinking I would run downstairs and get something from the deli and come back up here and eat at my desk," Lashawnda said.

"Would you like to join me for dinner?" Cicely asked, as if Lashawnda had never caught her and Marissa having sex in their bed. As if they were supposed to still be a couple.

"No . . . thank you," Lashawnda replied slowly. She decided that there was nothing that Cicely could say, or do, that would have shock value.

"Lashawnda, we're going to be working together; we might as well try to be friends," Cicely insisted.

"Cicely, I will continue to work for you because I need a check and you need an employee, but I don't see how we can be friends, because every time I look at you now all I see is Marissa's breasts all in your face. I feel betrayed. I see you as a liar. How can we be friends when I see all of that?"

"I understand that you're upset, Lashawnda, and I apologize that things turned out the way that they did. I still care about you. It's just that Marissa was under a tremendous amount of stress, and she came on to me. I tried to resist, but you know what happens when you've had too much to drink. One thing led to another, and that's when you walked in."

Lashawnda burst into laughter. "Cicely, you think I'm some kind of a fool, don't you? I'm not the same person you rescued in front of the grocery store. I'm a full-grown woman. And I'm insulted that you would come to me with a lame story like that." Lashawnda shook her head in disgust. "You know what, Cicely, I was going to try to stay here through the week, but it's not even worth it. The money is not that big a deal."

"So you're quitting?" Cicely asked in disbelief.

"You know, I tried, but I can't stand to be in the same space with you."

"After everything I've done for you, you mean to tell me you're going to just leave me without any help?" She was beginning to lose control of her usually calm demeanor.

"I'm sure I've returned the favor in more ways than one," Lashawnda said, and got up out of her seat. "You weren't the only one giving."

"You'll be back, because who else would hire you? You're a thirty-year-old woman with no real skills or experience," Cicely huffed as she stood to her feet. Her face was contorted and flushed. It was the most out of control Lashawnda had ever seen Cicely. "You were nothing when I first met you. If it weren't for me, you would still be in the ghetto trying to scrape by. You're still a hoochy hood rat!"

"Cicely, with all your degrees and credentials, I'm sure you can come up with a better way to insult me," Lashawnda said calmly. She relished knowing that Cicely needed her much more than she needed Cicely.

"You know what, bitch, just get out of my office!" Cicely yelled.

"My pleasure, Cicely. I'm leaving," Lashawnda said, and walked toward the door. But she couldn't resist having the last word. "And by the way, your sex is not as good as you think. You're actually quite boring. I know men who lick it better than you could ever imagine."

Lashawnda walked out and closed the door behind her. Cicely was yelling something, but Lashawnda was so puffed up that she didn't hear. She gathered her things from her desk and found a small box to put them in. Then she stopped and took a moment to look around the office that had changed her life. She knew she'd never see that place again. She slowly walked out and closed the door behind her. Instead of being sad, she felt good inside and was confident about her possibilities.

She still wasn't sure about her sexuality. As things stood, she'd had a bad track record with both men and women. However, she was beginning to like herself, so she looked forward to getting to know Lashawnda and finding out what kinds of things she would fill her apartment with, what kind of job she would be able to land. She anticipated finding out what she'd like to do when she was alone, and she wondered what kind of person she would find herself linked to. Regardless of their gender, she knew that it would be someone she would choose out of want and compatibility instead of need or convenience. She was a grown-ass woman and knew it was high time to make decisions that reflected her age. She also knew that regardless of her recent losses and the uncertainty of her future, she was going to be just fine.

34

MY WAY

THE ALARM CLOCK went off at eight A.M. Alecia rolled over and hit all the buttons until she found the snooze.

"Today is your day," she groaned from beneath her covers.

Then she lay staring at the wall, attempting to find the motivation to get up before the alarm clock went off again.

"Today is your day," she said. This time louder.

The phone rang. She sighed and reached over her alarm clock to get it.

"This is Alecia," she said.

"So you are back," William said. "Tony told me he picked you up from the airport yesterday."

"He did. Is it a problem?" she asked, not really caring if it was.

"No, Jewel, not at all. I'm calling to see if we can meet for lunch today."

"Well, I have a list of things that I need to do today."

"But you have to eat sometime, right?" he asked.

"Hold on just a sec. I need to check my schedule for today. I'll let you know what time will be good for me."

"Okay. Check your schedule," he said sarcastically.

Alecia laid down the phone and counted to thirty. Just then the alarm clock went off. She knew the phone was near the clock so she took her time about turning it off.

"I'm sorry, William. I hope that alarm didn't bother you. Anyway, I can be available around one o'clock, I guess."

"Okay. One o'clock it is. I'll be by to pick you up."

"Why don't we meet out—I have some errands I have to run."

"I've got a taste for soul food. Let's go to Harold and Belle's."

"Soul food? I was thinking more like Sushi on Sunset, but soul food in Inglewood is cool."

"Are you sure that's okay with you?"

"I guess I am due a taste of some good ol' Cajun-fried catfish. I'll see you there," she said and hung up the phone.

There wasn't a reason to be angry at William. He'd had no idea his wife was going to show up in San Diego. Plus, her meeting him today would give him an opportunity to make things right and allow her to determine what she needed to do for herself and her life. In the meantime, she needed to do so much to get started with her day. She had numerous phone calls to make, but the first thing on her list was to get showered.

After getting dressed, Alecia began making calls. The first one was to a photographer whose work she admired. She set up a date with him for a photo shoot. She needed new head shots to begin working. Then she called up her old acting coach to begin lessons. That was no problem at all. As long as she was paying, she would be able to continue training. Finally she made the dreaded call to her old agent.

His receptionist answered the phone.

"May I please speak to Masden?"

"May I say who's calling?"

"This is Alecia Jewel Parker."

"Alecia. Oh, I gotta put you through," she said, laughing rudely.

Alecia wasn't surprised.

"Talk to me," Masden said.

"Hi, Masden. This is Alecia."

"Yeah, I know. So what are you doing calling me, wasting my time?"

"I'm ready," she said.

"Yeah, that's what I thought when you first walked through my door, but then what happened? You turned down every role I found for you. You said they weren't good enough."

"I know, but—"

"I got you speaking roles. You could have been SAG by now. You know Jada Pinkett-Smith? It should have been Alecia Jewel Parker-Smith. But no, you weren't willing to start from the bottom and work your way to the top. You wanted to begin a star. But nobody, and I mean nobody, not even Alecia Jewel Parker, steps on the screen and becomes an instant star."

"Masden, listen to me. I realize that now."

"I know you're not asking me to represent you again. You were my worst client ever."

"I've changed."

"Yeah, maturity works every time. But now you're too old! A has-been. How old are you now, anyway, thirty? There's no way I can get any work for you."

"I said I'm ready, and I'm not too old!" Alecia demanded. "Somebody out there has a part with my name on it, and if anybody can find it for me, it's you. I know that you're the best in the business. That's why I'm calling now." She hated groveling, but she knew what worked with him.

"Yeah, you've still got it, just enough bullshit know-how to make it in this crazy business. Now, you know your first jobs are not going to be leads, right?"

"I know!"

"Do you have your head shots?"

"Got a shoot set up for Friday."

"Okay. Bring the proofs to the office as soon as you get them. I want to have some say this time in the ones we use."

"Okay."

"What about classes? Have you been working on your craft? Because if you're dealing with me, longevity is the goal."

"I begin classes again on Thursday. Twice a week."

"Okay, we're set. You are still beautiful, right?"

"Even better than when you saw me last," she purred.

"That's what I want to hear. All right then, let's get to work," he said.

"Masden, thanks so much and I promise I won't let you down."

"All right Miss Alecia Jewel, we'll see about that."

"Oh, we will," she replied confidently.

———

ALECIA WALKED THROUGH the restaurant toward the table where William was sitting. Most of the patrons enjoying their meals were African American businesspeople on their lunch breaks.

She found William seated at a table in a corner in the far back of the restaurant. She wasn't surprised—they found secluded seating when dining in public whenever possible.

When Alecia approached the table, William stood up and pulled her seat out for her.

"So what are you in the mood for?" he asked.

"I don't know yet. It's been a while since we came here. I need to look the menu over."

"No problem," he said. "You're absolutely breathtaking."

Alecia opened her menu and replied with an unfeeling "Thank you."

After the waitress took their orders, William leaned forward to grab Alecia's hand, but she saw what he was doing, picked up her napkin, and placed it in her lap, leaving her hands underneath the table.

"I know you hate me," he said.

"I don't hate you, William. You know that. I'm in love with you."

"I'm in love with you too. I'm so sorry about what happened in San Diego. I had no idea Phyllis was going to be there."

"Of course you didn't," Alecia replied calmly. She was going to allow him to say everything that he felt necessary. She wanted him to say he was getting a divorce.

"I told her not to ever come anywhere that I was unannounced."

"I'm sure she didn't appreciate that."

"She was angry. We went to sleep hugging different sides of the bed."

"That must have been miserable for her," Alecia said.

"For me too, because I was wondering all night if you were okay."

"As you can see, I'm just fine," Alecia said with a dry smile.

"I can see that. But I want to know if everything is cool between you and me."

"I guess this means you have no intention of leaving your wife?" she asked, keeping her tone low.

William shot her a look of disbelief.

"I think that's a fair question," she said.

"Maybe so, but you've never asked before," he said.

"Well, I'm asking now. Are you going to divorce Phyllis?"

William took a deep breath, picked up his glass, took a sip of water, and cleared his throat. "Alecia, Phyllis and I have been married for fifteen years."

"I figured it had been about that long, William, but that still doesn't answer my question," she insisted.

"Does it really matter to you?" he asked.

"Of course it does. I am in love with you, William, and I don't want to—I will *not* share you any longer."

"Alecia, I give you anything you ask for. I bought you a condominium and paid off all your sky-high credit-card balances. I take care of you. I thought you were cool with our arrangement. You never said anything before. Plus you have a pack of boyfriends that I never say anything about. What's the problem?" he asked, seemingly confused with why they were having such a conversation.

Alecia composed herself, resisting her need to scream and cry and throw a tantrum. "The problem is that you've given me everything except *you,* and that's what I want. But I can't have you," Alecia said and lowered her head, "because you belong to Phyllis."

Just then the waitress walked up and served them their food.

"Can I help you with anything else?" she asked.

"We're just fine. Thank you," William said.

She walked off.

Reality was staring Alecia in the face. William never intended to leave his wife, and he would keep Alecia on the side for as long as she would allow him to. She had to be honest with herself. She wanted more than William, or any married man, could possibly give, so she had to get what she could and get out without feeling that she'd lost everything.

"William, I intend to keep my car and my condo."

"You can't afford them, Alecia."

She licked her lips and began, "But you can, William. It's over between us, but I expect you to write me a check right now to cover my mortgage and car note for the next six months. That's all I expect from you. You owe me that much. After that, I don't want anything else from you."

"And why should I do that?" he asked.

"You just sat there and told me that you loved me. Did you mean that or are you just putting together words to string me along?"

"So you're trying to say that you expect me to keep you for six months and you're not going to be spending time with me. Do you take me for a fool?" William asked.

"No, William, but I know that I had to mean something to you. All those long talks we've had and the way that you've looked at me and touched me—I couldn't have been just an expensive lay. No, William, I know the kind of man you are and surely you're deeper than that."

"I am and it was," William nervously replied. He looked dejected and vulnerable.

"Well, prove it!" Alecia said and stared him dead in the eyes.

William hesitantly pulled out his checkbook and began filling out a check.

"Fill in the amount," he said, "and it better be the correct amount, down to the dime."

"Six months, that's all I ask," Alecia replied.

William handed the check over to her. "So this is it," he said.

"It's your choice, not mine," Alecia replied, while examining the check to make sure the signature was legit. It was. She put it into her purse. Then stood up.

"If you ever change your mind . . ." William began, but he knew it was over.

"I won't," she replied and turned and walked away.

When she got outside, she gave the valet her ticket. He returned, rolling up in her SLK 32 AMG Mercedes-Benz and opened the car door for her to get inside.

When she closed the door, she pulled down the shade to look at herself in the mirror. She saw the disappointment in her eyes. She was heartbroken, but she refused to cry. After all, she had a blank check, and a life that had taught her that time heals all wounds. She checked out her physique, and everything was looking good as usual. She spoke to her reflection. "Hey, Alecia Jewel Parker, you might give him your heart, but he'll never take your common sense." She slipped on her Chanel sunglasses, pulled out of the lot, and headed to the bank.

35

CATARA IN THE CITY

ATARA SAT ON the subway after a long day of work at Saks. She lay back, closed her eyes, and listened to the radio, trying to block out the noise on the train and unwind from the day. Her clientele always increased their visits around Christmastime. It had been a long stressful day and everybody seemed to need a dress for a Christmas shindig at Tavern on the Green, but she took her day in stride. She had big plans, and although she wasn't sure how it was going to happen, she felt confident that she would get her turn in the design industry.

Her eyes were closed and she was mouthing the words to Toni Braxton's "Another Sad Love Song," when she almost missed her chance to get off when the train came to her stop. An elderly lady, who always sat across from her on the train but never spoke, tapped her on the shoulder.

"You're gonna miss your stop," she said smiling.

Catara looked around and noticed that the doors were about to close, so she jumped up and rushed for the door. "Thank you," she yelled behind her.

People never cease to amaze me, she said to herself as she took the steps up to the street. She had a half-mile walk to get to her apartment. It was freezing out and flakes of snow were falling.

Catara looked up at the snow. *This time next year, I will be a professional designer,* she promised herself.

Inside her apartment, Catara threw her coat, scarf, and gloves on the floor and walked over to her cordless phone to check her voice mail.

"You have one new message," the automated voice said.

"Catara, this is Cheryl. Give me a call as soon as you get this message," she said. "I have good news, so call me now. Love you, cuz."

Catara took a seat on her sofa and noticed how out of line she was for throwing her garments down, so she got up to pick them up as she dialed. "Hey, Cheryl. This is Catara. I got your message. What's up?"

"Are you sitting down?" Cheryl asked.

"No. Do I need to be?" Catara asked as she picked up her things.

"I would if I were you," Cheryl said.

"So what is it?"

Catara walked over to her closet, put her coat and scarf on a hanger, stuffed her gloves into a pocket of the coat, and took a seat on her bed.

"Catara, you're not going to believe this. Do you remember Lamont?" Cheryl asked.

"Yeah. The guy who took us to the airport before Thanksgiving."

"Yeah, him," Cheryl replied.

"He asked you to marry him?" Catara joked.

"Where would you get a thought like that, silly?" Cheryl said. Her voice was even mousier than usual. "No. He really liked the pajamas you were wearing when he came over that morning."

"I remember. He told me he liked them then."

"I mean he *really* liked them, to the point that he told his best friend about them, and he wants to see them," Cheryl said with excitement in her voice.

"Okay. That's nice to know, but what's so great about Lamont's best friend wanting to see my pajamas?"

"His best friend is one of the head lingerie designers for Victoria's Secret!" Cheryl screamed. "He wants to branch off and form an upscale plus-size lingerie line. He has created the lingerie but is interested in seeing your pajamas to possibly bring you and your line to the collection."

"Oh my God. Are you serious?" Catara replied. She fell back on the bed.

"Yes, and he wants to meet with you immediately and see the pajamas that Lamont saw, plus anything else that you have. He also wants to see any of your other sketches of lingerie."

Catara sat up. She was overwhelmed, ecstatic. She'd never sent a résumé or samples to Victoria's Secret, because she just assumed that they wouldn't be interested or that they'd discriminate against her once they saw her, because of her weight.

"So what do I need to do to contact him?" she asked.

Cheryl gave her his name and number and told her to call first thing the next morning.

"I'm so nervous. What if he doesn't like my work? No. I know he'll like it. He'd better like it," Catara said.

"All I know is that when I told Lamont about your background, he said his friend is looking for a designer and that your pajamas are going to blow him away."

"Unbelievable," Catara said.

"Yeah, cuz. It's happening for you," Cheryl said.

"It is, isn't it," Catara replied.

When the two hung up the phone Catara lay back on her bed with a broad smile on her face. She thought her previous interview had been the chance of a lifetime, but this one beat them all. Once she got her interview date, she was going to mark off that date from her calendar to make sure there would be no customers to prevent her from getting there on time.

The phone rang and interrupted her bliss.

She put it up to her ear.

"Hello," she answered.

"May I speak to Catara?" the male voice said.

"This is Catara. With whom am I speaking?" she said attempting to pep up her voice.

"This is Marcus Radford. I met you a few days ago on a flight going to Miami. Remember, you gave up your seat to me so that I could sit in the aisle."

"Of course I remember you," Catara said. She sat up.

"So how was your trip?" he asked.

"It was great. Thanks for asking. And you were traveling on business, right?"

"Yes I was. It was a productive weekend, but I did get down to South Beach one night. I had a good time."

"That's nice to hear. Marcus, could you hold on for just a second?" Catara asked. She put the phone to the side of her and stood up off the bed and covered her mouth, which was wide open, while jumping up and down beside the bed. She took a deep breath and picked the phone back up.

"Is everything okay?" he asked.

"Everything is fine," she replied calmly.

"So, Catara. The reason that I'm calling you is that I have tickets to see *The Producers* on Broadway. I hear the wardrobe is phenomenal. They actually won a Tony Award for costume design, and I figured that you, of all people, would appreciate going."

"Thank you, Marcus. That is really nice of you," she replied. She knew he was a good guy from their lengthy discussion during their flight together, but she never would have taken him to be the type who would call her up just to give her tickets to a show because he thought she would enjoy checking out the costuming.

"And I was thinking that maybe we could grab a bite to eat afterward and continue the engaging conversation we began on the plane."

"So are you asking me out on a date?" Catara asked.

He chuckled. "Well, I guess I am. Are you saying yes?"

"I guess I am," she replied.

They laughed.

"The tickets are for this Saturday night. I hope that date works for you."

"Saturday works well," she said.

"Great," he said and sighed. "It's been a while since I've gotten the nerve up to do something like this, so I'm glad you said yes. Well, Catara, you have a good evening and I do look forward to seeing you Saturday," he said, sounding rushed.

"Wait a minute. I want to share my news with you, if you don't mind," she said.

Catara told him about her interview and the possibility of other things. They continued talking that evening for an hour or so.

Catara hung up the phone feeling elated. She knew that every day wasn't going to be as sweet as the one she was having, but she embraced the good feeling of possibility, of what was yet to come.

epilogue

BIRTHDAY SHOUT-OUT

WHEN THE RED light flashed on, Melvin Green began speaking. "This is Melvin Green and the Morning Show Crew. I hope you enjoyed that list of songs we just played for you. I'm sure that last one, by Mary J. Blige, will help you get your day going. My girl, Louisa Montero, has something that she'd like to say to the ladies that she spent her birthday weekend with. Now, I heard that you took over Miami and caused so much chaos in the Grand Bahamas that they kicked you ladies off the island."

"And you know we turned it out, but in a good way! They're begging us to come back! This is Louisa Montero, and I just wanted to shout out to my sisters in spirit: Alecia, Catara, Elise, Lashawnda, and Tanya. Ladies, I don't know if the timing will ever be right for us to do it again, but let me tell you now, our Night Before Thirty birthday vacation was a moment in time I'll never forget. Each of you is special in your own unique way, and I wish each and every one of you a life filled with love and happiness as you embark on life beyond thirty. God bless each of you, and just know that there's a piece of all of you in my heart."

Melvin cut in, "Ah, ain't that so sweet. I think I'm gonna cry. I think I'm gonna have a birthday celebration of my own and call it the Night Before . . . Let's not go there with my age. Anyway, I bet you ladies had a good time. And on behalf of Melvin Green and the Morning Show

Crew, I'd like to play a song for you birthday girls. But I'm gonna also dedicate it to every lady out there who is about to turn thirty, who is thirty, or who has long since passed thirty—that's you, Mom. This song is for you."

Melvin sat back and grinned as "Isn't She Lovely?" by Stevie Wonder played.

Isn't she lovely? Isn't she wonderful!

ACKNOWLEDGMENTS

There are so many people who touch my life and help to make it possible for me to continue to write and promote my works. I will never be able to thank everybody, but would like to mention a few:

To my heavenly Father, God, who continues to protect, guide, and stretch me. Sometimes I lose track of what's truly important. I'm thankful that he has provided me with family and friends who have ways of keeping me grounded.

To my daddy, Raymond, thank you for being my role model and a constant reminder that good men still walk this earth. To my mother, Linda, I cherish your meaningful and loving advice. To my big sister, Kim, you never cease to amaze me. I remain inspired by your courage and your will. To my little sister, Tracy, you are so wise and considerate of others. Thanks for always reminding me to be thoughtful. And to my favorite niece, Jalyn, you are such a beautiful young flower. It fills my heart with joy just watching you blossom.

To my family: the Butlers, the Macks, Caren Handley, Keisha Kirkland, Athena Y. Reese, Artis "Coolio" Ivey, Phnesheia Works, Lorenzo A. Works, Ellis Schaffer, Byron Hueston, Courtney "Corey" Gunn, Lanetia Butler, Regina Weston, Joe Wilson, Edwardo Jackson, Crystal Jackson, Elisa Freeman-Carr, Angela Stephens, Monique Johnson, Ronda Cosby, Stacy Cohen, Melvin E. Banks, Jr., and my "peeps" in Hopkinsville, Kentucky. I am grateful for your friendship and support.

To Melody Guy, my editor, I value your direction, foresight, and patience. To Beth Pearson, Jynne Martin, and the rest of the Random House staff, thanks for putting such care into completing and promoting my novels. To Sarah Lazin and Paula Balzer, my agents, thanks for your commitment and efforts in guiding my career as a writer. To Sadeqa Johnson, I appreciate the experience and positive attitude you've brought to help organize and build my speaking career.

Also to RM Johnson, John Dunson, Tiffany V. Bradshaw, Vaughn Perry, Gary Hardwick, Pastor Kevin W. Cosby, Dana Pump, Larry B. Scott, Eric Garrett, Barry Tilford, Chris Whitney, Carlos and Stacey Wilson, Rodney Carson, Mitch Drone, Corey Wadlington, Roger Holloway, Cordele Rolle, Chris Taylor, Jihad Shaheed, Keith Adams, Thomas J. Flowers, Kalmin Fullard, and Dr. Mario E. Paz.

To the wonderful booksellers: Emma Rogers, Adline Clark, Jackie Williams-Folks, Malik, Esowon Books, Maleta McPherson, Felecia A. Wintons, Jackie Perkins, James Muhammad, Rasheed Ali, Jerry Thompson, Nkenge Abi, Donna Stokes-Lucas, Sonia Williams-Babers, Mututa, Vera Warren-Williams, Jennifer Turner, Jim Rogers, Michele Lewis, Brother Simba, and Robin Green-Cary. What would we do without you?

Also, L. Peggy Hicks, Miss Lina Catalano, Diedra Michele, Jolan Solis, Marjorie Pennell, Vivica A. Fox, Tina Andrews, Stanley Bennett Clay, William Cole, Dewayne Dancer, Michael "Hollywood" Hernandez and Kit, Sylvia Simone, Devetta J McIntyre, Jetie B. Wilds, Jr., Twanda Black, Albert Butler, Cliff and Janine, Rufus Beal, KJ in the Midday, LaRita Shelby, Richard Davis, Chastity Godfrey, and Collette Ramsey.

And finally, to Alpha Kappa Alpha Sorority, Inc., Delta Sigma Theta Sorority, Inc., Zeta Phi Beta Sorority, Inc., Sigma Gamma Rho Sorority, Inc., The National Pan-Hellenic Council, Inc., 100 Black Men of America, and the countless colleges and universities that have shown their support.

THE NIGHT BEFORE THIRTY

A Reader's Guide

TAJUANA "TJ" BUTLER

Reading Group Questions and Topics for Discussion

The following Reading Group Guide was created to enhance your group's discussion of *The Night Before Thirty* by Tajuana "TJ" Butler, a story about five women who are about to turn thirty and whose lives are about to change when a radio contest brings them all together.

1. Catara remembers a time in her past when she felt beautiful and self-confident. What happened? She claims her weight is at fault. Is she using it as an excuse?

2. Although winning the contest allows Catara, Lashawnda, Tanya, Alecia, and Elise to escape for a weekend, each woman spends a lot of time thinking about her own past and future during the trip. Why is this? What is it about the weekend getaway that sparks this kind of thinking? What perspective do the women gain about their lives?

3. Louisa asks each of the women to pick a question and share something about her own life to help everyone to get to know one another. Do their stories do more than this? What does each of the women learn from the other? About themselves?

4. Cicely helped turn Lashawnda's life around by giving her the education and ambition she might never have developed on her own. Did Cicely use her? Is Lashawnda really confused about her sexuality?

5. Nearly all the women approach their thirtieth birthday feeling as if they are missing something. What do each of the women want? What is it about turning thirty that makes people reevaluate their lives?

6. Although Alecia seems to have it all, does she? What is she looking for in her men? What does her relationship with her younger sister reveal about her?

7. One of the themes of *The Night Before Thirty* is finding the strength to believe in yourself and your ability to succeed. What do the women realize about themselves during the cruise? How do you think their lives will change?

8. Of all the women, Elise is the one who seems to have it all together. She doesn't allow her disappointment with her athletic career to drive her away from gymnastics or into the arms of a married man. Where do her strength and leadership come from? Why does she have such a hard time telling Allen how she really feels about him?

9. Tanya repeatedly involves herself with the wrong kind of man. Why? What effect did her experience with Steve have on her choices later on? Can her relationship with Chris succeed? Why does she want to move so badly?

10. What are some of the reasons Louisa chose each of the winners? How are the women alike? How are they different?

An excerpt from
Tajuana "TJ" Butler's new novel,

Just My Luck

Thirty-eight-year-old Lanita Lightfoot
is finally graduating from college. But first,
Lanita's husband treats her to a day of beauty
at an upscale black salon in Los Angeles, during
which she shares her story with the salon staff
and fellow patrons—a story of struggle,
sacrifice, and fortunate turns of luck.
And what a story it is. . . .

Chapter 1

As Lanita approached the salon, she could barely contain her excitement. It had been a long time since she'd had the extra time or money to even get her hair done, let alone indulge in the pampering she was about to enjoy, but her husband had insisted she spare no expense during her visit. Today was their special day. Today they would celebrate what had taken years of struggle and sacrifice to complete—their college education.

As Lanita reached for the salon door, she looked down and noticed four quarters scattered on the sidewalk. Smiling, she bent down to pick them up. *Another small gift to remind me of who I am and what I've accomplished,* she thought. She tossed the quarters from one hand to the other and then placed them in her pants pocket before opening the door.

Already feeling more relaxed, Lanita approached the receptionist, a pretty young woman with immaculately groomed hair and a cheerful, welcoming smile. "Hi, my name is Lanita, and I'm scheduled to see a stylist, nail tech, and facialist. I'm not sure in which order," she said with a small laugh, "but I know I'm supposed to begin at ten. I'm a few minutes early, but I believe it's better to be a few minutes early than a few minutes late, if you know what I mean."

"Sure," said the receptionist. "Have a seat over there. Someone will be with you shortly—but are you okay?"

"I'm fine," Lanita said. She touched a hand to her hair. "Why do you ask?"

"I saw you bending down outside. It looked like you'd lost something."

"Oh, that," Lanita said with another laugh. "Thanks for asking, but I haven't lost anything in some time. I was actually reaping my blessing, that's all." Smiling warmly at the receptionist, Lanita glanced around, noting the tasteful, expensive decor. "Wow, this is really a nice salon. It reminds me of the ones on those reality shows where they take people to get makeovers. This setting really makes a person feel like she's privileged to be here."

It was the receptionist's turn to laugh. "Well, we *are* one of the top salons in Los Angeles, the crème de la crème. Our clients include a number of celebrities and their families. I think you'll find our staff is top-notch." The young woman winked at Lanita, giving her a knowing smile.

"Well, it's been a while since I've been pampered—in fact almost twelve years—but believe you me, there was a time when I would go to places like this weekly." Lanita sat down, easing herself into her chair and unconsciously assuming the air of someone accustomed to the luxurious setting. A heavy sigh followed, and before she knew it, she had fallen into deep thought. As excited as she was about what the day would bring, she couldn't help but remember the events that had led her there. She shook her head, choosing to distract herself by enjoying her surroundings and focusing on the present. After all, that was what today was all about—the present *and* the future. "So what's your name?" Lanita asked the receptionist.

"I'm Natasha," she responded. "By the way, would you like something to drink?"

"Sure. What are my choices?"

"There's bottled water, sparkling or flat, red and white wine, or orange juice."

After a moment of thought, Lanita said, "I'll take the sparkling water. I'm graduating from USC today, and I don't want to begin celebrating too early, if you know what I mean." Lanita snapped her fingers, all but dancing in her chair.

"Congratulations!" Natasha said. "Are you sure you don't want a glass of wine? You should start the day off with a bang."

Lanita instantly felt somber. "To be honest with you, I never touch the stuff—alcohol, I mean. Not after what it did to my mother and me."

Natasha looked down at her phone, seeming unsure of how to respond. Then she said, "I'll get that water for you."

Across the room from Lanita was a large chrome-trimmed mirror. After Natasha left the room, Lanita got up and slowly walked over to it. Gazing at her reflection, she saw an aging woman wearing red Capri pants, a yellow T-shirt, and a silver chain with a silver-dollar pendant. Frowning at what she saw, she ran her fingers through her hair. "Girlfriend," she said, "you're in a bad need of a relaxer, and when was the last time your thirty-eight-year-old self had that dead skin removed from your face?"

She grabbed the pendant and kissed it. Then she placed it so that it lay just so against her chest. "Flat as pancakes," she said of her breasts. Sliding her hands over her body, admiring her trim figure that otherwise had curves in all the right places, she smiled. She then turned her back to the mirror, looked over her shoulder, and placed her hands on her hips, shaking her derriere in the mirror. She might be close to forty, but her backside still looked just fine.

Just then Natasha came back in the room, carrying a glass of water. She cleared her throat unobtrusively and Lanita abruptly stopped dancing. She was caught. She managed a nervous giggle, saying, "You'll have to excuse me. I'm usually more dignified, but I . . ."

Natasha laughed. "No need to apologize. Sometimes you just have to celebrate in your own way." She handed Lanita the water.

"I'm so embarrassed," Lanita said, feeling the flush in her cheeks.

"Don't worry," Natasha said, squeezing Lanita's shoulder. She lowered her voice to a conspiratorial whisper and said, "I won't tell anyone."

"Thank you," Lanita said, her cheeks still hot with embarrassment. She took the glass from Natasha and again turned to view herself in the mirror. "For the past few years, I've been doing my own hair. I use my husband's clippers to keep the ends trimmed. I'm not good at all, but I've gotten better." She smoothed her hand over her short-cropped hair. "Recently I've been going for the Halle Berry look, but I've had so much going on these past few weeks, with finals and all, that I'm definitely missing the mark by a long shot."

Still staring into the mirror, this time Lanita noted the effects of years of living. "Time waits for no one," she said under her breath before looking at Natasha. "I hope the stylist here will hook me up. You know, make me feel beautiful again."

"We have exceptional hairstylists, the best in town. I'm sure they'll do a good job of reminding you just how beautiful you are."

"I sure hope so, because my husband is a good man and he's spending a lot of money on me today, money we really don't have to blow." Lanita turned to look at Natasha. "Don't get me wrong," she continued. "We pay our bills. We've just been putting a lot back saving for another house." She took a sip of water. "He doesn't have much, but he treats me like I'm a princess. When I was a little girl, I used to dream of one day marrying a prince. Let me tell you, the man I married is as chivalrous as any of those men in the royal families over there in Europe—maybe even more so. He's handsome, considerate, loving, and dashing. You know what I mean?"

Natasha rolled her eyes. "I wish I did. They don't make many men like that anymore, especially not in Los Angeles."

"Girl, he's broke compared to the rich men I dated once upon a time. He doesn't have two pennies to rub together to make a dime. He cuts glass for a living, you know, for mirrors and tables and shelves. We've invested a lot of money into our education. We both decided to go for broke and get our degrees."

Lanita walked past Natasha and sat back in her chair. "We're gonna be just fine. After today I'll have my degree and he'll have his. We'll both be able to begin new careers."

The phone rang and Natasha rushed to pick it up, resuming her seat behind the front counter. After listening for a few moments, she said, "Okay, I'll let her know," and then hung up.

She turned to Lanita, saying, "You were supposed to be getting your facial first, but Miss Lina is running a little late, so you'll see Jimmy Choo first. He's going to style your hair. He should be here in a couple of minutes, just as soon as he's finished up in back."

"Jimmy Choo?" Lanita said. "You mean the guy who makes those thousand-dollar shoes does hair too?"

"Well, no," Natasha said. "They do share the same name, but they are two different people."

"Is Jimmy Asian?"

"Yes, he is," Natasha said. "Is that okay?"

Lanita almost jumped out of the chair. "I don't mean to overreact, but is he educated about caring for African-American hair? Everything has to be right today. I've had some real horror stories in the hair department. Once a French lady gave me a relaxer and my mane shed for weeks. I nearly went bald until my mother gave me a protein treatment." Lanita frowned. "I'm sorry, I'm just a little scared. I mean, I can't go across the stage looking all crazy. When I take off my cap, my hair needs to be bouncing and behaving, not embarrassing and shaming."

"Trust me," Natasha said. "Jimmy knows what he's doing. As a matter of fact, he does my hair." She reached up to fluff her smooth, shiny layered bob.

"Well, your hair looks good," Lanita said. "Now that I think about it, the guy who does Halle Berry's hair is Asian too, isn't he?" At Natasha's nod, Lanita said, "Now, that's a good sign. Maybe he'll be able to make me look as good as her."

"So, how late is he going to be? I have to meet my sweetie on campus at one o'clock sharp. Graduation begins at one-thirty."

"He should only be about ten more minutes." Natasha's warm smile put Lanita at ease.

"Oh, that's not bad at all," Lanita said, relaxing back.

Natasha took another call. When she was finished, she looked up and asked, "Do you have any plans after graduation, or are you going straight into job hunting?"

"We're considering a short vacation," Lanita said. "We hope to begin working at the end of the summer."

"Where do you want to go?"

"The French Polynesian islands," Lanita said, sighing.

"But how could you two afford that? I thought your money was tight. I don't mean to be forward . . ."

"That's okay. Yeah, the islands are pricey, but a girl can wish, can't she?" Lanita smiled, crossing her legs. "You'll be surprised at the amazing things that have happened in my life that weren't supposed to."

"But, Tahiti and places like that." Natasha shook her head. "That's a lot to wish for just out of school."

"You're right, but stranger things have happened in my life. My mother always said that just enough of King Midas's blood runs in my veins to turn hard luck into gold, but not enough to keep it."

"Really?"

"Yeah, really. I was born lucky."

"Lucky?" Natasha said, skepticism creeping into her voice.

"Yes. I consider myself an intelligent and levelheaded woman, but honestly, I've had a streak of luck that has followed me since birth. I was born during the Watts riots of 1965, and my birth prevented a man's store from being burned to a crisp."

"You were born in Watts, California, during the actual riots?" The skepticism in Natasha's voice was beginning to turn to awe. "That must have been crazy for your mother."

"Yeah, and because that man's store didn't get burned down, he gave me and my mother a place to live rent-free for years. Isn't that lucky?"

"Yeah, I suppose so," Natasha said. "I remember reading about the Watts riots back when I was in high school. It seems like your real luck was making it out of there alive."

Lanita tilted her glass and took another sip. She made herself comfortable and began easing down memory lane. "Since we have a few minutes before Jimmy Choo will be ready for me, I'll tell you about my birth. It's one of my favorite stories. My mother loved to tell it whenever she and her friends sat around and got drunk on cheap liquor. She told it so many times that I sometimes feel like I saw it with my own eyes."

TAJUANA "TJ" BUTLER is the founder of Lavelle Publishing and is also a writer, poet, and public speaker who discusses women's issues. She is the author of the novels *Sorority Sisters*, *The Night Before Thirty*, *Just My Luck*, and the number one *Essence* magazine bestseller *Hand-me-down Heartache*, in addition to the poetry collection *The Desires of a Woman*. She attended the University of Louisville, and she lives in Kentucky. You can visit her website at www.tjbutler.com.

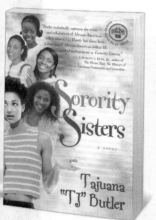